A PALACE OF ART

A PALACE OF ART

A NOVEL

by

J. I. M. STEWART

LONDON
VICTOR GOLLANCZ LTD
1972

(CF Stewart)

ISBN 0 575 01394 X

58600

Printed in Great Britain by
Northumberland Press Ltd., Gateshead

CONTENTS

Part One

Part Two

Part Three

Part Four

Part One

A PARTY AT NUDD

EVERY NOW AND then Mrs Montacute gave the sort
of party that was now beginning. She expected people to
come anything up to seventy miles (which was the distance from London) in order to attend. More often than
not they did, although all that was on offer was a glass or
two of indifferent champagne and a stroll round Nudd.
The stroll was the draw, for Mrs Montacute had contrived that the house should enjoy all the celebrity it
deserved. At least she had contrived that it should enjoy
this so far as the moneyed classes were concerned. It was
not her policy to set up turnstiles and admit the populace
to her collection at so much a head. Her solicitor, Mr
Thurkle, had urged upon her that there is a good deal
more in civic benevolence of this kind than the mere
takings at the door, since if you submit to the discomforts
of living virtually in a public museum it is only just that
you should conceive yourself entitled to attract less tax-
ation than if you do not. Mrs Montacute was scarcely the
sort of woman who needed such matters explaining to
her. She had a good business head. Her policy, she pointed
out to her adviser, was one of exclusivity—a hideous word
the hinterland to which was her belief that the very
wealthiest Americans have a fondness for competing in
markets inaccessible and even unknown to common collectors. It was wholesome that such should be persuaded
that the mere entrée to Nudd was to be achieved only by
means of quasi-diplomatic representations made through
their Embassy in Grosvenor Square.

This was not one of the musical parties. The musical

parties were grander affairs, and happened about twice a year. Although not herself musical, Mrs Montacute was careful to ensure that the strains dispensed on these occasions were the best that the market could supply, and moreover it was a token of that flair for blending and matching and harmonizing beautiful things which Nudd everywhere made manifest that at the musical parties the quality of the champagne distinguishably went up. The function of the musical parties was to suggest that Nudd was a centre of aesthetic cultivation in the widest sense, or in the widest sense compatible with an overriding dedication to an élitest view of things in general. Parties like the present were simply designed as a reminder that when Nudd went under the hammer everybody with money to burn upon the altar of art would want to be there.

Lambert Domberg (who would certainly want to be there) drew his car to a halt on the brow of the hill. It was not that they were too early, for guests could be seen already wandering on the low mellow terrace which alone Nudd interposed between itself and the tranquil Evenlode. It was rather that, being accompanied by Octavius Chevalley, who had recently become an employee of his firm, it was his impulse to afford the young man a leisured view of what might be called a 'prospect' in more than one sense of the word. Had Satan condescended to be accompanied by a stripling aide-de-camp on his hazardous reconnaissance, it would have been thus that, pausing upon Mount Niphates, he would have pointed to the beckoning spoil below.

'A palace of art,' Domberg said. Except to those of his clients who might be disconcerted by it, Domberg seldom spoke without irony. In the firm it was understood that, being a scholar by training, he found the whole business of chaffering in masterpieces demeaning, and that it was a sensitive spirit which was defending itself in this way.

Nobody in the concern took offence. For one thing, Domberg was effectively the boss. For another, everybody was prosperous, and therefore tolerance was easy.

'I don't call it much of a palace,' Chevalley said. 'It's just a manor-house on rather a large scale.'

'If not a *palazzo*, a *palazzina*. Or, say, a *palazzotto*.' Dictionary patter of this sort was also characteristic of Domberg; Chevalley, who had put effort into learning Italian genuinely and well, didn't care for such paltry displays at all. 'It's all very compassable, no doubt,' Domberg went on concessively. 'But there's not much that isn't superb. A kind of Mauritshuis, say.'

'But surely not full of boring Dutchmen?' Chevalley was dismayed. 'Cuyp, and all that—globular women milking rectangular cows?'

'No, no. Simply the impression of things decidedly picked. The *salon carré* effect.'

'So I've heard.' Chevalley, who was not very much attending to these exchanges, fell silent as he studied Nudd Manor.

It was apple-pie all around and spick-and-span all over, as such places in the Cotswolds tend to be. Pitched at a just remove from the village over which it presided, its finely proportioned intricacies of buffy stone nevertheless gave the appearance of having generously broadcast the influence of their own high amenity. There were several other houses of some consequence and an equal antiquity, and in point of up-keep each might have been described as very consciously up-keeping with the others. Everywhere the lawns were velvety, the shrubs clipped, the trees (like not a few of their owners) assisted by unobtrusive surgery to preserve shapeliness into old age. The humbler dwellings—or those in which there had been some original intention of housing the industrious poor—were well-groomed rather than neat, and their little gardens had been gentrified as effectively as had their low

parlours, large-ovened kitchens, and garret bedrooms hazardous to the heads of all save dwarfs. The entire spectacle
was very much *en suite*, and viewed from a slight elevation
could thus be suggestive of the superior accommodations
of an ocean liner or the lounge of a large hotel. Alter-
natively, you might suppose that you were in the presence of an expensive toy, and that each of these smaller
architectural gems was pick-uppable, and fittable into or
around the main fabric of Nudd Manor itself—to the
achieving of something like a palace after all.

And the palace-image must, it seemed, have remained
in Chevalley's head.

'Your palace of art,' he asked, '—does it run to a high-
born maiden?'

'Ah, that's to get your poets mixed up, isn't it? But,
roughly speaking, yes. There's a daughter, although I
don't recall her name. I've had a mere glimpse of her, indeed.' Domberg made to drive on, and then thought better of it and produced a cigarette-case. 'But a mere glimpse
authenticates her maidenhood—or at least its extreme
probability. As for being high-born, that pitches it a little
steeply. Say respectably connected, like the rest of us, my
dear lad. And her late father, Nicholas Montacute,
achieved moderate affluence in the City.'

'Moderate? Then where did the money for all that
come from?' Asking this, Chevalley made a gesture designed to penetrate within Mrs Montacute's dwelling
rather than wave around it. 'Even if this woman has an
eye like a hawk, and phenomenal sensibility, and heaven
knows what training, and is an inspired snapper up—'

'All that is complete rot. I've forgotten if you smoke?'

For a moment Chevalley appeared to have forgotten too.
Then he shook his head.

'Thank you, no.... *Rot?*'

'Between you and me, yes. Our Mrs Montacute is an

aesthetic imbecile. There's no more crassly tasteless woman in England.'

'Then, dash it all—' Chevalley's tone signalled indignation as well as surprise. His companion had made quite a thing of having gained permission to present him to the chatelaine of Nudd. 'You mean she *isn't* what she's supposed to be—a genius who puts one pot beside another and achieves—'

'Absolute poppycock, but a useful piece of mythology. Increasingly, the collection as a whole becomes more valuable than the sum of its parts—because of this wand she waves over it all. Or, better than wand, say the finger of taste. Nudd as a going concern, a composed entity, might one day fetch the moon. One thinks of all sorts of possibilities. The University of Texas might buy it absolutely on the hoof—they probably go in for hooves in the largest way in Texas—as a rest-home for jaded professors.'

'I'm told the bottom is dropping out of that foreign campus racket. American universities are running short of cash.'

'True enough.' Domberg reinforced his agreement with a gesture. 'Still, the place has capabilities, as Mr Brown would have said.'

'The woman's on the make?'

'Tremendously. She is a culminating point in the whole shambles, my dear Octavius, to which your young life is beginning to dedicate itself.'

'Well, thank you for bringing me down. Mrs Montacute ought to be worth meeting.' Chevalley spoke cautiously, as if not sure how to regard a stance in the shambles so double-faced as that of his principal. 'And at least it's a nice day—and a pleasant scene.'

'Meaning a well-heeled scene,' Domberg said easily, and sent a puff of Turkish tobacco in the direction of Nudd and its demesne. 'But familiar enough, I suppose. Those little *rentiers'* paradises—you've been brought up to them, haven't you?'

'Anything Nudd-like *I've* known—and it was quite a bit, I agree—has all gone up the spout.' Chevalley laughed awkwardly. 'And no less vulgar phrase will do. Although my grandfather, as a matter of fact, was known in the family as the Grand Hypothecator.'

'Very amusing,' Domberg said—and added sourly: 'If you are to redeem his pledges by peddling pictures, you'll have to work damned hard.'

'Oh, I quite mean to do *that*. An eighth child, you know, decidedly confronts the world.' Chevalley stretched himself demonstratively—an exercise which the ample dimensions of Domberg's car made feasible as he sat. 'And now explain to me, please. If the late Nicholas Montacute was something short of a millionaire, and if his widow is as you say she is, how do we come to be confronted with what we *are* going to be confronted with when we run down this hill and up that dressy little drive? I'm all agog to know.'

'Nudd and its contents came to Mrs Montacute from an eccentric uncle—horribly eccentric, he appears to have been, but savingly wealthy as well. He'd travelled, and he'd collected—intelligently and pertinaciously, and with no shrinking from writing what, for the period, must have seemed pretty big cheques. Then he got it into his head that his niece had married a man of taste.'

'Had she?'

'In a very limited way, yes. Nicholas Montacute was of a type still much around, and which you will be meeting up with often enough. He had a fancy for the sale-rooms, and for being known there, and known by people like ourselves. He'd pick things up, and get the hang of them, and then pick up a few more. There must have been some faint grace in him, I'd suppose, although I doubt whether he'll be accounted more than a straight Philistine at the Last Trump. It was probably to people on golf-courses that he boasted of the last bit of Limoges, or the last Tompion, or the last Palmer or Varley or whatever, that he'd sunk money in.'

'How awful! And his wife's eccentric uncle was taken in?'

'Apparently so. Hugo Counterpayne—that was his name —left the Montacutes Nudd and all the art stuff—and nothing else. To a nephew, Cedric Counterpayne, his only other relation, he left a considerably more substantial fortune in the prosaic form of stocks and shares. But since then, the objects you will presently be admiring must have increased in value by ten or twentyfold, whereas the other fortune is averred to have done not too well. There's said to be family dissension as a result. But that's no concern of ours.'

'Obviously not. And the Montacutes hung on? They didn't realize on their windfall?'

'Not on a single scrap of it, so far as anybody knows. Just an occasional astute addition here and there.'

'It must have come uncommonly expensive.'

'It must, indeed. She's a strong-minded woman.'

'Was he a strong-minded man?'

'That's improbable. Mrs Montacute master-minded the thing. Or mistress-minded it.' Domberg paused on this joke, and appeared not to approve of it. 'Of course they had only one child: your high-born maiden. *She* probably wasn't all that expensive. And then, before Nicholas Montacute could get restive, he died.'

'The stuff being legally all his wife's?'

'Certainly. No death-duties yet—which is why everything is still intact in the house down there.'

'Well, *she*'ll have to die. How old is she?'

'Not nearly old enough to make the fact of her mortality particularly interesting. Moreover, it isn't her plan. Too unspectacular to attract her, I'd say.'

'Dying? Then what *is* her plan?'

'Selling out—at the top of the market. She studies it like mad. And does all this'—Domberg eyed the guests on the distant terrace—'in the interest of the projected exercise.'

'Have you much of a notion of what it would knock down at now?'

'I'd suppose it would top the three million mark.'

A statement like this is liable to produce silence. Chevalley's lips discernibly rounded, indeed, as if it was his intention to offer a low whistle. But he opted for the more restrained effect of elevating his eyebrows.

'But the insurance!' he presently said. 'If there *is* insurance.'

'Quite so. And the woman is said to have pinched and scraped. It has become a consuming passion with her.'

'But not of the high aesthetic kind?'

'There *is* almost something aesthetic about it.' Domberg paused, and switched on his engine. 'Because of its purity,' he added gnomically.

'Is it all because of her daughter, would you say?' A fresh aspect of the matter appeared to have struck Chevalley with some force. 'Mrs Montacute is determined to make the high-born maiden a great heiress?'

'The child must be called that already—provided she is to inherit all this wealth, whether in one form or another. But I suppose Mrs Montacute can do what she likes with it. And as to the extent of her devotion to the girl, I just don't know. One doesn't see how holding on—holding *out*, as it pretty well is—will be of much ultimate practical advantage to anybody. It's a matter of pride, it seems to me. The Nudd sale is going to mark the very crest of the wave. After that, the deluge.'

Having achieved this somewhat confused water-imagery, Domberg slipped into gear and drove down the hill.

As he drove down, a girl walked up. She might compassionately have been called a stoutly-framed girl—so stoutly-framed that it was surprising she tackled the acclivity as buoyantly as she did. When she paused momentarily—as she was observed to do now—it was for the purpose, not of taking breath, but of disentangling a double leash of juvenile fox-hounds surrounding her. She must be puppy-walking, Octavius Chevalley thought—thus recalling, dimly beyond an urban adolescence, a childhood in some contact with rural pursuits. The activity made her, he conjectured, a red-faced daughter of a red-faced gentry—and not, as her general *tenue* might suggest, the equally red-faced daughter of some boor or hind.

This social discrimination was, no doubt, insignificant, but may have been in Domberg's mind too when he made rather a ceremonious business of slowing his car to a crawl. The girl struggled with her canine charges, among whom some indiscipline appeared to have broken out. She cursed them heartily, and seconded this with physical exertions and contortions which made her, for the time, chiefly a spectacle of generous gluteal muscles sheathed in faded jeans. She straightened up, to reveal her high complexion as balanced by light blue eyes, almost flaxen hair, and a flash of teeth not merely perfect but deserving to be called imposing as well. Chevalley found himself in imagination stripping off the jeans and everything else on the spot. That this state of mind was not lascivious in intention appeared in the fact that he immediately dowered the pinkish object thus conjured up with a tiara, several pearl necklaces, and an answeringly pinkish cloud upon which to perch. The result might have been a spectacle thrown on canvas or ceiling by Rubens himself. It was at least more agreeable than a globular milkmaid by Cuyp.

The girl with the puppies waved the car on, decisively and with a hint of impatience which she apparently saw no need to dissimulate. Chevalley, although his own glance at her had been a little too amused, was disappointed at not seeming to receive the briefest glance in return. She was, after all, an abounding Flanders mare of a wench. Domberg offered her a grave salute. The car purred decorously past. The six puppies yelped at it derisively.

'Well, there you are,' Domberg said. 'You've seen her.'

'The village Juno? Or one of Diana's nymphs alarmed, and about to produce a thundering displacement in a forest pool?'

'The daughter, Octavius. Your high-born maiden from her palace-tower. And now I remember what she's called. Gloria. Gloria Montacute.'

'What a God-awful name!'

Domberg responded to this consciously coarse ejaculation with a curious glance. In a not particularly interesting way—he reflected—there was something slightly problematic about Chevalley. Perhaps he hadn't coped too well with what a current jargon called the identity-crisis of adolescence. Certainly he did at times appear to dislike himself, although at other times he could be rather amusing. And to dislike oneself struck Domberg as an incomprehensible folly—particularly in one who has been fortunate enough to secure a job in a first-rate firm. So Domberg followed his swift look with a disapproving silence. They had passed through the gates of Nudd Manor before he spoke.

'She's cutting her mother's party,' he said. 'What do we learn from that?'

2

HARRY CARTER'S THREE-PIECE SUITE

GLORIA CONTINUED TO climb, first up the dusty secondary road and then, when she had passed through a field-gate, across deserted pasture towards a hazel spinney. The puppies, unconscious of the serious pursuits to which their adult lives were to be devoted in such surroundings, circled and tumbled innocently at her feet. It was late afternoon but the day had been hot; it was still warm even in the airy beech-wood beyond the hazels; had a forest pool indeed presented itself, Gloria might have been tempted to plunge, hounds and all. As it was, she strode straight through, to emerge upon a stretch of bare hill, down-like in character, upon the ridge of which stood a ruined barn.

It was the first untidy object her path had encountered. At one end a stretch of battered brick and mortar survived, but in the main it had been a weatherboard and thatch structure, and this—whether accidentally or in an exuberance of rural malice—had at some late period been burnt down. An oblong of charred uprights suggested the carious maw of a prehistoric monster of the wold— or perhaps, to a more exotic imagination, the surviving evidences of a minor *auto-da-fé*. This latter fancy would have been supported by the appearance here and there of bits and pieces of abandoned agricultural machinery suggestive of preliminary torments conscientiously carried out. What might have been tightly faggoted fuel for the godly bonfire was effectively represented by cubes of straw, gathered and compacted by ingenious mechanical means, but then abandoned in disordered heaps like the build-

ing-blocks of a bored child. Some of these had been shifted since Gloria's last visit here. They had been formed
into a semi-circular breastwork as if by an imagination
having cowboys and Indians in mind, or perhaps with the
more practical object of commanding the approaches to
the place from a view-point itself concealed. Gloria was
directing upon this innovation a thoughtful regard when
a figure rose up behind the barricade and vaulted it. The
figure was that of a young man.

'There, now!' the young man said. He spoke as if re-
suming an argument from a moment before. 'You've
come.'

'And so have you, Harry.'

'Of course I have. Although I had a chance, as a matter
of fact, of playing for the Fifteen.'

'Then it was stupid of you not to take it.' If the young
man called Harry had expected approbation or gratitude
he was disappointed. 'It's pretty good—being asked to
play for your college in your first term.'

'Even a grotty agricultural college?'

'Don't be silly. I'll bet you could give any Oxford college
points. And you'll feel a fool if they find somebody else.
There's only one full back in a rugger team.'

'Oh, I expect they'd let me shove in the scrum. I can
shove quite hard when I want to.'

'I expect you can.' Gloria regarded her rural admirer—
for it was this that Harry Carter might be called—attentively. He was her own age, the younger son of the tenant
of the manor farm, and had been one of the facts of life
—although not an absorbing fact—during the couple of
years in which he had doggedly worked to get his college
entrance. Having gained it, he had gained confidence as
well—so that one didn't know in what direction he
mightn't now show rather more of the quality than he
ought to. This made Harry interesting, as did his having lately grown quite as much a man as his elder brother.

Gloria could remember peeping through a hedge (for she had a country girl's habits) and seeing the elder brother get some sort of wrestler's grip on Harry and push his head into a cattle trough. This exciting event wouldn't happen again. Or, if it did, it would be the other way round. On this hot September afternoon Harry had rolled up his shirt-sleeves to the armpits, and beneath the skin, golden-bronze as barley, his muscles rippled pleasingly. 'But you must go on being a full back, all the same,' Gloria said seriously. 'You must practise your place-kicking like any-thing. Particularly from near touch and on your awkward side. It's what counts most of all in the end.' Gloria paused, and saw that Harry was accepting this counsel attentively; indeed, he was looking at her with the brightest interest. This gratified her very much. Although not a visionary girl, she suddenly saw him at Twickenham, bringing off the vital conversion in the last fifteen seconds of the match. Against France, she decided—for there was an ad-ditional and patriotic glory in that, absent from merely defeating Scotland or Wales.

'Come and sit down,' Harry was saying. 'These bales are quite dry, and I've made a kind of sofa out of them.' He held out a reassuringly brotherly hand. 'A couple of chairs too, as a matter of fact.'

'That's very industrious of you.' Gloria wondered what she would have found to say if Harry's second announce-ment had been: 'And a perfectly enormous double bed.' She knew, but did not approve, several young men who would run to a joke like that. Harry didn't make venture-some conversation. It wasn't, she suspected, his conception of going seriously to work.

But now Harry was looking not at her but at the puppies. They had flopped down on the straw-strewn floor of the barn, and two or three of them were putting on an ostentatious turn as deserving canines in distress. Their

tongues lolled out and their fat little tummies were behaving like bellows.

'Humbugs,' Harry said. 'But they'd do with a drink—
a small one—all the same.'

'No water.'

'Yes, there is. I got the ball-cock working in that rusty
trough outside. Had a wash, as a matter of fact.' Harry
held out, with conscious pride, remarkably clean hands.
'An old pannikin, too. Just half a jiffy.'

Harry vanished from the barn—or round the corner of
what remained of it—so that Gloria was virtuously left
deserted in favour of a job of work that ought to be done.
She didn't know whether this was engaging in Harry, or
merely clever. There was a clatter and a swish of water—
and then he was back, laughing and triumphant, with the
brimming pannikin balanced before him. For a moment
there seemed to be a great deal of sunlight in his hair.
He'd taken to wearing his hair student-length, and it too
gave the effect of a very recent wash. Gloria studied him
appraisingly as he stooped among the puppies and
straightened up again. Twickenham was still in her mind.
Harry's shoulders were broad but not heavy. His hips were
admirably slim.

He in turn, she saw, studied her. Under a fallen lock of
the hair—dark chestnut hair—his dark eyes were very
bright. She wasn't able to suppose that he was visualizing
her in any situation, appropriate to her sex, which at all
corresponded to an international rugger match. But at
least Harry's gaze didn't give, somehow, the effect of a
stare. And now he had turned away again, walked across
to his schoolboy stockade, and was peering over it with
all the caution that an expected cloud of redskin arrows
might prompt.

'Not a soul in sight,' Harry announced decisively. 'Come
on.'

The sofa and twin chairs were a fact, and the effect was rather touchingly domestic. Being built up out of cubes of straw, they had the appearance of the sort of 'three-piece suite', chunky and over-stuffed, displayed in the windows of cheap furniture shops. Gloria liked them at once. There was nothing of the kind at Nudd. And the whole effort was an unexpected flight of fantasy on Harry's part.

'Sit down,' Harry commanded, and Gloria sat down—on the sofa because it might hurt Harry's feelings if she chose one of the chairs. The action unfortunately hurt *her*, since jeans are very inadequate protection against the spiky assault that baled straw can contrive. But she bore this stoically, and a wriggle presently caused the agony to abate. Harry sat down beside her, at what appeared to be a precisely—indeed, premeditatedly—calculated interval of eighteen inches. And for this a motive appeared at once. He reached behind him and produced a paper bag. 'I brought you some chocolates,' he said with satisfaction; and from the bag produced a sizeable box. Gloria saw that Harry was not a sophisticated purchaser of such things. Quantity rather than quality had been his idea. But now, without the idle preliminary ceremony of handing her his handsome gift, he tugged the box open and set it down between them. 'Have one of the round ones,' Harry ordered.

Gloria, although she knew she oughtn't to eat chocolates, had one of the round ones. Harry, remarking that for every couple of chocolates he ate it was easy to do a fast quarter-mile, took a round one too.

'Oh, Gloria!' Harry suddenly exclaimed. 'Gloria, you are the most gorgeous girl!'

Harry had given 'girl' a rustic roll of the tongue so attractive that Gloria didn't at all resent the fact that this spontaneous outburst was a rehearsed effect. The mere alliteration would have told one that—in addition to which (she reflected sagely) Harry Carter would never make much of an actor. So now she didn't merely take another chocolate she didn't particularly want. She spoke with marked kindness as well.

'Harry, dear, don't be an ass. And tell me about things. Is it very hard work?'

'Oh, I don't mind *that*!' Harry, if checked, was cheerful. 'There are a couple of idiots from public schools, and half a dozen chaps from higher up their grammar schools than I ever got. But they've got no practical know-how. They wouldn't know a pig's behind if you shoved it at them.' Harry paused in self-appreciation. This was about as far in coarse speech as he would go with a girl like Gloria, he appeared to be saying—and it was a bond between them that he could go so far. 'So I expect I'll make do.'

'I'm sure you will. But what about after that? Is there any chance of getting a farm?'

'Not an earthly. I'd need forty thousand flat.'

'I suppose that *is* rather a lot of money.'

'I suppose it is.' Harry gave a satiric laugh, and accompanied it with a mocking glance. This struck Gloria as quite a complicated response from so simple a youth.

'What about the manor farm? If my mother—'

'Your ma could do nothing about it, my dear. Any of my father's sons will have a title to the tenancy. But Ted's the eldest and Ted will take it. I could wring his bloody neck.'

'I suppose so.' Gloria, of course, didn't really suppose so at all. She was astonished by a sentiment so lacking in fraternal regard. Here was just another of the gaps between Harry's world and her own.

'So it sounds like Australia, my dear.' Harry had taken a fancy to this form of address. He probably thought of it as affectionate without being familiar. 'A wonderful country, some say. A man came and talked about it at the Young Farmers. With ciné-films.'

'Shouldn't you need that forty thousand there too?'

'I've got an uncle well established on the land. He'd see me in. Hard work, of course. But I'm up to that.' For the moment, Harry's voice had the ring of perfect truth. 'Gloria, do you think you'd like Australia?'

'I don't know enough about it to say.'

'Gloria, dear, if you and I—'

'No, Harry. It isn't sensible.'

Harry was silent, as if really dashed. One of the puppies appeared to have resumed panting. Only it wasn't the puppy. It was Harry himself, to whose breathing something was happening. Gloria reflected on whether she ought to feel alarmed.

'Take the big one in the middle,' Harry said in a perceptibly changed voice.

'No, thank you.' Gloria had looked at the big one in the middle and judged that it would be full of unpalatable marzipan. 'I don't think I want another just at the moment.'

'Do as you're told.'

This was Harry going into a routine. The sequence was masculine command, feminine disobedience, masculine discipline. It wasn't exactly sadistic, she supposed. It was just that Harry's notions of courtship, being what her mother would have called plebeian, included a kind of skylarking rough-and-tumble. The ritual had amused and excited her once or twice, although Harry's hand was heavier than he knew. But she wasn't going to dig it again now, or perhaps again ever. So she stopped him, not by dodging (since she knew there was no eluding Harry's lightning grab) but with a straight look.

'We're not kids, Harry.' She said this by way of easing the situation, but for some moments Harry didn't respond. He looked first baffled and furious and then sheepish and awkward, so that she wondered if she liked him in the least. After this, however, he grinned cheerfully, picked up the big middle chocolate, bit it in half, and held up the other half to her mouth.

'Halves,' Harry said, and watched with alert pleasure as Gloria's notable teeth accepted this token of peace. Then he threw himself back on the sofa (demolishing a large part of it in the process) in an admirable posture of relaxed ease, so that Gloria did for a moment find herself wondering whether he was not a bit of an actor after all. He cocked his thumbs into the band of his breeches and spread his fingers over a belly as flat as a shove-halfpenny board. Down this vista, and from beneath a further tumble of chestnut hair, he contrived to gaze at Gloria with the lazy satisfaction that a man might bend upon a submissive six months' bride. 'What's on at the big house?' he asked. 'Another of your ma's parties?'

'Why do you insist on calling my mother my ma?'

'To make fun of you, my dear.' Harry's laugh was that of one who has regained control of a situation. 'A party for looking at all those pictures and things?'

'Yes, of course. All our parties are like that. I was passed by some of the people coming up. In a car, I mean. A man who buys and sells pictures, whose name I forget. And a younger one with him.' Gloria was not clear why she was going into all this. 'The younger one didn't see I was looking at him. But *he* was looking at *me*—'

'He had no business to be looking at you at all. But just *how* was he looking at you?'

'As if I was a ludicrous spectacle, I suppose.'

'Just point him out to me some time, Gloria, and I'll belt him till he snivels.'

'And won't that be gay?' It came into Gloria's head as she made this mocking response that Harry meant what he said. She wasn't clear about him as a husband, but he would make a good guard dog. 'I'll have to be going back,' she said—and as she spoke stood up and looked down at him. His shirt was open over a small dark nipple, and there were coils of dark hair on his chest. 'Walk down with me,' she said. 'You can take one lot of those tiresome animals.'

From his supine and super-extended position upon the straw, and without moving a leg an inch or stirring his thumbs from their negligent cache, Harry in slow motion came upright at the hips. It was childish, Gloria thought, to be so proud of one's belly muscles. Or perhaps not. To enjoy thus possessing oneself—and in ways that would stop happening when one ceased to be young—was perhaps more sensible than to enjoy possessing a whole palaceful of *objets d'art*.

They walked downhill together, Gloria carrying the chocolates. Harry shouted at the puppies like a huntsman, or whistled the airs of popular songs. These activities were designed to give the impression that all was well, and that nothing had failed to go as he wanted it. Gloria, since she was inclined to be in love with Harry, felt disturbed by the small extent to which she trusted him. She wondered whether he had already enjoyed successes with village girls. Something—it was perhaps again a matter of that indefinable possessing of himself—hinted to her that he had. Quite possibly, and with a healthy instinct to be trading up, he had put her next on his list.

Gloria was ashamed of this crude thought, and startled that Harry had stopped whistling at the very moment it occurred to her. It was part of his being rather splendidly an animal that intuitive things seemed to happen inside his head. This had nothing to do with intelligence. Harry, she had estimated, was a little brainier than she was—but he could be that without its amounting to much. She was at least clear-headed about him to *that* extent. And now, when he spoke, it might definitely have been to mark his sense of her social remove.

'Oughtn't you to have stopped for the party, Gloria, and

helped your ma to entertain her guests? In your position in the county, you have responsibilities.' Harry appeared to have adopted this terminology quite seriously. 'Although it's awfully nice of you to come and talk to me instead.'

'I don't think we have a position in the county, exactly. It's mostly townees.'

'And now you insist on being a townee yourself. Why don't you live at home for a bit, my dear? I would, if I had a place like Nudd.'

'One ought to earn a living.'

'You don't even come home every week-end.'

'I'm on duty some week-ends.'

'I don't understand this job. It seems funny, with your education.'

'Harry, I just didn't have a proper education, as you had. It was fairly expensive, I expect. But what it came to was damn-all.'

'Accomplishments,' Harry said, with a glint of humour. 'But I still don't see why you need be a tea lady.'

'It's rather good. I meet all sorts.'

'Who do you dish it out to, anyway?' There was now a pleasing hint of jealousy in Harry's voice. 'Medical students? Young doctors?'

'Sometimes. But just to anybody who'll take it, really. Patients, nurses, visitors, cleaners. And particularly the men in the morgue. It seems to be awfully thirsty work, washing corpses.'

Harry, who wouldn't have turned aside from slaughtering swine, made a disgusted noise. He was genuinely shocked.

'But you can't go *on*!' he exclaimed. 'Not at a thing like that.'

'Oh, I'm thinking of a change. I could become a lollipop lady, and see kids over crossings. It's a more open-air life.'

Harry fell silent. Perhaps he was wondering whether

the theme of an open-air life might be developed so as to
re-introduce the subject of emigration to Australia. Or
perhaps he was just feeling that his tryst with Gloria was
over, and that he was down by the price of a large box
of chocolates.

'It looks as if I shan't be back even for the tail-end of
it,' Gloria said, and came to a halt. Nudd Manor was now
in full view below them, sunlit but surrounded by length-
ening shadows. 'They're calling it a day—earlier than
they usually do. Perhaps the champagne's run out.'

'Champagne?' Harry echoed. He was impressed.

Gloria made no reply. The puppies, impatient to be
returned to their kennel and enjoy some evening refection, yelped idiotically. Faintly up the hill came the sound
of a single car clumsily changing gear. But moving down
the drive, rather slowly, was a whole file of cars: big
cars mostly, but with a little one here and there. One of
the big ones she seemed to recognize as the impressive
affair that had brought to Nudd the superior young man
whom Harry, at some future time, was going to belt until
he snivelled. And now the first of the line of cars, passing
through the lodge gates, rapidly and as if in obscure relief
picked up speed on the high road, leaving a cloud of dust
behind it.

'Harry, come with me.' Gloria, who had been glancing
at her follower's face, heard herself with surprise utter this
command or invitation. 'Guise will have a bottle or two
hidden away. We'll find one.'

'But would you say I'm presentable?' There was naïve
astonishment in Harry Carter's voice, and his eyes were
sparkling in a way that would have done credit to the
promised Nudd champagne. 'I've never—'

'There are straws in your hair. Apart from that, you're
all right.' Gloria had looked Harry up and down, thus
firmly delimiting the nature of the presentability at issue.
'So let's hurry back.'

3

WALKING ROUND
WITH MRS MONTACUTE

CHEVALLEY HAD HEARD about the fountain—her *fontana minore*, Mrs Montacute liked to call it by way of a side-glance at its big brother in Perugia—so at least he was prepared for that. It was planted bang in the middle of the hall at Nudd, and what ought first to have struck one, no doubt, was the incongruity of such an appearance in a Tudor manor-house. But in whichever of three directions one looked—and three vistas did notably radiate from it—the small complex achievement somehow remained in perfect keeping with its background.

Waiting to pay his respects to his hostess, whose agreeable custom it was to receive her guests beside this valuable possession, Chevalley recalled Domberg's assurance that the *fontana minore* had recently been most rigorously researched, and that several of the figures were attested as Nicola Pisano's without a doubt. So it was quite a prize to have in one's pocket. Somebody had stolen it, one gathered, from many-fountained Viterbo, but too many centuries ago to make its recovery by a despoiled municipality a viable proposition.

'Considerable subtlety of design,' Domberg was saying. Indoors, he spoke in a rather loud but confidently well-bred voice. 'Notice, Octavius, that whereas the lower basin is a twenty-sided polygon, the upper basin has nine sides and not ten. As a consequence, it is a perfect example of Op art—something that young people believe themselves to have invented a few years ago. But, of course, all art is Op. It *involves*, my dear lad: And here, you see, because of this twenty-and-nine relationship, one is constantly edged round the thing in quest of a visual symmetry that isn't there. Delightful. Very delightful. Only we shan't ourselves be able to circumambulate it at the moment, because of the stance the good lady has taken up.'

'It ought to give the place the air of a museum at once.' Chevalley spoke in a voice more discreetly lowered than that of his principal. In the apprenticeship which he was undergoing it seemed to be expected of him that he should learn to conduct much of his conversation through the medium of what used, he supposed, to be called persiflage. 'A fountain's an absurd object to be asked to hang one's hat and coat on. It's playing, too! Or at least dripping. One feels one ought to open one's umbrella—not abandon it.'

'Ah, yes—but then you can't, in this day and age, thrust the labours of the Pisani and their kind into the garden among the plastic dwarfs and china gnomes.'

'Are there plastic dwarfs and china gnomes?'

'It wouldn't surprise me to hear that the late Nicholas Montacute had picked a few up from time to time. And there are numerous nineteenth-century terra-cottas from L'Impruneta, which is pretty well the same thing.'

'What you called the finger of taste is certainly evident.' Chevalley was peering beyond the fountain. 'Vigorously stirring in every pie.'

'Yes, Octavius—but whose finger of taste? There is a small mystery there. It cannot be the poor lady's. Remark her attire.'

Chevalley remarked Mrs Montacute's attire—cautiously, since it was now no more than a yard away. He and Domberg were, in fact, next in the short line of the later arrivals. Mrs Montacute (whose dress was certainly striking rather than felicitous) had elected to converse at some length with a Japanese gentleman who was bowing vigorously over her every sentence. Domberg seemed not im-

patient; he regarded the spectacle with complacency;
nothing of late years had been more gratifying, after all,
than the bobbing up (and down) in the sale-rooms of
London of industrial magnates from the Orient disposed
to collect in a big way.

'Hakagawa'—Domberg quoted, wittily if much too
loudly—'bowing among the Titians.' And then he was
himself bowing over Mrs Montacute's hand. 'You wave
your wand,' he said gaily, 'and Nudd is around me once
more. How very, very kind! And this is my young colleague, Octavius Chevalley, whom you have been so
gracious as to allow me to bring along.'

Mrs Montacute was a handsome woman. On this particular afternoon, being keyed up for her party, it is possible that she was looking even more handsome than
usual. Anyone wishing to hint a critical note in describing her might have murmured that dear Fenella was
almost obtrusively in rude health. Her daughter had inherited her complexion and, for that matter, her teeth,
but not her boldly cut and somewhat masculine features.
These Mrs Montacute chose to accentuate by wearing
spectacles massively framed in what could be called a
board-room taste, and jewellery which, although genuinely
barbaric and Scythian in origin, might have been more
readily conceived as draped round Tamburlane than Zeno-
crate. She had large hands, and the habit of holding them
out slightly in front of her thighs—thus presenting the
appearance of a lady wrestler or of a piece of outmoded
sculpture of the Epstein era: this according to the particular cultural context one brought to her.

'You shall walk round with me,' she said to Chevalley,
when she had dismissed his companion until some later
moment.

'That's awfully kind of you.'

'Nothing of the sort. Everybody new walks round with

me. Did I hear you say something about the Titians?'

'Oh, no! That was Lambert Domberg.' Chevalley was alarmed. 'He was quoting *Gerontion*.'

'Gerontion?' Mrs Montacute glanced suspiciously at her guest. 'I never heard of him. I can't believe that he is any sort of authority on Titian.'

'T. S. Eliot's *Gerontion*.' Chevalley attempted this piece of sorting out not too hopefully.

'I don't see that his being the protégé of an American poet can affect the matter.'

'No, of course not.' Chevalley would almost have liked to feel he was being made fun of. Nudd as aesthetic *tour de force* was now all around him, and there was something monstrous in the thought that its guardianship was in the hands—the great hammy hands—of a totally moronic woman. 'I think you have two Titians?'

'Yes, I have—and very troublesome they are.'

'Troublesome?' Chevalley felt his head begin to swim. Mrs Montacute might have been speaking of a couple of valuable but hopelessly over-bred and delicate dogs.

'Certainly. Titian wouldn't have kept his place in a decent Rotary Club a twelvemonth. "Self not Service"— that was Titian. No ethical standards whatever. He marketed as his own—complete with signature—no end of pictures he had never touched. But there were others just as bad. Signorelli—I've had trouble with him. Not with Raphael, but that's probably only because I don't possess a Raphael. I wouldn't touch a Raphael. Could you believe it! He signed a Madonna he'd simply had painted by Giulio Romano. And you know about *him*.'

'Giulio? Well, he's mentioned by Shakespeare.'

'He may be mentioned by T. S. Eliot, for all I care.' Mrs Montacute gave this the effect of withering repartee. 'Giulio was a painter of straight porn—for cardinals and people of that sort. Raphael, who had a wholly reputable line in Madonnas and Saints and Donors, ought to have been ashamed of himself for associating with such a shady person.' Mrs Montacute paused. 'And don't suppose, young man, that I can't give you what you people call references. *The Study and Criticism of Italian Art. Second Series. Rudiments of Connoisseurship. By—*'

'Yes, of course.' Early Berenson, Chevalley reflected, was not exactly up to date. But it was evident that the woman did, in a brutal way, know her onions. And *that* was just the right expression for it. Domberg had not exaggerated. Mrs Montacute regarded her treasures as a greengrocer's wife would regard the coarsest of her marketable commodities.

'And here the Titians are,' Mrs Montacute said.

Chevalley surveyed the Titians. They weren't large Titians, but they were by no means small. They weren't excessively famous, but they were undoubtedly important: Chevalley recalled how often bits and pieces of them were reproduced for learned purposes. Unless Mrs Montacute's Titian-trouble was bad Titian-trouble— which he didn't believe—just these two pictures alone would account for a large dollop of Domberg's notional three million pounds. He decided to say something bald and professional to this effect.

'The brace of them would knock down for a pretty packet,' he said—and at once wanted to retract so gross a turn of phrase.

'Unless somebody started whispering.' Mrs Montacute was unoffended. 'And Titian's credibility *is* a worry, one has to admit. It's like those showy companies with a bunch of directors you don't somehow hear much of elsewhere. A little invested in a quarter like that is all very well; you sometimes take quite a profit even if there's trouble brewing. But it unbalances a portfolio if you go in at all deep in that way.'

Chevalley nodded agreement with this proposition—or, rather, bowed agreement, since he was picking up the

archaic graces that went with his trade. He then trans-
ferred his attention from the Titians (he was constantly
seeing such things, after all) to adjacent aspects of what
might be called the Nudd portfolio. 'Balance' was certainly
the appropriate word for it. For example, and to an instructed eye, not much less remarkable than these two
canvases themselves was the richness and incredible pre-
servation of the Venetian velvet with which the wall behind
them was hung. And indeed, as soon as you got out of the
lofty hall—stripped to its stone in the interest of com-
posing with the *fontana minore*—you were everywhere
conscious of backgrounds of fabulous stuffs. Not of tap-
estries, which are boring things, but of subtly figured,
napped, damasked, shot, brocaded fabrics of the sort
which, because perishable, is priceless when it survives.
These backcloths were, for the most part, sombrely toned.
Against them the fine cabinets were insubstantial, were
ghostly except where sparely picked out in gold, so that
the glowing, smouldering, gleaming porcelains and
enamels they guarded seemed to float like mysterious
chalices, holy grails, in air. It came to Octavius Chevalley,
as upon a sudden note of sobriety, that Nudd was not a
joke. It was only this absurd woman who was that. And
the widow of the late modestly prosperous Nicholas Montacute wouldn't be around for ever. But much—even if
unhappily not all—of what she presided over was as nearly
imperishable as made no matter.

Not that there was anything about Mrs Montacute to
suggest imminent demise. On the contrary, she was growing upon Chevalley as a creature of preternatural vitality.
There was something sinister about it. It was as if she
battened, vampire-like, upon the aesthetic essences around
her to what would be an ultimate effect of leaving Nudd
an exhausted vial, an empty shell, and herself some hideous
extreme in the mere exuberance of the flesh.

This was a fantasy so pleasingly macabre that it distracted Chevalley's attention from the actual presence and conversation of his hostess, and it was abruptly that he became aware of her as asking him in what his present interest lay. He had a wild thought of replying 'Your daughter'—which would at least have been true to the extent that the fat girl with the puppies had lodged herself as a curiously disturbing image in his consciousness. But being a circumspect young man, he switched on his modesty-persona and explained that, although the Venetian *cinquecento* was his chief interest, he had lately been endeavouring to improve himself in the field of ceramics.

'Excellent!' There was a sudden warmth of approbation in Mrs Montacute's voice. 'A thoroughly sound choice. A most rewarding sector. Really amazing growth. I must show you my top camel—a quite exceptionally large camel.'

'You have a camel that's been growing amazingly?' Vaguely in Chevalley's mind was the confused notion that Mrs Montacute must run her artistic treasure-house in double harness with a private zoo.

'A T'ang camel. Size is very important in T'ang camels. Whereas with things like Tou Ts'ai chicken cups it's quite the other way: the smaller they are, the better—rather as with toy dogs. But, as I was saying, the overall growth-rate in oriental ceramics at present is most gratifying to anybody with large holdings. Particularly Sung. I am thankful to say I have several Ju and Kuan pieces from the imperial kilns. Blue chips, if ever there were any.'

'Blue chips—?' It was a moment before Chevalley recalled that this was not a technical term in the discussion of Chinese pots. 'But yes, of course. Most impregnable investments. I congratulate you.'

'Oriental painting, now, is quite a different matter. And particularly the Chinese. Wang Meng has been a great disappointment to me. And so have my river scenes by Wu Pin. Wu Pin is absolutely stagnant.'

'I'm very sorry to hear it. But of course, despite Heracleitus, one can't expect everything to flow all the time.'

'And now you must see the ikons.' Mrs Montacute had ignored or failed to comprehend Chevalley's brilliant joke, and this naturally disappointed him. 'Ikons have been very active of late, as you know. Several may be said to have worked miracles—chiefly in New York.'

Having communicated this surprising piece of thaumaturgical intelligence, Mrs Montacute led the way through several apartments to a farther corner of Nudd. Here and there she indicated to perambulating guests—mainly through the bold flourishing of a champagne glass—her resolute intention of conversing with them ere long. Chevalley, although he felt proper gratification at being kept so firmly in tow, found himself inwardly acknowledging that a modicum of artistic discussion with his hostess went quite a long way. As a consequence, when the Byzantine aspect of the portfolio had been honoured, he ventured to strike out a line of his own.

'I'm sorry not to have had the pleasure of meeting Miss Montacute,' he said. 'Domberg pointed her out to me as we were driving up. She seemed to be marching off with her dogs.'

For long enough to disconcert one so self-conscious as Chevalley, Mrs Montacute made no reply to this. Perhaps she was marking a legitimate sense of impertinence in this young man's hinted amusement at having detected a decamping daughter. Or perhaps her mind had merely drifted back to brood darkly over the gelid Wu Pin. When she did speak, however, it was in a conciliatory tone.

'I hope Gloria may have returned before our guests leave. When she is at home I encourage her to be as much in the open air as possible. Unfortunately there are many week-ends in which she has to remain in London. Gloria is quite devoted to her hospital.'

'Is she a nurse?' It didn't seem probable to Chevalley that the florid and lumbering, if curiously haunting, madonna of the fox-hounds was a rising young lady doctor.

'Gloria's responsibilities,' Mrs Montacute said, 'are on the catering side.'

4

ENTER A DISTRIBUTIST AND
EXIT A COLLECTOR

DOMBERG WANDERED ROUND by himself. Although
acquainted with many of his fellow guests, he had no
present wish for their conversation, and he therefore in-
timated that kind of aesthetic abstraction which nicely
bred people know must not be broken in upon. His head,
slightly inclined to one side as he studied Titian's rough
satyrs wooing nymphs in shady places, or as he estimated
the unsatisfactoriness of the wretched Wang Meng, might
have been one of those notices which hotels provide to be
hung on door-knobs with the injunction *Do not disturb*.
Or (in a figure more appropriate to Nudd) he might have
been murmuring the musical Italian equivalent of this—
Però non me destar—which Michelangelo imagines as
proceeding from the marble lips of Night in the New
Sacristy of San Lorenzo.

Mrs Montacute didn't run to anything by Michelangelo,
but she ran to the devil of a lot. It was borne in upon
Domberg that even three million was an underestimate
of the likely knock-down total one day to be achieved at
the great Nudd sale. It wasn't so much a matter of the
really major things—the Titians and the Velazquez and
the tremendous La Tour—as of the innumerable articles
of vertu which the luck of the draw seemed almost invariably to have brought out at the top of their class.
Domberg held that sort of bric-à-brac in no very high
regard. He had a special expression of amused disdain,
indeed, for those marks of high authenticity at times triumphantly discoverable on the underside of old plates.
Still, in an age in which a soup-tureen might fetch more

than your grandfather would have given for a Rembrandt or a Claude, it was not for a prudent man altogether to neglect such matters. So Domberg peered about him with care. He reminded himself, moreover, that even a mania for collecting soup-tureens was meritorious—always provided that, within a reasonable number of years, the collector tired of his treasures, sold up, and started in on something else. It is only public-spirited conduct of this sort, after all, that keeps art going.

But in this regard there was plainly nothing to expect, so far as Fenella Montacute was concerned. A glance at the old girl told one she was booked to live into her nineties, and even then she would probably die while still holding on. Which would mean that young Chevalley might see the great Nudd sale, but that he, Domberg, would not. And in the interim depressingly little would be happening. Mrs Montacute's instinct for investment would no doubt prompt her to occasional adjustments in her holdings here and there. But these would be minimal, and would doubtless be conducted privately, as between collector and collector, in the course of convivialities very much like the present party.

This thought caused Domberg to scowl—into the recesses, as it happened, of a dark cabinet within which there subaqueously swam, like scraps of seaweed, various objects in ancient jade. His scowl deepened—he chanced rather to dislike jade—and then he became aware that there also floated in the cabinet a kind of ghostly jellyfish. But this was only the reflection in glass of a human face which had hove up behind him. He turned, still scowling, and found himself more or less eyeball to eyeball with a much more ferociously scowling young man.

The young man was untidily but colourfully dressed. Save for the improbability of such a person's being present at Mrs Montacute's party, Domberg would have taken him for an artist. He had picked up from a side-table what appeared to be a delicate little sea-horse in *faience*, and this, to Domberg's horror, he was lightly and absently tossing in air. Some protest was essential.

'I think,' Domberg said firmly, 'you had better put it down. These things break easily.'

'Oh—are you the detective?'

'No, I am not.'

'Sorry. You looked a bit bored.' The young man, despite an alarming wildness of regard, spoke inoffensively enough. And he had even restored the sea-horse to its place with decent care. 'So I thought you might be a private eye. They probably hire two or three for an affair like this. Bloody lot of junk it is, isn't it?' The young man's scowl became fleetingly an engaging smile, but he made no pause to receive either agreement or disagreement. 'Can you tell me which is the old woman herself? Is she the one dressed like a Christmas cracker?'

'Yes, she is.' Veracity constrained Domberg to this reply, although he disapproved of Mrs Montacute's being thus insultingly referred to by a guest. 'Did you neglect to make her acquaintance on your arrival?'

'Christ, yes! I gate-crashed, man. Old Fenella wouldn't care for the idea of my being here at all. I'm a kind of relation, you see. Are you?'

'No, I am not. I am merely'—Domberg stretched a point, being curious about the young man—'an old friend of the family.'

'Then you must have heard of the Counterpaynes. I'm Jake Counterpayne. How do you do?'

'How do you do?' Domberg accepted this irregular introduction grudgingly. 'My name is Lambert Domberg.'

'Comberback and Domberg?' A return to ferocity on Mr Counterpayne's part accompanied this question.

'Yes.'

'Well, I'm buggered!' The young man evinced a kind of savage cheerfulness as he offered this extravagant information. 'I've never met one of the top operators before. Quite your sort of thing, all this must be. And I'm bound to say it staggers *me* a bit. Of course I've heard a lot about it, since it's a family affair, and I thought I'd come and see. Waiter!'

This shout had been directed at Mrs Montacute's butler, whom Domberg knew to be named Guise. Guise had been passing with a bottle of champagne, and this shocking young man was now waving an empty glass at him. What made his conduct peculiarly deplorable was the evident fact that his manner of summoning Mrs Montacute's chief retainer had not in the least been an innocent solecism. It had been an outrageously tasteless joke. Domberg felt that he ought simply to move away. As it happened, however, Guise's manner of coping with the situation was to relegate Counterpayne to second place. So Domberg watched with satisfaction the bottle being emptied into his own glass, and stayed put.

'One up to you,' Counterpayne said without animus as Guise retreated. 'I know what *I'd* do with it.'

'The champagne?'

'The collection, or whatever it's called. Chuck it out.'

'Chuck it out?' This conception eluded Domberg. 'Disperse it,' he added hopefully, 'in a series of sales?'

'Pitch it through the windows, and let the villagers come and take their pick. If there are any villagers, that is. A bit here and a bit there might liven up some dull interiors. But all this purse-proud accumulation in one house is disgusting.'

'I suppose'—Domberg spoke with his accustomed irony —'you are what, when I was young, was called a distributist.'

'Was that a kind of pointilliste? You're quite right that I'm a painter.'

'I am interested to hear it, Mr Counterpayne. But I was referring to what appear to be your political persuasions.'

'Maoist.'

'Dear me! Do you carry that little red book?'

'Here you are.' With a promptitude disconcerting to Domberg, Mr Jake Counterpayne fished a small volume out of a baggy pocket. 'Care to borrow it? I doubt whether it would do you much good. Excuse me just a moment!' This time, there had appeared in a corner of the room a female assistant of Guise's bearing a trayful of brimming glasses. The young man's capture of her was so rapid that Domberg had no chance to move on before he was back again with a glass in each hand. 'The foaming grape of eastern France,' he said poetically. 'And I asked for one for my wife.'

'Mrs Counterpayne has gate-crashed too?'

'Not married, man.' Counterpayne deftly secreted his reserve refreshment behind one of Mrs Montacute's less considerable camels. 'By the way—is the young wench here, do you happen to know?'

'I suppose you mean Miss Montacute.' Domberg's tone was severe. Charity is elusive, but decorum it is always possible to preserve. 'I believe she is exercising some dogs.'

'Ought to be exercising herself, from what I hear. Gloria's said to turn the scale at fifteen stone. Would you say that's about right?'

'I have had no occasion to consider the matter. But I should judge it to be an exaggeration.'

'It was partly to have a dekko at her that I barged in.' Jake Counterpayne was perhaps approximating his vocabulary to what he judged an old-fashioned colloquial note. 'Gloria and I are cousins of a sort, of course, but we haven't met since we were kids. There was a family row, and it rumbles on. Cash-nexus stuff. The strains and contradictions of an acquisitive society. Montagues and Capulets, you might say. And here I am at the party.'

Domberg received these final odd remarks in silence. They would not have been offered to a stranger, he judged, had the young man not been briskly at work on the champagne for some time. Counterpayne had been far from speaking of the daughter of the house as one who could teach the torches to burn bright, or even who showed as a rich jewel in an Ethiop's ear. But Gloria Montacute, if not a Juliet, was very much an heiress, and her cousin must know it. Domberg doubted whether the possession of the most pronounced Maoist principles would render such a circumstance wholly uninteresting. So it was not improbable that Jake Counterpayne had come to Nudd on a reconnaissance of a mercenary sort.

Certainly the young man didn't appear to take much interest in what he had called a bloody lot of junk. This was unsurprising in itself. It was very much within Lambert Domberg's knowledge that the attitude of young artists to the labours of their predecessors through the centuries is frequently a compost of arrogant indifference and rapid theft. You can see them in the National Gallery or the Tate every day, and wonder why they have indefinably the air of pickpockets. It is because their every instinct is plagiaristic rather than contemplative.

These opinions of Lambert Domberg's are not to be judged illiberal. He had nothing against young painters and the like considered simply as human beings. It was merely that he held a strong conviction that artistic activity was best regarded as a definable historical phenomenon which had come to an end with the eighth Impressionist Exhibition in 1886. After that, when considered from a professional point of view, the continued coming into being of further works of art was mainly a nuisance. At least it had to be called that as soon as anything of the sort achieved some spurious and assuredly evanescent celebrity. To date, Jake Counterpayne was probably innocent here; it was unlikely that anybody had got round to paying for his empty sardine-tins, or abandoned motor-tyres, or whatever it was he painted, money adequate to the purchase of, say, a perfectly respectable little Calvert or Cotman.

But now, and quite suddenly, Counterpayne struck Domberg in a new light. A penny dropped, so to speak, that ought to have dropped several minutes before.

'I think,' Domberg said, 'that you must be a grand-nephew of Hugo Counterpayne, who formed the collection?'

'And left it all to old Fenella. You're quite right. And that was the start of the row, you know. My father—he's Cedric Counterpayne, old Fenella's first cousin—resented it. Old Hugo left him quite a lot of lolly instead, but he doesn't seem to have managed it very well. And he still gets steamed up about all this stuff—doing nothing but hang on the walls or lurk in the cabinets or piddle like that glorified cattle-trough in the hall, and yet appreciating in value like mad all the time. I feel for my father. He's rather dotty, of course—but harmlessly enough.' Jake Counterpayne paused to negotiate his switch of champagne glasses. 'He and I get on not too badly, all things considered. I'd say I quite like him, on the whole.'

'That must be most gratifying to you both.' Domberg's own father had died forty years before, and Domberg in consequence possessed, if faintly, all the right feelings about him. He was therefore offended by this somewhat casual expression of filial regard. 'Do I gather that, although Gloria was known to you as a child, you have never so much as met her mother?'

'Correct. Gloria once came on a visit to us, and I suppose it must have been a manoeuvre by our parents towards a reconciliation. The angel-children were to do the trick. But it didn't come off. When the time for it came I refused to do a return visit. I said I wasn't going to waste my holidays living with a beastly girl. It's wonderful how one's inclinations change.'

'No doubt. But it isn't, you know, too late for a re-

conciliation now.' Domberg said this because he had become aware of his hostess as only a couple of paces away
from him—and because of a sudden impulse either meritorious or malicious according to one's point of view. He
put a hand on the young man's elbow and swung him
round. 'Dear lady!' he said. 'May I have the pleasure of
introducing your kinsman, Jake Counterpayne?'

Mrs Montacute's gaze was blank. For a moment at least,
this seemed quite natural. She had been confronted by
something surprising—and this through the instrumen-
tality of discourteous, or at least *outré*, behaviour on the
part of a customarily circumspect trafficker in the fine
arts. But the blank gaze unnervingly continued. It would
have been fair to inform Mrs Montacute, as Macbeth informed the ghost of Banquo, that she had no speculation
in those eyes that she did glare with.

Then Mrs Montacute spoke. Or rather she didn't exactly speak; she merely emitted sounds that might be
held compatible with the state known as being speechless
with indignation. But was Mrs Montacute really indignant?
It didn't seem quite like that. In fact, Mrs Montacute was
smiling pleasantly—or was so smiling until a curious
sliding or gliding movement made itself perceptible over
one side of her face. She then sat down, also in a sliding
way, and not without a certain appearance of conscious
grace. Unfortunately the chair that she had chosen owned
the status only of what the learned call an eidetic image.
In brute fact it wasn't there. What Mrs Montacute sat
down on, therefore, was the floor; and on the floor she
lay supine a moment later. Not many seconds had to pass
before it became evident that she was dead.

5

A SENSE OF SHOCK

NOTHING SINISTER OR even, in the strict sense, un-expected attached to Mrs Montacute's sudden death. It was to turn out that the family doctor (who was at the party as representing what Mrs Montacute called local society) had foreboded it, or at least something approximating to it, for a year or more. Such conclusive cerebral disasters threaten and occur. And if Mrs Montacute herself had fully understood the extent of her own vulnerability she had very successfully kept mum about it. Were the news to have got around, it is very probable, after all, that she would have been increasingly pestered by sundry persons evincing a disinterested concern for the well-being of the fine arts.

But, of course, so sudden a stroke—or *coup de théâtre* —as Mrs Montacute had achieved came to many as a considerable shock. It was certainly a shock to Lambert Domberg, who spent some time under the distressing impression that a mild and unwonted impropriety on his part had proved instantly lethal to his hostess. It turned out, however, that Mrs Montacute had been behaving oddly—had, to put it crudely, been gibbering instead of talking—for some minutes before her clouding gaze had been solicited for her long-lost kinsman, Jake Counterpayne. It was a shock to Jake. Never before had this young man been invited to make his bow to one whose death-rattle was more or less in her throat.

But, naturally enough, it was chiefly a shock to Gloria.

6

WALKING ROUND WITH
GLORIA MONTACUTE

YET GLORIA HAD, to some extent, experienced a premonition. Or perhaps it had been Harry Carter who had done that—who had picked up some hint of a message from the manner in which a departing motor-car seemed impatient to shake off the dust of Nudd behind it. Gloria was to recall this later as an instance of that feral alertness—so decidedly to be reckoned with—which distinguished Harry from the rest of her acquaintance.

They had walked down the hill contentedly enough. Gloria, as was her habit, revolved various practical issues in her mind and came to a decision on each. She chose the train by which she would return to London next day. Exercising her imagination to practical effect, she estimated the likely weight of her suitcase and concluded that it would be unnecessary to hire a taxi at Paddington. She pondered taking Harry's barely rifled box of chocolates as a present to the assistant tea lady, but judged she didn't know the assistant tea lady quite well enough as yet to render this impaired gift appropriate. Fortunately Mrs Bantry, her mother's cook, could be relied on to be pleased with it.

The puppies had to be returned to the kennels, a quarter of a mile away, and some words exchanged with the kennel-man. This took time. Nudd, when they reached it, was in a state of unnatural quiet, all the same.

'They've gone, my dear—every one of them.' Harry, who was a little awed by the big house, produced this gravely. He even came to a momentary halt.

'So they have, and I'm afraid it looks rather dull.' Gloria

had a sense of wanting to be alone. 'Perhaps, Harry—'

'I'm coming in, my dear—like we said.' Harry was striding ahead again.

'Yes, of course. But something must have happened, it seems to me.'

'Yes,' Harry said unemotionally. 'Something must.'

The family doctor had remained, and so had a strange young man who introduced himself on a subdued note as Gloria's cousin Jake Counterpayne. Nobody else had felt sufficiently an intimate of the household to do other than depart at once. Jake, having said something reasonably appropriate and quite without mumbling, neither lingered nor gave any effect of being anxious to bolt. Gloria, dimly conscious that this forgotten kinsman was what her mother would have called *un garçon farouche*, chalked him up a mark for decent manners when he did leave. Harry saw him out of the house. Gloria was amused by the spectacle. Only when she became conscious of her amusement as very shocking did she seem to realize that her mother was dead. She went up to her bedroom and wept.

It was late in the evening when she came downstairs again. Guise had turned on lights sparingly here and there. Most of them were designed not for general illumination but to pick out particularly notable stretches and hunks of art. Mrs Montacute's top camel—the outsize T'ang one—glowed within a nimbus of its own, as if raised to sainthood among its kind. The small boy called Don Balthasar Carlos, joyously caracoling on a rocking-horse which the courtly tact of Velazquez had transformed into a live and prancing steed, was held in a mild radiance perhaps grateful to a child booked for the gloomiest of thrones. And the mysterious candle-lit world of La Tour, being hung in a recess in which there now glimmered other points of light, made an effect which would have had to be judged theatrical if it hadn't somehow triumphantly (in a favourite phrase of the late Mrs Montacute's) 'come off'.

But these and similar appearances Gloria passed by without much, or indeed any, regard. This was not attributable to her grief. She had ceased paying attention to the priceless contents of Nudd from the moment at which she had successfully rebelled against her mother's notion that she was an appropriate person 'to take people round'. Had she recalled at this moment the positiveness of her stance on that occasion she might have blamed herself bitterly. But that would have been irrational, as guilt-feelings at times of bereavement commonly are (or are declared by well-balanced people to be). Certainly the job of cicerone wouldn't have been at all Gloria's thing. It hadn't, for that matter, been quite her mother's either, except with visitors themselves owning a lively sense of how markets move.

She came into the hall, that area of Nudd which was fortunately so spacious as to present an uncramped arena for the *fontana minore*. The *fontana minore* still splashed and trickled, and a beam of light from below undercut the sharp features of Henry of Cornwall—whose murder, in sacrilegious circumstances, by Guy de Montfort was the most spirited of the small spectacles on view. Harry was viewing it now. Harry had stayed put.

'The doctor went off,' Harry said, rapidly and by way of explaining himself. 'So really there's nobody around, is there? Except all those servants.'

This was an exaggerated expression. Guise and Mrs Bantry did, it was true, require supporting presences, but all except two of these were unassuming females who came in from the village on a daily basis. Nudd couldn't be called a great household. It was a considerable place, all the same. Perhaps a sense of its mere dimensions was troubling Harry.

'Haven't you got any relations?' he said on a demanding note. 'An aunt or something?'

'I have some elderly cousins I never see. They must be the parents of that young man you saw off the premises—Jake Counterpayne.'

'What silly names the aristocracy have, my dear.'

'We haven't anything to do with the aristocracy—not any of us.' Gloria often had to wonder whether Harry Carter was quite the social innocent he seemed. 'We're just plain money. But didn't you think Jake looked as if he might be a bit reacting against it?'

'At least he didn't say he'd got a job as a tea lady.' Harry had achieved one of his rare strokes of wit. 'I don't think I liked him much, Gloria. He said something a bit odd, just as he drove away. He said he'd been gate-crashing, which had made things awkward. I don't think it's manners, to go where you're not asked.' Harry looked comfortably round the hall of Nudd Manor. He *had* been asked—and (it was to be supposed) by the Manor's new proprietor.

'If he *felt* it to be awkward, that was quite nice of him.' It wasn't clear to Gloria why she was engaging in this defence of her virtually unknown cousin.

'I thought we were well rid of him, Gloria my dear. A kind of hippie, he seemed to me. I don't expect his mother would be much use to you. Look, Gloria—shall I ask *my* mother to come across? She could stay the night easily.'

'Oh, I don't think—' Gloria checked her first impulse to turn down this proposal. It sounded like making a fuss (which you mustn't do when people die) and moreover she wasn't certain that there didn't lurk in Harry's offer, whether guilefully or not, his unslumbering instinct to prosecute his suit (if it could be called a suit). But Gloria was a tea lady, and tea ladies in great hospitals are a secular priesthood, perpetually holding out a cup of communion to persons often for one reason or another in deep states of feeling; and this develops in tea ladies a sensitiveness which their outward seeming may not betray. So Gloria was aware of Harry's suggestion as having an impersonal source in the mortuary ritual of the folk. This was the big house, and in the big house it would be peculiarly shocking that only hired people should assist at a wake. 'Yes, Harry—please,' she said. 'I'd like your mother to come.'

'Then I'll go and fetch her right away.' Harry paused on this; he didn't, in fact, seem ready to move. 'Oh, I forgot to tell you. The vicar came. But I told him you were asleep, and cleared him out.'

Gloria didn't know how to receive this surprising news. Chiefly she felt relieved. Not believing that her mother was now in heaven (or anywhere else, for that matter), she was disposed to feel (perhaps fallaciously) that there would have been only awkwardness in a precipitate encounter with a person professionally committed to the contrary persuasion. On the other hand it was undeniable that Harry Carter, perhaps assuming, once more, even greater social innocence than was actually his, had acted decidedly out of turn. It wasn't Harry's business to chase away clergymen from a house of mourning in which he himself had no standing whatever—which, indeed, he had never before entered in his life. But yet again there hovered for Gloria on the edge of all this a ludicrous yet attractive vision of Harry taking charge of the whole thing: sending for the undertaker, and notifying *The Times,* and ordering the funeral baked meats, and tipping the sexton. It was wrong to be amused, whether by this or anything else. She owned, however, a curious feeling that just at this moment, within hours of her mother's death, moods and responses were possible which would not be possible on the following day or for a good many days to come.

'Harry,' she said suddenly, 'did Guise get you anything?'

'Get me anything? No, of course not.' Harry appeared startled.

'But you've very kindly stayed here for hours! You must have a drink—before going back to the farm for your mother. Come on. We can still find something.' Gloria divined a possible occasion of shyness on Harry's part. 'And without bothering the servants.'

'They seem to be keeping away.' Harry's bright eyes were searchingly on Gloria across an angle of the fountain. A sense of propriety had prompted him to button his shirt almost to the neck, and to roll down his sleeves. But he still looked like something which Gloria found it diffi-cult to put a name to. It was something heathen, she vaguely supposed: some minor divinity having to do with vintages and harvests. Titian could have made quite something of Harry.

'Oh, they'll come around when you leave,' Gloria said —meaning Guise and Mrs Bantry and the housemaid.

'Has that man been here for a long time?'

'Guise? He's been with us for ages—in fact he be-longed here before we came to Nudd. He'll be very good and comforting. But, of course, it will be wonderful to have your mother for the night, if she can really manage it. Now, come along.'

The dining-room at Nudd opened into the drawing-room through wide folding doors, and it was in this com-bined apartment that a light collation had chiefly been on offer at the late party. Much had been hastily cleared away by injured caterers, unaccustomed to the impro-priety of sudden death at a banquet. But there was still a long table at the far end of the room, draped in Nudd's best linen. Fishing under a corner of this as one who knew the customs of the house, Gloria produced a silver bucket in which floated, in what had recently been ice, an unopened bottle of champagne. She mopped the bottle with a table-napkin, handed it silently to Harry, and turned to find clean glasses in a basket near by. Harry eyed the bottle doubtfully, as if feeling involved by a suddenly unaccountable Gloria in monstrous indecorum. Gloria enjoyed this, although she knew she ought not to be enjoying anything. Harry, bracing himself, applied strong fingers to the wire and thrusting thumbs to the knobbly and obscurely fascinating cork. In the silent house the cork came out with the effect of a cannon-shot and flew across the room. The bottle foamed at the neck as Gloria pushed a glass under it. Harry—such was his sense of a wild indecency—had gone pale, like a harvest more than ready to reap. And then they were drinking together, soberly enough.

'May I walk round?' Harry asked surprisingly.

'Yes, of course—and I'll come with you. Only, you mustn't ask me about all those things. I'm not clued up on them at all.' Gloria paused, aware that Harry was puzzled. 'Except,' she added defensively, 'that I do some-times know just the names.'

They walked round, much as the late Mrs Montacute's guests had done. Italian condottieri, French courtesans, Spanish beggar-boys, English soldiers and bishops and bluestockings looked down on them from the walls, and the camels fastidiously averted their noses as they went by. Harry stared for a long time at a picture of a lion eating a horse, and said that only a fool would let a lion get within a mile of a horse like that. This was his sole comment on the collection. Gloria found such continence comfortable.

It was rather a forlorn perambulation, all the same—and would have been so quite apart from the waves of misery which, like birth-pangs, were now coming to Gloria with accelerating frequency and force. Two children who

had paid their penny for Punch and Judy and had become spectators, instead, of *Polyeucte* or *Sejanus His Fall*
would have been in an analogous situation. At length
they came back to the drawing-room and the champagne,
and Harry asked a simply wondering question.

'Gloria—if you have only those Counterpayne cousins,
does that mean that all this stuff is now going to belong
to you?'

'Oh, I don't know at all.' It surprised Gloria to realize
that this speculation had never entered her head. 'Perhaps it's going to be given to the National Gallery, or
some place like that.'

'People say it's enormously valuable. I suppose that's
so?'

'Yes, I know it is. My mother was rather keen on all
that.'

Harry was silent for a moment, perhaps judging a pause
respectful after the mention of Mrs Montacute. But when
he spoke again, it was to continue on a practical note.

'She mayn't even have made a will—dying suddenly
like that. Then you certainly *would* have everything.
That's the law.'

'I suppose so. Yes.'

'And you'll be a tremendous catch, my dear. So God
knows who will be after you.'

This, in the circumstances of the evening, seemed
much more indecent than drinking a glass of champagne,
and it was Gloria's impulse to bring her wake with Harry
to a close. But she didn't want to snub him. Furthermore
she had sensed, in his manner and tone rather than his
words, something that was insidiously pleasing even if
perplexing. It could be put, she thought, like this: if she
had pointed at little Don Balthasar Carlos and said 'That
one alone would pay several times over for the largest
farm in England' Harry would thereby be presented with

an idea which at present wasn't remotely in his head. Her probable future proprietorship of the collection, and her consequent extreme eligibility as a bride, were indeed matters upon which he had just touched. But it had been distinguishably in a disinterested spirit, or at the most out of what might be described as a brotherly regard. Not that his *look* was brotherly; his glance under that tumble of chestnut hair remained much more unbrotherly than was proper at the moment. But it did seem as if no mercenary shadow fell across Harry's bright passion, unreliable though that might be.

Gloria (although the point is doubtful) might have taken a useful further step in the analysis of the situation had not Harry interrupted her train of thought by picking up the half-empty champagne bottle.

'Have some more, my dear.'

'No, thank you.' Gloria was as clear about this as she had been earlier about the chocolates. 'And now I think perhaps you'd better—'

'Yes, of course.' Harry was all decent alacrity, and together they made their way back to the hall. The *fontana minore* was still at play. Harry stopped before it. 'Can't that thing,' he asked brusquely, 'be stopped from peeing?' His sense of the impiety of champagne-drinking had not much affected his actual conduct in the matter. And he clearly owned a poor opinion of a *trecento* fountain as a twentieth-century domestic convenience.

'There's a tap just at your foot,' Gloria said meekly. She herself had always been impatient with the *fontana minore*: this dated from the moment in her childhood at which Mrs Montacute had vetoed the keeping of goldfish in it.

Harry turned off the water. The pattering sound produced by the fountain at its accustomed half-cock was negligible. Yet the silence that now fell was shattering. It was as if the vital pulse of the entire house had stopped. Gloria burst into tears.

It was perhaps to make up for this foolishness that she committed the further foolishness of accompanying Harry some way down the drive. Dusk was deepening into darkness, and there was no moon. Harry's misinterpretation of the state of the case was disastrous. When his right hand crept up from Gloria's waist to cup her right breast she said 'No' in a tone he ought to have listened to. But Priapus himself must have been whispering in Harry's other ear, since he was now prompted to explore expertly with finger and thumb. A moment later Gloria found that she had not merely broken away from behaviour crudely outrageous at such a time. She had slapped Harry's face very hard as well, and was striding back to the house. Harry made no attempt to follow.

Half-an-hour later Harry's mother turned up, all the same. She was a woman of strong character and robust practical sense. Her people had farmed in the adjoining parish for centuries, and in Harry's world she was regarded as superior to the Carters and at the same time reasonably unblemished by pride. With all this, she was a motherly woman as well. She comforted Gloria quite a lot. It was only when she had brought her a hot drink in bed, however, that she said something the actual sense of which much caught Gloria's attention.

'It was an unfamiliar situation for Harry to find himself in,' Mrs Carter said.

'I suppose it was.' Gloria realized that the words probably meant almost nothing at all; were intended as a conventional acknowledgement that a big house remains a big house in any circumstances. Or wasn't it quite that? Had Harry confessed his bad conduct to his mother, and asked her to put in a good word for him? Gloria felt a stab of unaccustomed feeling as this possibility came to her, and was surprised to have to identify it as jealousy. Certainly she didn't want Mrs Carter to know anything that had happened between Harry and herself, and she wouldn't have dreamt of revealing to her the unfortunate incident on the drive.

But Gloria did dream during the brief spell of sleep she got that night. It was a confused dream. Only in the morning she could just recall that Harry had been present in a corner of it.

Part Two

7

THE FINGER OF TASTE

THE SHUTTERS WERE up at Nudd. Or rather the lattices were down: steel contraptions of the kind long favoured by jewellers and silversmiths, and latterly much adopted by private householders of the more substantial sort. Various types of burglar-alarm go along with them, and any attempt to tamper with those at Nudd was supposed to ring a bell both in the nearest police station and in the cottage of the local constable.

Mr Guise the butler and Mrs Bantry the cook, who were now alone in the house, slept securely behind these devices. At the instance of Miss Montacute's solicitor, indeed, the lattices remained locked in position all day. But as they admitted as much direct daylight as was normally allowed to play upon the treasures of Nudd, this caused no inconvenience.

Guise—'Be pleased to pronounce it like "wise",' he would tell the uninstructed—looked after the air-conditioning, as he had always done. Mrs Bantry looked after Guise. From the village two women continued to come in to do the rough; and twice a week two others of somewhat superior station performed the more responsible cleaning directly under Guise's eye.

Guise's eye was the only particularly notable thing about him—or was so to those who did not also remark a certain precision of movement, and notably of the hands, which indefinably failed to be butler-like in character. The eye would have suggested nothing but a commonplace concern with the tangible and visible surfaces of life but for a perceptible steadiness and concentration of regard,

and for an oddly arresting effect which an opthalmolo-
gist might have explained as the habit of making minute
changes of focus all the time. The late Mrs Montacute
had been rather proud of Guise. Like herself (she explained) Guise possessed the inestimable gift of natural
taste, and this had been refined in him by the position
he had for long occupied. There had been occasions (she
would add) upon which she had not hesitated to consult
Guise on aesthetic issues. His responses, although
necessarily untutored, had been positively helpful from
time to time. But one must not exaggerate, and Guise
was fortunately not to be thought of as owning an intelligence inappropriate to his condition in life. By this
reservation Mrs Montacute meant that her butler had no
understanding of, or interest in, the movement of the
market.

Both Guise and Mrs Bantry had received several picture
postcards from Gloria—signed 'Gloria' in acknowledgement of their status as ancient retainers (or perhaps only
because Gloria, if quite unconsciously, was of an egalitarian turn of mind). They might have been called blue
postcards, since they chiefly depicted lakes and skies.
Gloria was in Italy and enjoying it very much—particularly, she stated, since discovering that it was not necessary
to eat *pasta* twice, or even once, a day. Gloria was always
candid about the problem of the weighing-machine.

Mrs Bantry ranged her postcards on her kitchen
mantelpiece. Guise shoved his away in a drawer in his
pantry. He wasn't, he informed Mrs Bantry, fond of
blue. It was the most unstable of colours. From Giotto in
the Cappella degli Scrovegni to Reynolds at the Tate,
there could be only one verdict on *that*. And if you
wanted to know whether any good could come of the
monkeying by restorers and cleaners with God's natural
malediction upon blue—well, you need only go to the

National Gallery and take a glance at Bacchus and Ariadne.

It was partly on the score of remarks of this kind that Mrs Bantry (who had never been to the National Gallery, let alone to Padua) held Guise in high regard. It was a regard which she sought to express in terms of the best fillet steak and similar dishes categorized as 'tasty' in her quite unassuming culinary vocabulary. Guise accepted these tokens of respect with proper expressions of appreciation, for he was a well-mannered man. Often, however, Mrs Bantry had to suspect that he was without much consciousness of what he ate, his mind being preoccupied with matters remote from the grosser pleasures of sense. A shrewd if simple woman, she was aware of the presence in Guise of some passion beyond her ken. Whatever it was, it fortunately didn't express itself in any sort of conduct likely to generate disapproval in the neighbourhood of Nudd.

In addition to the postcards, Guise had received a couple of letters from Gloria, presumably in response to reports he had despatched to her on the state of affairs at home. Guise did not communicate the content of these letters to Mrs Bantry, and this Mrs Bantry accepted as inherent in their relationship. Guise's sense of his status as higher than hers was quite unforced and inoffensive, and it retained these qualities now that, in some indefinable way, it was increasing fairly rapidly. 'Mr Guise,' Mrs Bantry would say comfortably in the small society of her own equals round about Nudd, 'is quite somebody. Mark my words.' Her words were marked, and invariably without even tacit disagreement. The superiority of Guise, like that of Harry Carter's mother, was a generally accepted fact. And, like Mrs Carter, he was himself punctiliously discreet about it.

It wasn't only Gloria who wrote to Guise. The volume of his correspondence had suddenly increased. Mrs Bantry was the more aware of this since it was prescriptively among her duties to receive the letters from the postman. Some of these had begun to declare themselves as coming from the United States, a distant territory in which it wasn't within Mrs Bantry's knowledge that Guise owned relatives. Besides which, the envelopes were typewritten, and frequently had printed on them the titles and addresses of what Mrs Bantry took to be business (or even, she might dimly have conjectured, learned) concerns.

A morning came upon which it was with one of these that she entered Guise's pantry.

'"The Curator, Nudd Manor",' Mrs Bantry read from the envelope. 'Would that be for you, Mr Guise?'

'Certainly, Mrs Bantry.' Guise put out a hand and received the letter. It was observable that between these two close associates of many years there was preserved a certain formality of appellation. 'You will remember it being distinctly stated by Miss Gloria that I was to regard myself as caretaker of Nudd during her absence.'

'Of course, Mr Guise.'

'"Curator", Mrs Bantry, is simply "caretaker" in the Latin tongue. A more dignified form, of course, and judged appropriate by some, it seems, to the importance of what I am in charge of.'

'Very proper, I'm sure,' Mrs Bantry said. 'Would there be a more dignified form for me?'

'"Curatrix", perhaps.' Guise offered this distinguishably at a venture. 'But I would not advise the adopting of it. Not at present. We have to be cautious, have we not?'

'Oh, certainly, Mr Guise.' Guise's question, which might have been detected by a more acute intelligence than Mrs Bantry's as escaping from some inner region of Guise's mind, impressed Mrs Bantry, as all slightly mysterious remarks were apt to do.

'And by the way, Mrs Bantry, I think we must now expect callers from time to time. Please tell the women that should they chance to answer the door-bell and be asked for the Montacute Curator, the callers are to be brought to me. Or rather they are to be shown into the library, where I shall come to receive them.'

'The library? Yes, of course.' For a moment—and surprisingly—Mrs Bantry's innocent regard might almost have been taking in certain slight modifications which had lately been manifesting themselves in Guise's attire. 'The Montacute Curator?' she added.

'Just that. And another thing. There must be the utmost discretion about such visitors. They are not to be gossiped about in the village. Definitely *not*.'

'Certainly not. And would these callers be from America, perhaps?'

'That is as may be.' Guise had pursed his lips. 'Some of them may wish, incidentally, to inspect our domestic arrangements. The number of bedrooms, and so on. In default of a housekeeper, that will fall within your province.' Guise paused. 'Be your job,' he added in an explanatory tone.

'If you say it's in order, Mr Guise, I'll be quite agreeable, of course. Everything is tidy enough, I'm happy to say.'

'Naturally it is. There may also be an architect from London. Or several architects. But nothing of that kind is to be talked about, either. Miss Gloria would not wish it.'

'Nothing of the kind is my habit, I'm sure.'

'It would be most improper, if it were. I am thinking, Mrs Bantry, of the servants.'

'Of the—?' Briefly, Mrs Bantry had the appearance of almost blinking at this. 'Yes, I see.'

'I am sure we shall continue to understand each other very well.' Guise offered this reassurance apparently out of sincere, if vague, benevolence. 'But I am detaining you, Mrs Bantry. And it is time that I took my walk through the rooms.' With some gravity, Guise had consulted his

watch. 'And checked the instruments, Mrs Bantry. I confess to a shade of anxiety about humidity in the East
Wing.'

The nature, the *quidditas,* of aesthetic experience has
through a good many millenniums perplexed the speculative intelligence. It is improbable that any clear ideas
on the problem obtained in the valley of the Dordogne
during the post-glacial era, or that other than obscurely
animistic and magical notions touched the minds of those
incomparable artists who there laboured in the *grotte de
Lascaux.* Rather later, say 15,000 years later, Aristotle
judged that grown men remain sufficiently childlike to
delight in imitations, and that the pleasure they thus
obtain is not necessarily as pernicious as his master Plato
—himself very much an artist in the broader sense of the
word—had been inclined to suppose. Quite shortly after
that (in terms of the time-scale such reflections involve us
with) Sigmund Freud held a roughly similar opinion. Artists, by thus delighting people, can more or less harmlessly
do themselves a bit of good, gaining wealth which will
obtain for them a fulfilment of desires that otherwise
might have eluded them. More importantly (for Freud
was a scientist) art, like a tomtom or a psychotropic drug,
can loosen up the mind of an individual exposed to it,
lulling some bits and activating others, so that interesting
observations on how we really tick can be made. Later
still (and only a few seconds ago in the effluxion of anthro-
pological time) much was said for the existence of a simple
Aesthetic Sense. There it is, and that's that. But this was
perhaps to throw up the philosophic sponge.

We are not likely to arrive on firmer ground here by
following Guise round Nudd, or even by attempting an
excursus into the past history of this not unremarkable
man. Mrs Montacute's theory of natural taste is a respectable one, and may be supported by much observation. It

is demonstrable that in all classes of society there are people who like art and people who do not; and the American lady who declared enthusiastically her conviction that art is beautiful surely hints the more or less random distribution of vulnerability to aesthetic impression. One house-painter simply decorates your room; another is passionate over the potentialities of yellow and grey. Of course, frequentation and familiarity are important, and nobody will ever know what sort of person Guise would have been had he not as a boy, and at a humble level, entered the employment of that Hugo Counterpayne who had been among the most perceptive and diligent collectors of his time. When Nudd passed to the Montacutes Guise was part of the package. Promoted, he had made himself competent in the management of wine, and had been esteemed accordingly by Nicholas Montacute, Gloria's father. But if below stairs he had kept an impeccable cellar-book, above stairs he had looked about him to what advantage he might. Yet one doesn't really know why. We are back where we started.

Here he is, however, taking his daily walk through the late Mrs Montacute's ever-appreciating treasure house. Although the market does not really interest him, he has a fairly accurate notion of the size of the cheques that might pass. No strategy, however disinterestedly conceived in the service of a passion, of an idea, can afford to neglect economic facts. He cherishes a reasonable confidence that he could hold his own with them if required. Lately, too, he has been picking up a certain amount of legal knowledge—or if not knowledge, at least relevant information and useful tips. But nothing of this is in his mind as he moves about Nudd at present. Nor is he quite the man who, only a few minutes ago, has been in conversation with Mrs Bantry. Were he to speak now—and it could be only to himself—it would not be as an upper servant, finding dignity in formal utterance and composed command. It would be—we can only say—as a lover, a worshipper, a guardian, a tutelary spirit. This is the queer fact about Guise.

The humidity has been controlled, as is immediately evident from the finely pointing needle on its dial. The air-conditioning plant, though moving, seems asleep; its low breathing answers the soft splash of the fountain in the hall. Guise finds himself satisfied with the light-level in the various rooms. To everything of this sort he gives careful attention, although his continental pilgrimages (for generous holidays have made him a well-travelled man) incline him to a sceptical view of the necessity for scientifically cosseting paintings. There are plenty of places in which masterpieces accept the play of the elements—hot or cold, moist or dry—and appear none the worse for it. He even has a sense—for he is in some degree an imaginative man—that these mysterious creations touch us most nearly when breathing with us a common air. You can be too pernickety with art, he thinks sagely, just as you can be too pernickety with wine. The way the French treat their wine! Without ceremony, you might call it. But the same stuff is better there than here, all the same. A living relationship is what's involved. It might be the same with art. Finer if handled more freely. Not made a thing of, you might say.

But here we have arrived at a rather deep level of Guise's thought or feeling. It may conflict, one day, with his predominant attitude: the attitude his long service at Nudd has bred into him. This attitude has to be called hermetic. Nudd is a *hortus conclusus*, a shrine. Above all, Nudd is integral, is almost something organic. This conception controls Guise and his policies.

He halts before the Titians. These, he tells himself grimly, are at the greatest immediate risk. The lawyers are cagey—and he has no standing with them, after all; can only fish respectfully for information when they come around. But he knows that those two paintings can go under the hammer for an enormous sum, realizable if an export licence is subsequently granted by something called the Reviewing Committee. He suspects—although it is obscure territory, on which he knows he can go wrong— that this stage may become a spring-board for further manoeuvre: a fund to 'save' them, or a move to make them over to the nation in lieu of estate duty. He does know that Mrs Montacute, at least until recently believing her middle years robust, admitted no measure that would have taken the collection out of her absolute ownership and control. So the undertaker's bill is not exactly the principal liability occasioned by her death. He wonders what attention Miss Gloria, her mother's sole heir, is capable of giving to the problem. He even finds it possible to wonder whether the Philistine child would so much as notice the disappearance of the Titians from the wall.

Guise moves on. This morning these considerations have not commanded him quite so urgently as they have been doing of late. He has something else on his mind. It is a problem so momentous that he hesitates, that he defers confronting it. In the peacock drawing-room—a nomenclature he has never much liked—he pauses, and takes a second turn round the impressive place. It might be better called the caravanserai drawing-room, he tells himself with a very rare incursion into humour, since it contains a concentration of camels. The largest of them, which he can remember Mrs Montacute as showing off to a young man from London on that fatal day, is virtually sniffing at a gay and fussy *Famille Rose* jar of the Ch'ien-lung period. It is a small incongruity of which Guise has long been aware. T'ang porcelain is unknown, but at least the camel can be accommodated with Sung. Guise walks off with the

jar to a far corner of the room, and returns holding
between his hands all the depth and softness of a *céladon*
piece in yellowish green. The camel takes to this at once.
And the whole balance of the room has subtly altered.
Its every relationship has been affected by this small
harmonizing act. Guise pauses for a few moments before
the mystery, and then walks on. Here has been no more
than a skirmish, a delaying action. And now the La Tour
is in front of him.

He flicks a switch, and momentarily takes refuge in
such reflections as an ardent amateur *Kunsthistoriker*
can command. Extraordinary that out of the agitated
chiaroscuro of Caravaggio, and by a route leading through
coppery Honthorst and his farthing dips, should come
this monumental, mathematical thing. La Tour's women
have brought a single candle to the Tomb. The Magda-
lene holds it in her left hand. Her right hand, raised in
the simple act of masking the small flame, commands
stillness, is a hieratic gesture sealing the solemnity of the
scene. At the centre, of necessity, is emptiness; La Tour
is painting what isn't any longer there. The light picks
out a crease in the napkin lying folded and apart; dimly
silhouetted in the foreground is the curve of the great
stone. But it is as if the light shines out further; catches,
here and there on the sides of some cavern within which
the sepulchre lies, a stalactitic gleam that frames the
sacred spectacle within vast reaches of geological time.
This is the effect of the two or three minute lamps which
Guise has switched on in the alcove where the painting
hangs. Guise has been proud of his device, and Mrs Montacute was enchanted by it—declaring to visitors that the
only comparable experience is turning to view *Las
Meniñas* in the great mirror which the authorities of the
Prado provide for the purpose.

But Guise has been uneasy for a long time, and now
he acts. He switches off the lights, crosses the room, draws

up first one and then another faintly translucent blind. Clear daylight floods in, and strikes directly upon the canvas. The late Mrs Montacute's butler takes a deep breath. Yes, mystery has withdrawn where it belongs, which is within the picture-space which Georges de la Tour alone has created. And *The Two Marys at the Tomb* has become more moving and more beautiful—and these, Guise thinks, are one and the same thing.

Guise's, then, is once more, as it has always been, the finger of taste at Nudd.

8

A JOURNEY PROPOSED

'IT'S NOT TO be denied,' Lambert Domberg said, 'that a finger of taste has been operative at Nudd.' Domberg had grown attached to the phrase he had employed to his young colleague Chevalley some months before. 'But it has certainly not been your client's.'

'I am no judge of these matters.' Mr Thurkle frowned as he offered this disclaimer—and since he glanced round Domberg's office at the same time might have been thought to be disapproving of it. But in fact it was not unlike his own office in Gray's Inn. Comberback and Domberg were far from being the sort of people to go in for what property promoters hopefully call prestige premises. Most of the objects permanently on view declared themselves as solid, respectable, old-fashioned, and even worn out. Only, what lay around here in apparent casual disorder was not obsolete legal journals, forgotten briefs, bundles of yellowing letters tied together with faded red tape, empty ink-wells and useless quill pens; rather it was Rembrandt etchings, Beardsley drawings, maquettes by Rodin or the assistants of the aged Renoir, obscurely rare maps, incunabula, and dim coins in faded velvet trays.

'And it is proper to say,' Mr Thurkle went on severely, 'that my calling on you is in pursuance only of one among a number of enquiries which I feel bound to make. So please consider everything as tentative at this stage. There is no cause for precipitancy. Only to one or two matters does a certain measure of urgency attach.'

Domberg received this judicious speech with a bow the

gravity of which must have made the crispness of his succeeding utterance a surprise.

'Death duties,' Domberg said.

'Ah, yes—that among other things.'

'Tricky territory, Mr Thurkle. You find the Controller reasonable—but then the Treasury Solicitor turns out to be in on it too. And *then* there may be a Minister, so that purely political factors obtrude. I've never known anybody embark on this business of payment in kind who didn't feel he ended up with a raw deal.'

'There is talk of just two pictures—extremely valuable works by Titian.'

'It would be surprising if there was not.'

'Then you advise against discharging almost the entire liability to estate duty in that way?'

'Certainly I do not.' Domberg was smoothly wary. 'For one thing, you haven't sought my advice—not in so many words—and it would be quite improper for me to volunteer it. If you ask us in writing for an expertise and valuation, that, of course, would be another matter. Even so, our position would be a morally delicate one. If you were to decide on a sale—'

'If Miss Montacute were to decide on a sale.'

'Quite so, quite so. If there were to be a sale, and you consulted the best informed opinion as to who should conduct it, you would undoubtedly be told—I speak quite frankly—that it would be to your disadvantage to employ any firm other than Comberback and Domberg. And Comberback and Domberg would stand to earn a very large sum of money in commission, should such an exercise in fact come their way. I confess I simply haven't found the ethical answer to this one, although it isn't all that infrequently that it turns up.'

'Most interesting,' Mr Thurkle said. He was not impressed by this candid parading of the obvious. 'I believe you used to see Mrs Montacute from time to time. Perhaps your delicacy won't prevent your telling me whether *she* had a sale in mind.'

'Decidedly she had.' Domberg was unruffled. 'Everyone knew it was what she was working towards. So if Miss Montacute wants to do the filial thing, she'll instruct you to sell up—lock, stock and barrel. There need be no delicacy in telling you *that*, my dear sir.'

'It seems curious, all the same. I am not well-seen in artistic matters, Mr Domberg, as I believe I have explained. Such leisure as I command is devoted to antiquarian pursuits which it would be irrelevant to particularize. But it has been my impression that the outstanding feature of all these valuable things at Nudd—'

'Is the way they come together. The finger of taste again—eh? And—as I said—it wasn't Mrs Montacute's. She was aware of it; she was proud of it; but it was no part of her passion. Her passion—to put it crudely—was simply the staggering total that a well contrived dispersal would bring in.' Domberg shook his head sombrely, as one who views an unworthy universe.

'Then an unknown—'

'Old Hugo Counterpayne, I suppose, who formed the collection in the first place. Or it's possible that, later on, Nicholas Montacute hired somebody with the necessary flair for arranging rooms and galleries. Not that I recall hearing of such a thing.'

'You are yourself, I believe, familiar with Nudd?'

'Oh, certainly. I was there, along with my assistant, Octavius Chevalley, at the party the poor lady died on.'

'Indeed?' Mr Thurkle's tone disapproved the final preposition. 'And you met Miss Montacute?'

'We saw her, but didn't meet her. She was setting out to walk some dogs. More her line, I imagine, than gushing over Chinese pots. In fact, we must frankly agree that Miss Gloria Montacute is a Philistine.'

'I don't know that I will agree to anything of the sort.' Mr Thurkle showed a proper disposition to defend a client. 'But it is certainly true that she appears not to have directed much of her interest towards the arts. Her choice of employment, moreover, did for a time strike me as eccentric. One might suppose that an element of what they call social protest has been involved.'

'In sloshing out tea in an East End hospital?'

'She would not, I believe, slosh it. She is a careful, as well as in many ways an unusually sensible, girl. Incidentally, I understand that the tea-urn has been taken from her.' Mr Thurkle produced his first smile. 'Rather against her inclination, she has been promoted. To the supervision, one supposes, of some part of the domestic arrangements of the hospital. That is why she has taken a holiday abroad. It is to be before entering on her new duties.'

'It still seems odd. Looked at any way you please, the girl's a great heiress. Isn't that right? You're the authority, I know.'

'The position is a perplexed one, Domberg.' It was reluctantly that Miss Montacute's solicitor bowed to convention in adopting this informal manner of address. 'There is really very little—except Nudd and its collection. At present, she isn't drawing a penny from the estate.'

'She could sell just that fountain—nothing more—and be well set-up for the rest of her days.'

'The point has not escaped me.' Thurkle said this so drily that he appeared to repent and seek a more companionable note. 'Of course I have to advise the child on the legal side. And of course there are some guide-lines that are clear enough—'

'Obviously. You have to maximize what can be got out of it all. That's why you've come to see me.'

'Prudence is essential, certainly. But one mustn't forget

there's a human side to the situation. She's very young, and she's the sole owner of all those extremely valuable things—without possessing the ballast, so to speak, of having any feeling for them. Suppose we do sell up. Whether she comes out of it with two million or three is of very little significance, I'd say.'

'Perfectly true. She'd scarcely be felt as a better catch with the one sum than with the other. In fact—'

Domberg broke off. The door of his room had opened, following upon a knock he had failed to distinguish.

'I'm terribly sorry!' It was Chevalley who had appeared. 'I oughtn't to have barged—'

'Not at all, my dear Octavius. Come in.' Domberg was benign. 'I'd like you to meet Mr Thurkle, who is Miss Montacute's solicitor.'

'The fat girl?' Chevalley asked—so that Thurkle produced his frown. But Chevalley had spoken less with a contemptuous intention than at random, and while still uncertain as to whether he should withdraw. Not— Thurkle might have reflected as he shook hands—a particularly decisive young man.

'Sit down, Octavius. Mr Thurkle tells me that Miss Montacute has forsaken the cup that cheers, and is travelling on the continent. As the owner of a great collection, she possibly feels it incumbent upon her to perform the Grand Tour.'

'Nothing of the kind.' Thurkle hadn't taken to this joke. 'She's on Lake Garda at present, and going on to Venice in a few days' time.'

'Venice?' Chevalley had become alert.

'Yes. Her forwarding address, as it happens, is that of the pensione once inhabited by Ruskin. But I doubt whether the fact is in her head. And a girl needn't be made fun of'—Thurkle produced a flash of asperity— 'simply because she isn't a prize student from the Courtauld.'

'Certainly not.' Domberg shot a warning glance at his assistant. Amusement at Miss Montacute's expense was out. 'And we mustn't be thought to take a narrow view, confined to our own interest. It's not simply the remarkable collection we must try to consider; it's the collection as Miss Montacute's property, and as Miss Montacute's problem. What ought she to do with it, that she will eventually take genuine satisfaction in having done?'

This elevated view of the matter perhaps surprised Chevalley, since it was Thurkle who next spoke.

'She might present it to the nation.'

'Like the estimable Sir Henry Tate.' Against both his better judgement and a further admonitory glare from his principal, Chevalley plunged into the frivolous. 'Only, she'd have to build a gallery as well. Tate did that, on the site of a prison given him by the government. They might give Miss Montacute Wormwood Scrubs.'

'Or she might give them Nudd.' Thurkle was suppressing irritation. 'And the collection could remain there.'

'It would be a magnificent gift,' Domberg said in a tone as reverently admiring as if the vague suggestion were already accomplished fact. 'But I fear it wouldn't work. The government—certainly this present government—would be far from enthusiastic. An independent picture gallery and museum in the depth of the country would be a considerable charge, and the number of visitors attracted to it might not be all that impressive. In fact, the government would expect an endowment thrown in—and that I understand to be something which Miss Montacute is not in a position to provide.'

'Most assuredly she is not,' Thurkle said.

'Of course the nation would almost certainly accept the collection—or the collections, to speak more accurately. But the spoils would then be divided: this and that to the National Gallery; this and that to the Tate; this and that to the V. and A. Poor Mrs Montacute would have hated the thought of it.'

'Not if her attitude was what you have declared it to be.' Thurkle looked at Domberg stonily. 'You said she was simply holding on for the peak of the market.'

'Yes, that is quite true. But didn't I also say she took a certain pride in the total achievement we call Nudd? However, I much hope this is purely hypothetical talk. I much hope Miss Montacute will not give away the collection—either to the nation or to anybody else.'

'Why do you much hope that?' Chevalley asked innocently.

'Because, my dear Octavius, I think the young woman ought to have the money—the enormous sum of money —that the collection can bring in.'

'A most interesting view.' It had been after a short silence that Thurkle spoke. 'And it brings us back to a sale, or a series of sales, conducted by your excellent firm.'

'Incidentally, yes. But you must credit me—you really must credit me, Thurkle—with my own interest in what you have called the human side of the thing. It *is* rather fascinating: this girl—an idealistic girl, perhaps, coming in so big a way into just this sort of property. Suppose that she simply unloads all those beautiful things on anybody who will accept them: national collections, municipal galleries, Lord knows what! What would she be doing? Giving away what she doesn't herself care for or value in the interest of securing for the public at large a kind of pleasure she knows nothing about.'

'Most interesting,' Thurkle repeated. But this time he uttered the words without sardonic intention.

'So she ends up with having achieved a gesture of vague and undirected benevolence—nothing more. When she comes to maturity—for she is as yet a child, as you say— will she take much satisfaction in that? I doubt it. I doubt it because of something you have told me yourself about Gloria Montacute. "An unusually sensible girl," you called her. And I suspect your standard in such matters to be distinctly high, my dear sir. Now, a thoroughly sensible girl is likely to be disposed to accept responsibility —and to be felt by others as fit for it. Do I begin to make myself clear?' The philosophic Domberg paused for a moment on this note of serious interrogation, and was rewarded by Thurkle with at least the ghost of a nod.

'You seem to mean,' Chevalley interpolated, 'that she should sell out, display herself as a genuine millionaire, and take what chases her up in consequence. In fact, you want to expose her to fortune-hunters. As a test of character, I suppose.'

'You put it a little crudely, Octavius.' Domberg spoke in a fatherly way. 'And I don't envisage Miss Montacute precisely as "taking" anything. I envisage her, with all this wealth at her disposal, in some decidedly active role. Consider her work in the East End.' Domberg now contrived to lend to what he had termed sloshing out tea the suggestion of years of selfless toil in the service of the submerged classes of London. 'It speaks of a strong sense of dedication, does it not? Social betterment, and so forth. And with wealth at her disposal, and decisions to make—'

'She would go from strength to strength,' Chevalley said—and was immediately uncertain whether he had said something merely inane or had honestly punctured this sanctimonious rubbish on his chief's part. 'I think,' he added weakly, and thereby sinking yet further in his own esteem, 'there's something in what you say.'

'But does Mr Thurkle?' As he asked this, Domberg glanced in modest challenge at his visitor.

'At least I think that a certain element of realizing on the collection is inevitable.' Thurkle seemed disposed to turn rocky again. 'No family solicitor, knowing how things stand financially, could responsibly advise otherwise. Nor should I in the least care to see a spectacular giving away

of an immensely valuable property. At present Miss Montacute may be an independent young woman, laudably
wishing to live on the fair return of her services to society.
But her future is necessarily unknown.' Thurkle paused
to frown—this time perhaps upon glimpsing an unnecessary orotundity in the enunciation of so massive a plati-
tude. 'She may marry. She may marry some worthy but
by no means affluent young man. Her present contacts,
after all, are in the field of the social services. And one
knows what sort of screw labourers in *that* vineyard command. She may bear children in considerable number—'

'I'd put money on that,' Chevalley said. 'For she's a
monument of the flesh, with divine fecundity written all
over her.'

'No doubt.' Thurkle had been put a little out of his
stride by this—and not the less so because it had revealed
in this rather disagreeable young man a flash of feeling
one somehow felt to be surprising in him. 'She may have
children and grandchildren. And seeing them struggling
in the common mill, she might regret having stripped
herself of the means to lift them out of it.'

'Very true,' Domberg said gravely. 'And you express
it admirably.'

'Thank you. And now, perhaps, we may turn to the
technical matters upon which I am appealing to you.'
Thurkle paused for a moment to let this sink in. 'Export
licences, for example. It is clear to me that American
and other overseas buyers...'

Briskly and cogently, Mr Thurkle put the questions he
had in mind. Domberg's answers were equally to the
point; for one whose training (like Chevalley's) had been
as an art historian, he had a notable grip on the mundane
side of his present trade. Mr Comberback himself, who had
built up the business but was now a background figure
drowsed in port, had scarcely been better at it in his
heyday. Mr Thurkle departed feeling that these fellows,

although they had shark written all over them, knew their job.

The two sharks were left confronting one another. Chevalley didn't really feel extremely shark-like. But the whiff of the thing was in the air, and he supposed it was his business to play. Moreover, he had a plan.

'It would be a tremendous sale,' he said.

'It would, indeed.'

'And at a time when comparable affairs look like being thin on the ground?'

'Perfectly true.'

'His mind seemed to be inclining that way.'

'Yes—but I doubt whether it's his mind that's in question. I suspect this ignorant girl of having a mind of her own.'

'How unwarranted and deplorable.'

'Don't be flippant, Octavius. We must take this matter seriously—in the interest of the firm.'

'I suppose so.' As Domberg pretty well *was* the firm nowadays, this seemed to Chevalley another piece of humbug. But since his own future clearly depended on his becoming a partner one day, it was necessary to be discreet. 'I think,' he said suddenly, 'I'll make our Gloria's acquaintance.'

'Make her acquaintance?'

'If the firm will pay.' Chevalley heard himself say this in a quite unnecessarily brazen manner. 'Call it just a small speculative outlay.'

'Getting introduced, and taking her out to dinner—that sort of thing?'

'Nothing of the kind. Flying to Venice at the end of the week.'

'I see.' Domberg stared doubtfully at his employee. 'I don't quite know how you could—'

'We know where she is. It's a pensione on the Zattere.

And there's another one next door.' Chevalley, who knew a lot about Venice, paused momentarily. 'You don't suppose she's under the protection of a male travelling-companion?'

'No, I do not.' Before this facetious expression, Domberg wondered what, if anything, Chevalley knew about such things. 'She's probably with a girl, or a couple of girls, of her own age. Perhaps from her hospital. They'll be going about in quite a simple way. And I doubt whether you'll cut much ice by breezing up in a confident fashion, claiming their acquaintance, and taking them for a blow-out at the Gritti Palace.'

'I'm not a fool,' Chevalley said shortly.

'My dear Octavius, I am suggesting nothing of the kind.' It was a point, Domberg thought, upon which his assistant might usefully develop a more unflawed confidence. 'Only, you know, *she* may not be, either. A false move, and you might do more harm than good.'

'Perfectly true. Of course I'd be in Venice in a professional way—studying Carpaccio, or a project of that kind. It's something, after all, I'm rather entitled to do.' Chevalley, like Domberg a long time ago, was rather prickly about having taken to commercial courses.

'Abundantly,' Domberg said. 'In fact, we all hope you'll be publishing another paper soon. You have your reputation to make. And we are all behind you.'

'Thank you. My point is that, if we did get on friendly terms, it might all go swimmingly. Wandering around a place like Venice, the business of the collection would naturally crop up. And I might influence the girl towards a sensible view. In which case we'd have the sale in our pocket before the end of the year.'

Lambert Domberg sighed gently—a man of fine feeling, subdued to what he worked in. He pointed to the telephone on his desk.

'You'll need travellers cheques,' he said. 'Get the bank.'

9

THE COUNTERPAYNES AT HOME

THE DOMESTIC RITUALS of the Counterpaynes were undeviatingly upper class. The lower the higher, Jake would say to his sister Mary, meaning that the rituals tended to be further accentuated every time the dividends shrank. But were they really shrinking, Mary would ask, or was their father merely indulging himself in congenial gloom? Certainly the imagination of disaster—an endowment said to be invaluable to a novelist, but of little use in the world of practical affairs—was Cedric Counterpayne's in the largest measure. He would predict economic calamity, public or private, with all the sombre glee of a weather man reiterating over the air his dismal tale of depressions everywhere closing in upon the British Isles. Jake gave it as his own opinion that their father, like the weather chap, was, if only marginally, more often right than wrong, and that to some extent it must therefore be objectively true that things were going from bad to worse. Mary didn't care for such a state of affairs at all; she had rather a wide variety of interests in the pursuit of which ready cash is indispensable. Jake wasn't much bothered. For one thing, he was dedicated to tearing down the fabric of society, and it would have been illogical to deplore the misfortunes, whether real or fictitious, of an individual *rentier*. For another thing, when he wasn't thinking about tearing down *this* fabric, he was much more absorbedly engaged in covering other fabrics, suitably disposed on out-size easels, with bold expanses of time, when quite broke) made do, amiably enough, with acrylic paint. So Jake (who lived at home from time to even the more vexatious practical consequences of his father's persuasions.

One of these consequences was the port, which now always came from the grocer. It was disgusting stuff, and Cedric Counterpayne didn't fail to make, so to speak, a poor mouth about it. Jake would reply cheerfully that all port was disgusting, and at the same time treat himself to a private grin at the absurdity of a proponent of cultural revolution engaged in taking dessert in a formal way with his papa. It happened every night. His mother and Mary (having eaten a date or shared a banana) would withdraw, and the decanter would then make its second and final round. It really was a round, at least to the extent of circumambulating the single candle that burned in the centre of the table. Jake would draw the decanter in its coaster towards him from what was roughly the position of three o'clock, replenish his glass, move the decanter a foot to the left, and then shove it to the nine o'clock station—from which it would be retrieved by his father and brought finally to rest until the two gentlemen, having concluded their dignified occasion, rose, trundled everything into the kitchen, and did the washing up. This last as a masculine activity was another instance of upper-class *convenances*. Jake didn't suppose it happened that way in China. But then when you don't live in China it must sometimes be more or less in order not to do as the Chinese do. The same thing applies, for that matter, if you don't live in Clerkenwell or Golders Green.

The Counterpaynes lived at Olney, in a Georgian house of some impressiveness which, over a period of at least twenty years, Cedric Counterpayne had been constantly announcing must be put on the market at once. In a rural situation it is still possible to find those who come in to oblige, and the Counterpayne ladies were thus assisted in their domestic tasks fairly liberally from 9 a.m. till noon. Jake suspected, and Mary confirmed, that a semi-nocturnal presence of this kind would also have been feasible enough. Thus the washing up was rather a matter, perhaps, of showing the flag. In a general way showing the flag was an activity which Jake much approved. So—although he was often as lazy and self-absorbed as most artists of any sort are—he had never protested against this conclusion to the day.

It was happening now. Cedric Counterpayne had donned a butcher's apron, and was rinsing plates in cold water as a careful preliminary to getting down to the serious detergent job. Jake, whose turn it was to dry, filled in time stoking the stove.

'Nothing at all!' Cedric Counterpayne said. 'It's entirely out of the way.'

'Yes,' Jake said, in the tone of one who hasn't caught on to what is being talked about.

'Simply not done.'

'No—not done.'

'In more civilized times, even a man's mere acquaintances got something. Mourning rings, for example.'

'They must rather have piled up—at least if one lived to an advanced age.' Jake now knew what was to be discussed. 'And you couldn't exactly wear a dozen mourning rings. Perhaps you just stowed them away, and bequeathed them to your own pals in turn.'

'And I haven't even received the common courtesy of being shown Fenella's will.'

'They may have reckoned it would be embarrassing, since there wasn't a ring or a bean for you. Anyway, later on you can go and read it at Somerset House. Cost you a bob—if you can run to it.' Humorous reference to the perpetual *res-angusta-domi* theme was one of Jake's techniques for coping with his father's more tedious side.

'I wonder what the girl thinks about it.'

'Gloria? I don't suppose she thinks about it at all.' Jake took the first of the port glasses from his father, dried it with care, and then tossed it into the air and caught it again. (We have already met this bad habit of Jake Counterpayne's.) 'Why should she?'

'One ought to think about one's relations occasionally. And particularly at times of bereavement.'

'I suppose Gloria was bereaved, but it couldn't honestly be said that you were. The death of a first cousin isn't a bereavement—particularly when you haven't passed the time of day for thirty years.'

'You take a very unfeeling view.'

'Whereas you think you ought to be able to touch somebody.'

'And it isn't an occasion for wit—a death in the family. If only because there may always be another death at any time. We're in the midst of the thing. I might die tomorrow, Jake, and it would be the very devil. Even your mother's death would be distinctly awkward.' Cedric Counterpayne extracted a soup plate from the bubble-filled bowl with an air of comfortable gloom. 'Quite frankly, it would be a difficult corner to turn.'

'Whereas Mary or I would be expendable.'

'There you go again. A callous attitude to sacred things. Not that I wholly blame you, my dear boy. So long as one government after another pursues these utterly damnable fiscal policies, all decent and generous feeling will be virtually impossible to sustain. So I don't wholly blame Fenella, either. No doubt she was having a hard time— and that was why she neglected this gesture—it needed to be no more than that—of common family duty.'

'She didn't seem to be having too hard a time.' Jake was waiting patiently for the second soup plate. 'Everything brassed up all over, it seemed to me. It's true that the champagne wasn't too good. But then the thing was pretty well a garden-party.' Jake paused to produce, quite unconsciously, his peculiar effect of virtually simultaneous scowl and grin. He might have been reflecting that he had just achieved a discrimination which would seem a bit obscure to Chairman Mao. 'There was a butler and all that, and dabs of caviar on the *canapés*. In fact your poor cousin Fenella Montacute was very comfortably in the mun. From day to day, I mean, and quite apart from owning all that museum junk. Do get on with those plates. I want to watch the News on the box. There's been a big demo in Trafalgar Square.'

Cedric Counterpayne got on with the plates. He judged televised demos to constitute a poor form of spectator sport, but considered that Jake was entitled to his own estimation of such things. Buried beneath decades of fretful idleness in him there was enough intelligence to make him prize a working relationship with his son.

'Anti-something?' he asked jocosely, and produced a couple of plates in brisk succession.

'Yes—anti-something. Was there anything definite you were going to say about Gloria?'

'About Gloria?' Understandably, Cedric Counterpayne was a little struck by the slant thus given to the conversation. 'Well, yes. It seems to me up to her to make good this neglect—we'll be prepared to call it an inadvertent neglect—on her mother's part.'

'Gloria ought to send you that mourning ring?'

'Not *exactly* a mourning ring. For good or ill, that belongs to a past age. But a memento, say. Or a keepsake. Rather a charming word, keepsake.'

'Can be a charming thing too. There's a young doctor in Scott Fitzgerald—'

'Scott Fitzgerald?'

'Irrelevant. A young doctor who's jilted by a girl, and who goes into the morgue, and cuts out of a female corpse—'

'Jake.'

'Sorry. You're absolutely right. Well—what about Gloria?'

'If the matter were simply brought to her mind, I've little doubt she would repair her mother's neglect.'

'Send something?'

'Just that. But the *right* thing. Recall Lady Lumber.'

'Can't. Never heard of her.'

'My dear boy, she lived at Stoke Goldington. When she was dying, your mother used to go over a great deal. Read the Bible to her, and Lord knows what. And the old soul was very insistent she should have something. Just to remember her by.'

'I'd remember anybody I read the Bible to in these circumstances, without what you call "something" arriving by post afterwards. But go on.'

'Not by post. We're no distance from Stoke Goldington. You must remember *that*. A groom brought it over in a trap.'

'I see. And what was it?'

'Well, that's the odd thing. After the funeral, and so forth, the old girl's son rang up, and asked what your mother would like to have. Which shows that poor Lady L. must have been muttering about the matter with her dying breath. Difficult for your mother. She couldn't very well say a thimble or a pin-cushion on the one hand, or the prize piece of Lumber family plate on the other. But she remembered that the house was absolutely stuffing with footstools. Regency footstools, for what that's worth. So she said she'd dearly like a Regency footstool.'

'And the groom brought one over?'

'No. He brought a parasol.'

'A parasol?' Jake stared blankly at his father.

'A parasol. Small summer umbrella.'

'But one couldn't *say* "Regency footstool" and be *heard* as saying—'

'Quite so. It was very mysterious.'

Father and son had arrived momentarily on common ground. They might be described as having entered the theatre of the absurd. They regarded each other with gravity. With gravity (or against it) Jake sent a plate spinning to within an inch of the ceiling, and caught it again without giving it a glance.

'Well, well!' Jake said. 'Mary will have made the coffee.'

Mary Counterpayne had made the coffee, as usual, in a bulbous glass contraption, vaguely suggestive of alchemical enterprise, for which her father had paid half-a-crown in his favourite local junk-yard. It was perfectly efficient, and the memory of this unwontedly triumphant episode in his long struggle with economic adversity cheered him up regularly every evening.

'Jake and I,' he said amiably to the ladies, 'have been having a chat about Gloria Montacute. And I was about to tell him that I think he ought to go and pay his respects.'

'Well, I'm—' Being in the presence of his mother, Jake checked himself in what it was natural to say. 'What an odd notion.'

'You mean,' Mary asked her father, 'that Gloria's to be regarded as the head of the family?'

'Nothing of the kind. It would simply be the decent thing. After all, we none of us went to the funeral.'

'We weren't invited,' Mrs Counterpayne said over her embroidery. 'And they put "private" in the notice in *The Times*.'

'At least Jake may be said to have been in at the death,' Mary pointed out. 'In fact, poor Fenella died as he goggled at her, like the serpent-woman under the gaze of the philosopher in the poem.'

'Lamia didn't die, dear.' Mrs Counterpayne had long struggled in the interest of the literary cultivation of her children. 'But you are quite right, in a way. She screamed and vanished, which is more or less the same thing.'

'I have always been glad,' Cedric Counterpayne said

seriously, 'that Jake attended that party—unhappy though its outcome was. His presence indicated proper family feeling.'

'I gate-crashed,' Jake said, and gulped his coffee. He still had his mind on the Nine o'clock News. 'Vulgar curiosity.'

'It was that, was it?' Mary looked hard at her brother. 'I've another theory.'

'Which you can bloody well keep to yourself. As for that party, the girl wasn't there, and I got a bit tight—'

'*Because* she wasn't there?' Mary asked.

'Because the champagne was bad. And I shouted at the butler, and it was a bit of a shambles all round. I'd be *persona non* thingummy, you may take it from me, if I ever went near Nudd again.'

'But I understand you remained,' Cedric Counterpayne said. 'As a member of the family, you very properly remained, and had a word with your cousin—'

'It's rot that second cousins are cousins.'

'And had a word with Gloria after the sad news had been broken to her. I judge it unlikely that you made a fool of yourself.'

'Perhaps I didn't.' Jake scowled ferociously as he was obliged to make this admission. 'But what's all this in aid of, anyway? Mourning rings all round?'

'Mourning rings?' Mrs Counterpayne repeated.

'Father thinks it would show nice feeling in Gloria if she gave us something to remember her mama by. And nothing can be more benevolent in intention than encouraging the growth of nice feeling in what used to be called an unformed girl.'

'Unformed?' Mary said. 'Gloria, by all accounts, is far from that. Her having a form is the first thing one notices about her.'

'Mary, you do say the most dead common things from time to time.' Jake offered this opinion dispassionately.

'I'm to go to Nudd again, and ingratiate myself with the girl, and say your mother is uncommonly fond of Regency footstools.'

'Regency footstools?' Mrs Counterpayne echoed, perplexed. 'I suppose there are such things. But I can't remember ever—'

'Footstools are a joke,' Cedric Counterpayne said. 'But something—unspectacular, but good of its kind—I do think it would be pleasant to receive. And pleasant to *give*. That's what I chiefly have in mind. Once she'd done it, she'd be *glad* she'd done it. A picture, say. Something like that.'

'Is your memory good enough,' Jake asked mildly, 'for you to have any particular picture in mind?'

'I do remember a small boy in fancy dress and on horseback. Rather a delightful affair. And just about right, wouldn't you say? Appropriate and all that.'

'The small boy happens to be by Velazquez, and to be worth more than an unfortunate black would earn if he laboured without stopping for two thousand years.'

'An unfortunate black?' Jake's mother reiterated. She was clearly much puzzled. '*What* unfortunate black?'

But at this Jake Counterpayne made a gesture of despair and left the room.

In Trafalgar Square, Robert Dougall told him, eight youths had been arrested, but were understood to have been subsequently released. This mild end to the demo seemed to encourage Mr Dougall, who smiled cheerfully as he added that that was all from him tonight. The weather chap appeared next, but Jake was uninterested in weather and switched off. He then found that his sister had followed him into the room where the box was kept. It was their old nursery, and still used for any ganging up they did. Feud, indeed, was quite as much a part of its history as was conspiracy. A bold scratch across the middle of the hardwood floor still bore witness to the summary resolution of some boundary dispute long before. At one end there continued to hang framed snapshots of Mary jumping over unimpressive barriers on a fat pony, and at the other end the wall was a palimpsest of carelessly pinned up and overlapping photographs, drawings and posters commemorating the development —whether intellectual, moral or artistic—of her brother. There was a page torn out of *Babar and Father Christmas* upon which some ruthless raid on a family album, followed by an infantile but ingenious labour of *collage,* had resulted in the helpful Professor Gillianez, the celebrated Professor William Jones, and even Socrates himself, all having been transmogrified into a much younger Cedric Counterpayne. There was a faded, cardboard-mounted group in which a stripling Jake glowered cross-legged from between the knees of a beefier boy clutching a football. There was the standard poster-like portrait of Che Guevara. There were reproductions of various bits and pieces of contemporary art—all dating from before the astounding day upon which Jake had discovered and asserted that he was an artist himself. If anything was missing, it was what might be called tokens or manifestos of erotic interests. It was Mary's opinion (she was three years older than Jake) that this lacuna was rather far from testifying to her brother's sexual innocence. But she may have been quite wrong. It is a sphere in which young men develop more variously than can readily be deduced from the pages of the Modern English Novel.

'What an idiotic conversation!' Mary said. 'But might there be anything in it?'

'Getting something convertible into hard cash out of Gloria?' Neither brother nor sister was often astray as to what the other was talking about. 'It seems improbable. But you never can tell. We know nothing about her.'

'You don't mean that you *will* go to Nudd—and pay your respects, as Daddy calls it?'

'Why not?'

'Why not? It isn't exactly you, for one thing.' Mary didn't say this approvingly. Her mother was vague and her father was hopeless, so it would balance things up a little if only Jake would adopt a practical slant towards the family fortunes. She gave utterance to this feeling now. 'You care damn-all about money.'

'You couldn't be farther wrong. I'm a bloody Forsyte, if you only knew. Hardly ever think of anything else.'

'Half the year, you have to live at home like a kid—'

'So have you—and you're older than I am.'

'This is utterly stupid.' Not being able to say something like 'Girls are different, God help them', Mary was baffled for a moment. So she went off at a tangent. 'Just what was the set-up you found at Nudd?'

'Well, Gloria wasn't living half the year there.'

'Of course not. The Montacutes are rolling.'

'My dear child, neither was she putting in her time idling at St-Tropez. She was holding down a job. Think of that. Probably still is.'

'Then you must go to Nudd at a week-end.' Mary was instantly practical. 'Unless you exchange letters or something first.'

'Don't feel much like that. Laborious. Just drop in.'

'That would probably be best.' For a moment Mary looked as perplexed as her mother was accustomed to do. She had little faith in the emergence of anything that could be called a calculating or venal Jake. 'Tell me more about the place. And about the people. Are there other Montacutes? I'm not clued up on it at all.'

'I don't think there are any other Montacutes—except, perhaps, far away out. We seem to be her nearest relations. That's what Daddy's on about, wouldn't you say? Nearest relations should get their whack. Let's say we agree.'

'Let's say anything that comes into our heads.' Mary resented the mocking hypothetical cast of this proposal. 'Just who was at Nudd when Fenella died—apart, I mean, from all the people who'd come to stare at Velazquez, and all that?'

'Nobody at all. A butler and some hired waiters. It was a bit awful, really. Oh! There was a young man.'

'A young man?'

'A young prole. And you needn't grin. Social class exists. It's just something we have to cope with. So let's face it. I resented this chap, partly just because he *was* a prole.' Jake had flushed. 'At least I'm prepared to be suitably ashamed.'

'There was some other reason for resenting him?'

'He seemed to think he was running the thing. Poor old Fenella's death and its aftermath, I mean. He *was* running it. Quite competently, too.'

'Just who was he?'

'The local farmer's son, or something. I think he'd been out with Gloria. I wasn't sure I liked him terribly.'

'Because he *was*—'

'Not that at all.' Jake was suddenly confident. 'I had a feeling there was something rather cunning about him.'

'You mean he may be after the Montacute millions?'

'No, I don't think I do.'

'Then he must just be—' Mary checked herself. 'Let's face a bit more of it,' she said.

'Such as?'

'That you've always had a thing about this Montacute cousin. Ever since you funked her as a kid.'

'*Funked* her?' Jake stared at his sister. 'You're bats. We *were* kids. Do you mean that I failed in some lovely infantile romance?'

'Something like that. She came *here*. And then you refused to go and stay *there*.'

'I accept that, at least as a stupid family joke. I've even

repeated it. But you're not pretending it has left some
sort of scar, or something?'

'A trauma. You failed in masculinity, my dear.'

It would have been reasonable to call the Counterpaynes, brother and sister, clever young people. They
talked to each other like this. But, at the moment, there
was something not quite idle in the nursery air.

'Have you any memory,' Jake asked, 'of just how old I
was?'

'Of course I have. But what have *you* always remembered about *her*?'

'That she was rather a jolly kid.' Jake Counterpayne
had a considerable command of straight answers.

'There you are. And just why did you take it into your
head to gate-crash that party, and have what you called
a dekko at her?'

'I've told you. Vulgar curiosity.'

'You're crude, and rude, and egotistical, and variously
disreputable. You put on turns. You haven't the slightest notion of earning an honest living.' Mary Counterpayne
offered these remarks sweetly. 'But I wouldn't say you're
vulgar. Your little dreams and purposes aren't vulgar. Or
not exactly. And that's the difference between us.'

Jake Counterpayne appeared to feel that this was the
kind of point from which family conversations do not
usefully continue.

'I'm going out to the barn to square up a canvas,' he
said shortly. 'And I'm going to Nudd on Sunday.'

10

ENCOUNTER WITH RUSTIC LOVERS

SUNDAY CAME, AND Jake went. If he went, in the end, none too willingly, this was less a matter of his own deeper disposition in the affair (something pretty obscure to him, anyway) than of reacting to family fuss. His father made as much ado over the expedition as if he really expected Jake to bring home Velazquez's Don Balthasar Carlos in the back of his mini-van. His mother appeared to judge it more probable that what he would bring back was Gloria Montacute herself—and perhaps no longer just as Gloria Montacute, but as one whom lightning action on the part of the Archbishop of Canterbury had translated into a Counterpayne. Some dream of this sort even revealed itself as having been in Mrs Counterpayne's mind a dozen years before—upon the occasion, in fact, of the more or less infant Gloria's unreturned visit to Olney. So long ago, Jake realized, had his mother seen what might be called a solution in this grand alliance. So long ago, therefore, had the poor lady already been perpending what she was accustomed to refer to as 'your father's difficulties'. All this rather browned Jake off.

Ought Jake to take Gloria a present? Mrs Counterpayne distinctly remembered that Gloria, on the occasion of her historic sojourn at Olney, had brought Jake nothing less than an air-gun—a weapon discharging either small lead slugs or brightly tufted darts with equal velocity. The gift, having been a little beyond Jake's years, had occasioned some anxiety at the time. It was positively transformed into an augury now.

Jake had no intention of taking Gloria a present. Anything of the kind would render implausible the fiction under cover of which he was going to make his bow: to wit, that finding himself quite unexpectedly in the neighbourhood of Nudd he had thought he might as well drop in. Jake rehearsed the delivery of this twaddle to himself several times, being without a clue that it would be beyond him to deliver it. The young know singularly little about themselves. Almost as little as do the aged.

Jake drew to a halt on the brow of a hill. (It is a spot we have visited before.) He wondered who Nudd had been. The name suggested an uncouth personage in a saga, or something of that kind. Perhaps he had been a Dane who had gone in for a spot of rapine in these parts before grabbing some land in a more permanent way and settling down. In which case he would find his old territory not wholly congenial now. It suggested nothing more warlike than the domestication, in modestly genteel dwellings dotted all over the view, of retired Indian Army colonels lingering out their shivering span beyond any last residual warmth that might be at play upon them from the sunset of the *raj*.

Nudd Manor itself was all right. Jake found that, despite his social and political convictions, he quite took to it. What disturbed him was the larger, although still quite local, prospect. Where the hell had it come from? Why had it been allowed to come about? He reckoned himself —apart from the rudiments of his own profession—as being as superlatively uneducated as any other public-school boy. But he wasn't sure that there hadn't been history lessons to which he had sufficiently listened to render him now perplexed before this queerly gentrified scene. It couldn't have any historical roots, this unnatural concentration of ingeniously mellow-looking country houses (which was what estate agents would call them) all within shouting distance (not that anybody here *would* shout) of a genuine ye-olde parish church. Something had

simply gone wrong with history—with all that stuff about
the manorial system and what have you—to produce such
a result. *Modern England, or Death Warmed Up*. There
were depressed moments—for example, when he told himself he couldn't even learn to draw—in which Jake gloomily fancied he might one day find himself writing books.
Well, at least he'd write one with just that title.

These were Gloria Montacute's surroundings, and they
must a bit have rubbed off on her. Yet he didn't remember
her as like that. And he *did* remember her—very vividly
indeed. He'd never again in all his life stand, a complete
stranger, before a girl who minutes before had learnt of
her mother's sudden death. Once was enough. But a good
sort of girl she'd certainly been. That, as his sister had
acutely guessed, was what this was all about.

Scowling at his own incoherence, Jake put his hand on
the ignition-switch of the van, and then thought better of
this and looked at his watch. It was half past twelve, which
struck him as an awkward hour. If he drove up to Nudd
now, he'd pretty well be inviting himself to lunch. Not
on.

He looked behind him and to his right. Up there, and
with surprising abruptness, quite a different terrain appeared: something like a ridge of downland, with here
and there the hump of a tumulus or an old barn. It was a
beckoning leg-stretching prospect, so that on an impulse
he scrambled out of the van. Perhaps it was a cowardly
and delaying tactic, but he'd walk for the outside of an
hour and arrive on Gloria a little after two o'clock. He
reached back into one of the van's capacious pouches and
brought out a packet of chocolate biscuits. These, although
betraying a somewhat juvenile taste, would be a perfectly
satisfactory meal.

He climbed to the sky-line, which didn't take long.
And everything was suddenly as solitary as you could

please. The only visible work of man was some sort of large tumble-down shed and a few chunks of baled straw. You could sing at the top of your voice, or shout any scraps of poetry in your head, and nobody would be the wiser. Jake almost started singing and then, for some reason, refrained. Instead—which was to prove to be unfortunate—he decided to explore the not very interesting ruin in front of him. It had been a barn or cow-house: something like that. He vaulted a little rampart of straw, turned inward, and stopped dead. With shocking abruptness, he had come on a couple making love.

Love-making was not, for one of Jake's generation, quite invariably a wholly private affair. But to his own way of thinking it was certainly that, and this made it odd that he now stayed put and watched, in a paralysed but interested way, just what was going on. He had become, of an instant, a *voyeur*, and for some seconds, at least, the fact didn't at all trouble him. He realized intuitively, rather than saw, that the couple were very young: quite as young as he was himself. It passed through his head that this was obscurely a factor in his behaviour; that it somehow made his spectatorship innocent. But almost at once he wasn't liking the reaction of his own heart and pulse. There was something demeaning in that kind and degree of excitement, it seemed, when one wasn't oneself in on the act. So he was really turning away, or was about to do so, when the man rolled over and he glimpsed the girl. She was a sallow, narrow-hipped creature, who looked less in need of a lover than of a square meal. Jake was suddenly horrified—and in this instant the man sat up and looked at him. And Jake looked at the man. It was the farmer's son, or whoever, who had once seen him out of Nudd. The young man had arched himself awkwardly in air, and was furiously pulling up his trousers, as Jake mumbled confused words and walked very rapidly away.

11

THE MONTACUTE CURATOR

He walked for an hour, just as he had promised himself. Rather to his surprise, it took a good part of this time to sort himself out. He was quite clear that having paused to witness a spot of copulation hadn't in itself much worried him. Perhaps it ought to have, but it hadn't. A couple of times he deliberately ran the thing through his head again, as one might a length of tape on a tape recorder, and it remained merely exciting and amusing, with no overtones of guilt attaching to his own bad behaviour at all. He didn't even feel ashamed of not feeling ashamed.

It hadn't been exactly agreeable, all the same. In fact, it had gone bad on him, and in two swift stages. There had been an odd shock, for a start, in the sudden glimpse of the half-stripped girl. Perhaps that had been what he'd once heard somebody call the John Ruskin syndrome. Poor young John R., brought up on the classical Nude as it culminated in Ingres and all that, suddenly confronted with the real thing in the person of his bride, and making no recovery to the end of his days. But it couldn't be that. Jake hadn't been an art student for four years without seeing plenty of naked girls. He hadn't, of course, known *this* girl from Adam—or rather from Eve—and he'd never see her again. It had just been the sudden perception that she was, so to speak, one particular girl, one individual and unique human being, here tumbled in straw upon the bestial floor, that had revealed itself as a thoroughly shocking thing. Jake felt that this piece of enlarged experience was quite worth brooding over.

But the real rub—if it might be put that way—was that he *had* known the young man. There the chap had been, detected and ludicrously feeling that there might be restored dignity in pulling his pants up. Come to think of it, though, he might have had a more practical aim. He couldn't have scrambled to his feet and come *hobbling* at Jake without further ignominy. It had been his idea to get himself in fighting trim.

Jake rather took to this view of the matter. If they'd had a fight, he himself might be feeling better now. It came to him as he strode over the down that he was nursing a blind and baffled rage, and that there would have been salubrity in agreeing to have a punch-up. He'd himself have landed some stiff ones, since he wasn't by any reckoning a weakling. But he had a notion that his adversary would have had the edge on him, would have given a shade more than he'd got.

This still dodged the main fact. It had been this lecherous young yokel who'd believed himself in charge of things at Nudd—and 'things' in this context had included Gloria herself—in the hours immediately following the death of Fenella Montacute at that bloody party.

It was the party that was increasingly in Jake's head as he made his way back to the van, and it stuck there as he sat in the little tin box munching chocolate biscuits. He'd hated all that hoarded treasure and hated all those people, dripping real wealth and bogus responses, who'd been yattering their way through it. In particular—although it wasn't all that relevant—he'd hated the smooth peddling rascal who was one half of Comberback and Domberg. So he'd put on a cheap turn. And then there had been catastrophe.

He felt, in an extravagant fashion he condemned in himself, that he'd like a bath. If there had been so much as a puddle up here on the down he'd almost have stripped and splashed in it before going on to Nudd. But he *was* going on to Nudd. He was quite clear about that.

His first impression was that the house must have been sold. There had, so far as he knew, been no family communication with Nudd, so the thing might have happened without the Counterpaynes hearing about it. It had been sold and—quite clearly—turned into an expensive private lunatic asylum.

Jake's notions of the custodial care of the mentally infirm were not particularly up to date, and his conjecture was based on the fact that every visible window of the mansion was screened on its inside by a fine metal lattice. These lattices, it was possible to discern, were of considerable elegance in themselves, which showed a very nice feeling on somebody's part for the susceptibilities of the inmates. And this was further proof that they must be a well-to-do crowd, since sensibility does not survive insanity except among the prosperous classes.

Not intending, however, to retreat without inquiry, Jake drove up to the front door, got out, and rang the bell. There was a long wait. Then he heard footsteps, and received a distinct impression of keys being turned and bolts drawn. The door was opened—cautiously, he thought—and he was being surveyed by a heavily built girl of rustic demeanour.

'Good afternoon,' Jake said conventionally and not hopefully. 'Is Miss Montacute at home?' The girl looked bewildered, so that it was apparent the question had been an unexpected one. 'Or has she—'

'The Curator will receive you in the library.'

The girl had said this, it seemed to Jake, rather with the effect of an automatic device at the other end of a telephone line; he felt that she must be programmed to go on repeating the same phrase until, somehow, you cut her off. But in fact she now stood back and ushered him

into the hall. He didn't particularly want to be inter-
viewed by some sort of medical superintendent or head
keeper. On the other hand the girl didn't seem to be a
likely source of reliable information, so he decided he'd
better go ahead. It was queer being inside Nudd again;
it was queer to find himself skirting once more what he
had heard that poor old Fenella called her *fontana minore*.
But it was even queerer hearing what his conductress
said next.

'Another American gentleman was here only this morning, sir. There has surely been a lot of interest of late. Not
that I'm supposed to speak of it, mind you.' The utterance
of this female attendant upon the insane again had its
curious quality of going by rote. 'From Harvard, he was.
There's a lot there, it seems, as they'd like to send to
Nudd.'

Jake found this intelligence astonishing. He was inclined, it was true, to think of all universities as crackpot
places, but Harvard must be in a bad way if it had to
export its lunatics across the Atlantic pretty well *en
masse*. Perhaps Nudd had been taken over by some institution with a reputation for coping successfully with
demented professors and egg-heads generally.

He was shown into the library, and left alone. It wasn't
one of the rooms he had wandered through on his earlier
visit, and he tried to look round it with proper curiosity.
But it wasn't easy, he found, since there was really nothing but Gloria in his head. It was clear that no Gloria
was going to show up—and this, perplexingly, seemed to
be both a disappointment and a relief. He supposed he
was afraid that, if she had been at Nudd, he might have
come out with something impossibly presuming about
the company she had been choosing to keep on the day
of her mother's death. He'd like that beastly young man
to have receded a little into the background before he
saw her again.

The library door opened, and as he turned round he recognized at once the figure framed in it. It was simply the late Mrs Montacute's butler.

And Jake saw that the late Mrs Montacute's butler in his turn recognized him.

'I regret that Miss Montacute is not in residence, sir.'

'Oh! Then she does still live here?' Jake jerked this out awkwardly. For a start, the butler's form of words had been unexpected. Presumably Guise—he remembered that to be the chap's name—regarded it as appropriate to Gloria's new dignity as owner of Nudd, but to Jake's ear it sounded more the sort of thing you would say about an absentee duke, or somebody of that kind. Then again, here was the man he had shouted 'Waiter!' at when doing his thing as a young social iconoclast and scourge of the bourgeoisie. Guise wasn't likely to have forgotten it.

'Most certainly, sir. I know of no other intention at present, I am glad to say. I believe I may be speaking to Mr James Counterpayne?'

'That's me.' Jake was impressed that Guise should be clued up on family matters in this way. Of course his name had eventually transpired on the occasion of old Fenella's death. But it was smart of the chap to have held on to it, and moreover he now seemed to be comporting himself very properly. If you believed in the rules, that was. Jake added this to himself hastily. He had no intention of digging master-and-man stuff with Guise or anybody else. Still, it was useful to be recognized as having a kind of family status.

'Is Gloria going to be away for long?' Jake asked.

There was a brief silence. Jake saw that calling Gloria 'Gloria' had been a mistake. The intention, of course, had been to get on a reformed social footing with Guise, but Guise clearly received it as a familiarity.

'I'm afraid I have no information on that point, sir.

When she returns to Nudd, I will take occasion to inform her of your call.'

This sounded dismissive, but to Jake it carried some other suggestion as well. Butlers were cattle who seldom came his way. But did a real butler talk like a stage butler unless he was himself in some obscure fashion enacting a role? And there was something elusive about Guise's wave-length, anyway. It was partly that he was being watchful and almost wary, as if he suspected this visitor of being after the family spoons. But then—Jake asked himself reasonably—why shouldn't he? Jake's accent (which Jake couldn't help) was the only socially respectable ticket he carried around with him, and his previous appearance at Nudd had been pretty well in the character of a Bolshevik—a word which no doubt actually existed in this elderly lackey's vocabulary. So if Guise had calling the police at the back of his head—well, good luck to him.

But there was something else about Guise which Jake found himself completely unable to define or identify. The chap had an aura—although that was a silly term—that Jake didn't at all react against. It was something which, if it were to emerge more clearly, might take on the character almost of a link or bond. Perhaps, Jake thought rather wildly, he was himself by nature what might be called a servant-class person. Perhaps he ought to have begun life as a page or a bell-hop or a boot-boy. It was an ideologically alluring vision, this of himself as *anima naturaliter proletariana*, but he doubted whether he really believed in it. No—it was something different and wholly elusive that hovered between Guise and himself.

But now another puzzle came into Jake's head. He had entered Nudd to the accompaniment of some very unaccountable remarks. All that about lunatics from Harvard, for instance. It would be difficult to bring up just that, but there had been something else he could fairly have a go at. And he'd do so, he decided, by way of bold challenge.

'The woman who showed me in, Mr Guise, said something about a Curator. What was the meaning of that?'

'A Curator, sir? I hardly think so. Caretaker, perhaps.'

'Curator was the word.'

'A somewhat similar word. Confusion is no doubt possible. Miss Montacute has instructed me to act as caretaker here during her absence abroad.'

'Abroad?' This took Jake off at a tangent. He somehow didn't associate Gloria with foreign parts.

'Miss Montacute is at present travelling on the continent.'

'Oh, I see. Well, just where is she now?'

'On that, sir, I am unable to afford you any information.'

It was an impasse—and with the chap talking like a book again. Moreover Guise had distinguishably spoken with a deliberate ambiguity. He might have been saying, 'You don't get *that* out of me, young man'. Or he might not.

'And you don't know when she'll be back?'

'No, sir.'

'Didn't she have a job in London? Has she given it up?'

There was a silence which Jake was young enough to find unnerving. And Guise had raised his eyebrows. A moment later he moved to the library door and respectfully opened it. It would never have occurred to Jake that a door *could* be opened respectfully. But there the thing was.

'You have your car, sir?' Guise asked.

Jake had his car, or at least he had his van. And it didn't look as if more was going to be said. He didn't think he was going to say more himself. For not at all deeply buried in Jake Counterpayne was a sensitive and

misdoubting youth. He remembered his father's idiotic
notions about Don Balthasar Carlos. At home they were
rather endearing, but they wouldn't carry well. He had
no fancy for himself as a prowling and predatory relative.
He withdrew into dignity and allowed himself to be conducted through Nudd.

And that might have been all. But he did look about
him as he walked. You couldn't move among these things,
among these tremendous and imprisoned presences, without doing *that*. And—this time—there weren't all those
awful people. There was only Guise.

Suddenly Jake came to a halt. It was before a small
picture—a bit of Venetian *poésie*, it might have been
called—displayed on an easel. The easel had a swathe of
dark crimson velvet draped over the back of it. The
arrangement was effective, but rather suggested a shop.
There was a little tag on the frame—the late Mrs Montacute had owned a weakness for informative tags—which
read *School of Giorgione*. And Jake made a grab at his
own most *farouche* manner.

'George only, again!' Jake said. 'Well, well.'

In the resulting silence, Guise did a strange thing—the
stranger for being not in the least directed at Jake. It was
almost as if Guise had forgotten Jake, and as if he was
doing something he had long meditated doing. He walked
up to the easel, removed the velvet cloth, folded it, and
laid it aside. Then he stood back.

'Yes,' Guise said.

'Yes,' Jake echoed—and it was somehow the most expressive syllable he had managed to utter in Nudd.

'And *School of Giorgione* isn't right either,' Guise said
in a new voice. 'It was in the nature of some to have
Schools, you might say, and some not. I speak in ignor-
ance, sir, as you must know. But I suggest "Mystery" as
a better word. A mysterious business, Mr Counterpayne,
all that about Giorgione. Very mysterious, indeed.'

12

TWO YOUNG MEN IN CONVERSATION

HALF-A-POUND of chocolate biscuits, consumed neat, would probably constitute a somewhat burdensome refection to one of mature years. But to a young man lately emerged from his nonage—and masticating, moreover, in a condition of brooding cerebration—such a mere snack or nuncheon is likely to leave a feeling of inanition little more than an hour or two later.

This was Jake Counterpayne's state as—beneath the thoughtful regard of Mr Guise—he scrambled into his van before the august façade of Nudd and drove away. He hadn't, indeed, much idea of doing anything except distancing the mansion by some miles prior to starting to think. Gloria's absence had dashed him; the butler by whom he had been 'received' puzzled him a good deal; he couldn't get the pilgrims from Harvard, whether supposititious or real, out of his head. It was a case in which distance might lend a measure of clarity to the view.

In the village over which Nudd presided like a throned lady, however, he had to slow down. He was a careful driver, and there were a lot of kids fooling around in the road. It was thus that he spotted the tea-shoppe. Shoppe was not, in fact, what it called itself, but it was that sort of place. Frail gentlewomen of advanced years no doubt ran it for their health. More pertinently, displayed in its window, without (somehow) the slightest effect of grossness, was a handsome pyramid of out-size muffins. It is well known that muffins correct chocolate biscuits just as brandy corrects port—and particularly if accompanied by three or four cups of China tea. Jake brought the van to a halt and went inside.

It was a tiny place and almost empty—an unsurprising fact since it was not yet half-past three. Still, lunch (if the ladies did lunches) must by now be 'off' and tea correspondingly 'on'. In a just confidence as to this, Jake sat down. A lady appeared almost at once, and didn't seem in the least put out when he modestly admitted his persuasion that tea and muffin would be precisely it.

A man with a military bearing and a dog on a lead left the shop, and as a result Jake now found himself alone in it with only two other customers, a couple of women of uninteresting age who were in a window-recess just over his left shoulder. He ought to have sat down at a table a little farther away, but by this time his tea had arrived and he sat tight.

'Not yet awhile,' he heard one of the women say. 'No, we don't expect Miss Gloria—Miss Montacute, Mr Guise says I ought to say now—back just yet. It seems she's quite seeing the world—a thing very proper to her station, after all.'

The voice offering this information and opinion had somehow contrived to suggest communication of the most confidential kind, so that Jake realized with misgiving that he was listening in on gossip. Having so surprisingly done a peeping Tom act only a few hours before, he was quite without a fancy for eavesdropping now. For some minutes, however, it didn't seem avoidable.

'Where is she at present?' the second woman asked. She spoke in quite a different tone, one of brisk interrogation and of a certain authority. In a rural hierarchy of which Jake had some understanding, there was a distinction between the two women.

'Now, that I don't know, Mrs Carter. Mr Guise may know. Carrying the responsibilities he does, I'd say he must know. But he has always been a little close, Mr Guise has. Perhaps Mr Harry might know?'

This, plainly, had been a foray between the venture-some and the impertinent. It got no change.

'Harry would have no occasion to know anything of the sort, Mrs Bantry.'

'Ah, it would be my mistake—him being, like yourself, Mrs Carter, on proper visiting terms at Nudd. And so clever a young man, bound to go far. At college already! Who knows where he may go?'

'He works quite hard at times,' Harry's mother said. She didn't speak as if she judged her son exceptional among human kind.

'And knowing so many of the young people hereabouts. Very attractive to the young women, your son is said to be. And I'm not surprised, I'm sure. Such a well set-up lad! Thoughtful, too. For instance, that time that he brought you to Nudd—'

'Won't you have another pastry, Mrs Bantry?'

It was plain that the woman called Mrs Carter wasn't having more of this. Nor was Jake. He was bolting his muffin furiously and as fast as he could. He did wonder, however, why Mrs Carter was giving tea to Mrs Bantry at all. Mrs Bantry must be some sort of upper domestic at Nudd. There could be no doubt who Harry was. And if Harry was a farmer's son, then Mrs Carter was that farm-er's wife. She had wanted information out of Mrs Bantry, information as to just when Gloria was likely to come home. And she hadn't, somehow, sounded as if she'd be heartbroken if the mistress of Nudd remained abroad for quite some time. Jake felt that Mrs Carter was a sensible woman.

But he also felt, and much more vividly, that this just wouldn't do. As a lurker in other people's backgrounds he'd damn-well done his stint for the day. He jumped up, paid his bill, and charged out of the shop.

In the doorway he charged into somebody—somebody

who appeared to own the power, in these circumstances, of rooting himself to the ground. Jake recoiled, perceptibly jolted, and found it was Harry he was staring at.

'I've come to fetch my mother,' Harry said, and thumbed in the direction of a Land-Rover behind him. He spoke just as if he and Jake were acquaintances of a casual order. In a sense they were.

'You'll find her inside.' Jake was constrained to reply more or less on the same note. And with this he made to pass on. He found the encounter upsetting. There Harry Carter had been, after all, pulling up his pants in the straw.

'She can wait,' Harry said.

'Why should she wait?' Jake asked crossly. There wasn't quite room to get past.

'You and I might have a word. Come and have a look at our cricket field.'

'Very well.'

Jake spoke under what proved to be a misapprehension. It was a misapprehension generated by that last image of Harry Carter as struggling with a garment in the interest of unimpeded motion—no longer of an amorous sort but aggressively in his, Jake's, direction. Jake had really supposed that Harry was intending a fight. He had himself subsequently imagined a fight as he strode over the down. And he had now taken it into his head that the local cricket field was the prescriptive spot upon which the lads of the village had it out with each other. Although he still felt the odds to be rather stiffly against him, he was quite ready to muck in.

But Harry, now heading for the outskirts of the village, was glancing sideways at him without any belligerent effect. It was a wary and calculating glance, perhaps, but it seemed perfectly friendly as well.

'We met at Nudd,' Harry said. 'You're a relation of Gloria's?'

'We're second cousins.' Jake was a little startled by this directness.

'Have you come to these parts to look her up?'

'Yes.'

'She's abroad. Do you know where?'

'No.'

'She'll be in Venice by now. At least, that's what her last postcard said.'

Jake received this blow in silence. It had certainly been effectively planted. What Harry Carter was up to was a kind of gloat. He was in correspondence with Gloria, and letting Jake know the fact. Jake felt a spurt of impotent rage. The sensation reminded him oddly of some juvenile occasion when a beastly prefect had the whip hand on him and was demonstrating the fact.

'Here we are,' Harry said easily, and sat down sprawling on a bench. 'A peaceful spot.'

Naturally a village cricket field is a peaceful spot. But something in Harry's voice spoke to Jake of an ironical intention. Harry had guessed Jake had been thinking in terms of a punch up. And Harry was amused.

'But seriously,' Harry said suddenly.

'Seriously?' Jake echoed. He wasn't too pleased by his vacant repetition of a word. He was letting this assured yokel make all the running. Not that 'yokel' was exactly right. At Olney there were several Harrys (only perhaps less formidable) whom he had played around with on terms of honest equality all his life. It would be a bloody inferior thing to turn on class-stuff now—and most of all inside his own head.

'About that up at the barn.' Harry Carter was suddenly picking his words with care. 'It can be between ourselves, wouldn't you say?'

'Of course.' Despite what he'd just been thinking, Jake spoke very stiffly indeed.

'Girls don't understand those things.'

'I think *that* girl did.' Jake took some comfort in having got in this.

'Nice girls, I mean.'

'If you take to dividing girls into girls and nice girls, you're pretty well on the way to becoming a cheerful young blackguard, if you ask me.'

Here had been another good reply. Only, this time, Jake didn't care for it. It was probably just and true, but it had sounded a ghastly piece of priggery, all the same. And his own erotic experience, although not even a parson could have called it heinously murky, didn't license him to chuck stones quite in this fashion.

Harry Carter looked at him comically—they were sitting side by side now, and the effect was undeniably companionable—and then suddenly swayed backwards on the bench so unexpectedly that Jake thought he must have fainted, or something of that kind. But he had merely turned his body into a seesaw. His bottom, although obviously not a true centre of gravity, had become a pivot upon which for a moment he relaxedly swayed. His shoulders went down to the turf, then his heels, and then he was composedly upright again by Jake's side. Jake found it not easy to work out in terms of his own muscular structure just how it was done. But it had been a brief and effective appeal to the life of the body as something granted for his enjoyment to man.

Jake's impulse to self-criticism—an exercise to which Maoist principles should have inclined him, anyway—now strengthened. He'd been proposing to himself a kind of excommunication of Harry Carter from decent society —or from Gloria's decent society, which was the point— just because of what Harry called 'that up at the barn'. But wasn't this sheer hypocrisy? About girls and how they should be it was difficult and he didn't feel he knew: if most men still harboured a yen for marrying a virgin they weren't necessarily being virtuous and beautiful but might simply be wanting an extra kick for their money. About men, however, it was hard to get away from the immemorial thing, and he doubted whether women much in their hearts revolted from it. Nature—after all, and to put it crudely—didn't package up much extra kick with a virgin husband. Anyway, it was himself he had to judge. And he knew very well that he wouldn't regard having laid one girl in a barn one day as debarring him from looking another girl straight in the eye on another. So this treating Harry Carter as a leper was shocking humbug. Really and truly, they were cheerful young blackguards together.

Whatever the validity of these moral reflections, they now induced Jake to favour Harry with a grin.

'It comes to this,' he said challengingly. 'You're dead scared I'll tell Gloria you've had that girl—and probably others round about the village as well.'

'She'd have a fair idea of it already, if you ask me.' Harry produced his own grin. It had a cocky quality which momentarily brought back all Jake's hostility.

'It would be a bit different—actually being told.'

'That's true.' Harry accepted this at once. And he hesitated. 'Particularly—well, about anything of the sort happening up there.'

'I see.' Jake suddenly found his soul deeply troubled, and his sage reflections on sexual conduct of a few moments before blown away like cobweb on a gust of primitive jealousy. 'Do you really suppose I *would* tell?' he demanded coldly.

'Might do. All's fair in—'

'Man, one doesn't hoist oneself up by giving the other chap a kick in the balls.'

'Doesn't one? Not at Eton and 'Arrer, I suppose.' Harry produced this gibe rather weakly. He had been visibly impressed.

'I don't know anything about Eton and Harrow. And

they've nothing to do with the case, anyway. So don't talk like a bloody fool.'

There was a silence, in which the two young men found themselves regarding each other uncertainly and with no great enmity.

'If only the pub was open,' Harry said, 'we could finish it up on a pint.'

'A beery truce?' This homespun notion quite pleased Jake. 'Shaking hands, and so forth? You must read uncommonly wholesome fiction in your spare time.'

'I haven't got much spare time, mate.' Harry had taken what Jake realized was a silly gibe in irritatingly good part. 'When I do read it's most sci-fi.'

Sci-fi being a staple diet with a number of Jake's acquaintance, this bid to generate a little cultural antagonism fell flat. It became evident that the young men hadn't much more to say to each other. In addition to which, Harry's mother oughtn't to be kept waiting longer. So Jake stood up.

'By the way,' he said, 'why did you tell me that Gloria is probably in Venice? Was it a bit of playing fair?'

'Play fair my arse,' Harry said robustly. 'I was taunting you, wasn't I? It was what I meant to do. A mistake, perhaps. You're completely idle, and could go off to Venice at any time. Some kind of an artist, aren't you?'

'Not some kind of an artist. Just an artist. And I'm not idle. As for going to Venice, I reckon a bus fare to Margate would be beyond me at the moment. You know, I suppose, that Gloria's going to be enormously wealthy?'

'Yes, I do.' Harry too had stood up. He wasn't only good-looking, Jake noted. Plenty of those Renaissance characters who did sums about the human body would have given him high marks. 'And, what's more,' Harry said, 'you know it as well.'

'I'm not mercenary, as it happens.'

'I could do with forty thousand to buy a farm.' Harry

laughed suddenly—and almost as if some pleasing in-
wardness attended this remark. 'Do you know, I remember telling Gloria that? But, as it happens, I'm not—'
Harry hesitated. 'What's that word?'

'Mercenary.'

'I'm not mercenary either. Or not in this connection.'
Harry gave the same laugh. 'Can't think why. With an
heiress around, it seems just silly. Pride or something.
Spoils fun.'

Jake made no reply. He was puzzled by Harry, and less
than pleased. But he somehow believed what Harry had
said.

He returned home by a route so indirect that it involved getting into a lay-by and sleeping in the van. One
can sleep very well in a mini-van, provided one doesn't
mind a little curling up. So it was Monday evening before
he again shoved the port on to nine o'clock.

'Can you let me have £100?' he asked.

'Yes.' Jake's father accompanied this instant reply with
small, agitated gestures and a look of alarm. Jake was far
from criticizing them. Occasions like these abundantly
licensed the mild putting on of an act. 'Not that it isn't
a little difficult,' his father said. 'Rolls-Royce, you know,
and trouble with motor-bicycles at the other end of the
scale, and more trouble brewing.'

'Brewing where?'

'No, no. The breweries. They're in a ferment. Still, it
can be managed, my dear boy.'

'Lucky I haven't got a job in a brewery. But I'm going
to make ice-cream. In Rugby. I went there and saw a
friend this morning.'

'Ice-cream?' Cedric Counterpayne was bewildered. 'At
the school?'

'Nothing to do with the school. There's a town as well
as a school. You must remember *that*. I start in three

weeks and work for two months. So you get your money back, with proper gratitude, twelve weeks from today.'

'Isn't it rather unseasonable—ice-cream, I mean—with autumn drawing on?'

'Oh, it's for next summer. They put it in enormous cold-storage places.'

'It must mean locking up a lot of capital.' Cedric Counterpayne shook his head dubiously. 'Are you sure this won't interfere with your work?'

'Just the opposite. Tremendous inspiration in machinery. Ever since Léger.' Jake didn't feel too happy about producing this rubbish. But his father, a truly amiable man, was fishing out his cheque-book now, and it seemed decent to say anything that would preserve his peace of mind. Jake's work was important to Jake's father, who probably felt that over the past half-dozen years he had locked up a lot of capital in it. For that matter, it was important to Jake too—only at the moment Jake was responding to the tug of another mystery.

'Shall you be at home,' Cedric Counterpayne asked as he handed over the cheque, 'until you go off to this ice-cream?'

'Probably not.' His father, Jake reflected, could scarcely have expected an affirmative reply. Nobody would go through the discomfort of borrowing £100 from a professedly penurious parent merely for the purpose of continued residence in Olney.

'Time to wash up, don't you think?' It was the only further question this admirable man asked.

Not so with Mary Counterpayne.

'I've borrowed a hundred quid from Daddy,' Jake told her as soon as they had made their retreat to the nursery. It was unfortunately a point of honour between them that they reported to each other all financial transactions of this sort. 'Repayable in twelve weeks' time.'

'Good God! Do you imagine that in the next three months you're going to *sell* a picture?'

'Not for a moment. Not bonkers.'

'Then what?'

'Going to make ice-cream.'

'*What* did you say?'

'Going to make ice-cream. Job. J-O-B. Like our kinswoman Gloria dishing out tea.'

'You have our kinswoman Gloria on the brain, all right. I suppose that's what this is in aid of?'

'Correct.' Jake knew prevarication to be idle.

'You've said nothing at all about what happened at Nudd. How did you find her?'

'Didn't. Gloria's abroad.'

'So Jake sets out for Lyonnesse, a hundred quid away.' It was with considerable acuteness, Jake felt, that his sister thus travestied a celebrated lyric. 'Or a sprat to catch a whale.'

'If it *was* that, I'd jump up and pretend to be furious with you.' Jake was in fact sprawled luxuriously on a broken-springed sofa. 'A damned insulting thing to say, et cetera.'

'But at least perhaps Daddy sees it as that?'

'As a sprat? Nothing of the kind. He hasn't a notion what the money's in aid of.'

'You asked him for all that money without any explanation at all?'

'It's the best way.'

A short silence showed that Mary acknowledged this as true.

'But look,' she said. 'I just don't *understand*. You've only had one glimpse of this girl since you were a kid. And everybody knows she's less like a woman than a performing elephant.'

'It's an exaggeration.' Jake was totally unoffended. 'Gloria's simply a well-built girl. And, of course, these things are deeply and marvellously irrational.'

'And you're telling me it would make no difference if she were a pauper?'

'Not a flicker. I suppose that's very wrong. There's certainly no virtue in it. As a matter of fact, I met a chap yesterday who feels exactly the same about her. And he's nothing but a lecherous young yeoman.'

'Young *what*?'

'Yeoman. Respectable word for modified prole.'

'And used, I suppose, in your Little Red Book?'

'Oh, yes—or something like it.' Jake paused. 'So I'm off to Venice.'

'What, in heaven's name, is Gloria Montacute doing in Venice? I thought she spent her time walking through some London hospital with a Little Red Lamp. Under a kind of samovar.'

'I don't know what she's doing in Venice. That's what I'm going to find out.'

'On £100? You can get there, and stay there, and get back, on £100?'

'Of course. You have the most fantastic notions. I'm taking the van—'

'You can't drive that round the Piazza San Marco, or whatever it's called.'

'There's a multi-storey car-park. And I can get the van over the channel and back for under ten quid. I know a chap who does it in the dark.'

Mary Counterpayne made a gesture expressive of the fact that she gave her brother up. She had to admit that beginning the pursuit of a girl on a kind of black-market or at least cut-price ferry was quite something. She even had to admit that Jake might go far. But would it be as a painter? Being a loyal sister, she wished the idea well, since it seemed to be Jake's ultimate dream. But now up had bobbed this other dream of the fat cousin from Nudd. She was going to be enormously wealthy—which meant that, if Jake married her, Jake would to all intents and purposes be enormously wealthy too. He would be this even if he was now pursuing Gloria in the utmost purity of heart. Rather to her surprise, Mary found that she didn't take to the idea a bit. The last thing that would be any good to Jake as a serious artist would be any amount of money dolloped out by a Philistine wife.

Part Three

13

TWO YOUNG WOMEN
IN CONVERSATION

'EACH OF THOSE flags must be half as big as a tennis court.'

Sitting outside Quadri's—for Florian's was in the shade—Gloria made this discovery with the satisfaction of a traveller in antique lands who comes momentarily in contact with some familiar thing. Tennis had perhaps been in her head; she wouldn't at all have minded three brisk sets; she had been rather short of exercise—except of the tramping round sort—since coming to this astonishing city. You could swim on the Lido, and according to the guide-book it was the most fashionable seaside resort in Italy. But when she reflected that it was only a few miles away from all those canals she had her doubts about it. The idea that the Adriatic and indeed the whole Mediterranean had become one big cesspool was obviously modish rot, and into any sea that *looked* right she was willing enough to plunge without demanding preliminary bacteriological analysis. But the Lido she hadn't taken to at all.

She *had* taken to this enormous square, just as she was now taking to these enormous flags. Two were national flags, brightly banal except for their breath-taking size. But on the other two St Mark's winged lion (a ubiquitous creature, and frequently for some reason provided with a football) was blazoned in gold upon a maroon ground. But 'maroon' was ridiculous; here was a colour indescribably splendid which had been familiar to her, she nostalgically thought, on certain expanses of ancient stuff at

Nudd. And this didn't end the impressiveness of these two civic flags; each of them ended in six long points or tails which flared like comets against the background of the extraordinary church—not in the least *like* a church —beyond.

'*Wunderschön!*' Gloria said—still about the flags.

'*Wunderbar!*' Miss Christine Anderson echoed. Miss Anderson was Gloria's travelling companion.

'*Ausgezeichnet!*' Gloria brilliantly offered. On Garda there had been numerous Germans—hundreds of them, in fact—and their enthusiasms had amused the English ladies very much. Here in the Piazza San Marco (described by a more sophisticated traveller as the drawing-room of Europe) they were aware of, but not much disturbed by, their own unfurnished cultural condition.

'You'd think,' Miss Anderson said on a practical note, 'that when they take them down for the night they could use them as dust-sheets to cover the whole cathedral. For I suppose it *is* a cathedral. Basilica seems to be the local word. That's what's in the book.'

'What about another ice?' Gloria asked, on a note more practical still.

'They cost the earth in this square.'

'Oh, well!' And Gloria waved at a waiter. It was the wrong waiter, but he hurried obligingly over to them, all the same. During their wanderings it had come to be admitted that Gloria had no need to travel on twopence, and she and Kirstie were sufficiently good friends not to have to bother about small reckonings. Gloria's social conscience, which was robust but not fanatical, would even have stretched to decent hotels. But that would have required a different proposal at the start, and turned Kirstie into a kind of semi-paid companion, which would be absurd. So, on the whole, they were doing Italy on the cheap. Kirstie was a Theatre Sister; she slaved like a probationer and carried large responsibilities; they paid her,

Gloria supposed, about what they paid a dustman.

'The campanile looks quite new,' Kirstie said. She remembered to speak disapprovingly, although anybody who works in an East End hospital should have nothing but praise for a modern fabric.

'It *is* new.' This odd fact had caught Gloria's eye in her Blue Guide. 'The old one fell down, and this one was opened on 25 April 1912.' A respect for dates was something she had caught from her mother.

'Opened?'

'Yes—you go up in a lift. But if you want to pay less there's an easy sloping walk.'

'An easy sloping walk?' Kirstie echoed unbelievingly. She turned her gaze from the towering brick monster to cast an anticipatory glance on the second ice. It had arrived, complete with a glass of water and a hospital-looking spoon, with commendable speed.

'That's what it says. Do you think they have a band playing here all the year round? It's almost winter now.'

'It doesn't feel like winter.'

'An old man in the pensione told me it can turn wintry at any time. There are storms, and all this goes under water. It can even freeze.'

'Think of those flags frozen hard. Like the tin ones they leave on the moon.'

The flags were almost like that now. A brisk breeze, cunningly insinuating itself into the drawing-room of Europe by way of the Mercerie, was blowing them stiffly out in the direction of the Piazzetta. It was four o'clock. The *mori* on the Torre dell'Orologio, as if abruptly awakening to the fact, phrenetically banged out the hour on their bell. A thousand well-trained pigeons rose obediently in air. The lady peddling *granturco* in the middle of the Piazza (she was without commercial rivals now that the high holiday-season was over), encouraged by this activity on the part of the beneficiaries of her zeal,

waved her wares and uttered shrill cries in competition
with the band. The band, playing Gounod, played Gounod louder. On the shady side of the vast space ranks of
cleared tables and empty chairs suggested a deserted
theatre, but without much affecting the general anima-
tion of the scene. It would be another month before the
tourists finally departed and the Venetians themselves
became distinguishable again.

One Venetian, however, in addition to the waiters and
the *granturco* lady, was identifiable now. He wore, indeed, in addition to a pair of ragged shorts, a T-shirt upon
which the word 'Oxford' was imprinted in large letters
beneath a representation of three crowns and an open
book. But this appeared to be a tribute to, rather than a
claim to residence within, a celebrated place of learning,
since its owner was a boy of eleven or twelve. He was
selling newspapers. And as that is an occupation commonly reserved in Italy for male citizens of mature years
he was rather pleased with the job.

Kirstie bought a paper. She bought an Italian one, although this was difficult to achieve and even seemed a
little to offend the young Oxonian. At school she had
done Spanish, since at that time she had appeared doomed
to a commercial career, and she could work her way
through Italian sentences as a result. This useful accom-
plishment impressed Gloria a good deal. But for the
moment Kirstie deferred intellectual exercise, to occupy
herself alternately with her ice and the astonishing edifice
beyond the flags. The light was changing—in Venice it
never does anything else—and the Basilica was changing
with it; it seemed to claim less and less to be a building,
and to admit itself more and more an exhalation merely.
The spectacle has never been described. 'Clear as amber
and delicate as ivory,' Ruskin tried, and went on to evoke
'marble foam', 'sculptured spray', and similar bold tropes.
Competent authorities aver his to be the best shot, but it

still won't quite do. For one thing, amid all this ethereal delicacy a certain high-handed mastering of architectural and decorative incongruities is an element in the effect, and analysis of this is difficult to achieve. Kirstie arrived upon the fringes of it with her next remark.

'Isn't it very odd,' she asked, 'to stick horses on a church?'

'It must be something to do with their religion.'

'I don't see why—not even for Catholics. Jesus travelled by donkey as a baby, and on an ass, which I suppose is the same thing, later on.' Kirstie had been well brought up. 'But I don't remember that he ever had anything to do with horses.'

'They're good horses.' Gloria shifted, as it were, the angle of appraisal. 'And .they must be nearly twenty hands.'

The four superb creatures on the loggia were certainly that, for proportions and perspectives are tricky before such a scene. And even from this distance their noble bronze glinted with residual gold. Mounted on them— Gloria suddenly thought—there ought to be four splendid young men.

'Read about them,' Kirstie said. She was a conscientious girl.

'Greek work of the time of Alexander.' Gloria had obediently rummaged in her guide. 'Possibly from the Rhodian Chariot of the Sun at Delphi.' Gloria looked up. 'What does *yours* say?' she demanded. Scepticism had been growing in her over matters of this sort.

'Oh, very well.' Kirstie too had a book: one devoted entirely to this unmanageable city. She consulted the index and turned to the appropriate page. 'Made in Imperial Rome,' she presently announced, 'and later sent to Constantinople. And—do you know?—it says they're loot. Pretty cool, putting loot on a church. They ought to be in a museum, if you ask me.'

'Or sent back to Constantinople.' Gloria fell silent. Perhaps the *fontana minore*, she was thinking, ought to be sent back to Viterbo.

Quite soon—if unbelievably—it was going to turn chilly. The fact would not be acknowledged in their pensione. And you have to go to rather a grand hotel in Italy before finding anywhere much in which to sit comfortably around. Undeniably, an awkwardly long evening stretched before them.

'Do you think there's a cinema?' Gloria asked.

'Of course there must be cinemas. It stands to reason.'

'I haven't seen any. But look in your paper. That ought to tell.'

Not without alacrity, Kirstie embarked on this alternative line of research. Sure enough, Venice—throned on her hundred isles—did have cinemas. There were at least half-a-dozen of them.

'*L'Assassino di Rillington Place: Numero Dieci,*' Kirstie read. 'How about that?'

'I don't think so.' They hadn't come nine hundred miles, Gloria felt, to plunge into London affairs not wholly remote from the professional experience of either. 'Isn't there something about Italians?'

'*I Licenziosi Desideri,*' Kirstie read slowly and laboriously, '*di una Ragazza Moderna con il Complesso della Verginità.* I've no doubt *that's* about Italians. And pretty permissive, if your taste lies that way.'

'It doesn't. Try again.'

'*Il Prigionero di Zenda.*'

'That's it! We've got the book at home.'

'In Italian?' Kirstie, having heard about the mysteries of Nudd, wasn't surprised.

'Of course not. It's an English book. *The Prisoner of Zenda,* by a man called Anthony Hope. When I read it as a kid, I thought it absolutely fab.'

'We'll go to that.' Kirstie put down her paper, and was then struck by a sudden thought. 'But I say! Do you think that in Italy girls go to cinemas and places of that sort without an escort?'

'What utter rot!' Gloria was astonished by this positively medieval question. 'You don't imagine we can't look after ourselves? And I didn't notice you much minding when those sailors whistled at us down there on the Riva.'

'They were rather nice sailors.'

'Well, perhaps the young males at the cinema will be rather nice too. And, even if the worst comes to the worst, it won't do you much harm to have your bottom pinched. It can happen in London on the Underground.' Gloria offered these flippant remarks because she was really rather startled. Kirstie Anderson was several years older than she was and to be presumed rich in worldly wisdom.

'It's just a thought,' Kirstie said. 'Perhaps one of those ancient American women in the pensione—'

'Excuse me,' a voice said from the next table. 'It's frightful cheek to butt in. But would it be too absolutely shocking and improper if I asked whether I might come along?'

They stared at the young Englishman who had made this incredible speech. He had been listening to their conversation—and as at least a scrap of it had been what is conventionally called indelicate he hadn't chosen too tactful a moment for announcing the fact. On the other hand, his boldness had something attractive about it. It wasn't boldness in the sense in which the word can mean assurance or impudence. He was looking at once lively and alarmed. It was evident that they had only to utter a word—or *not* utter a word—and he would acknowledge his outrageousness and bolt.

'It's very kind of you to have taken an interest in us,' Kirstie said drily.

'I'm terribly sorry!' Thus mildly rebuked, the young

man blushed. This was definitely engaging. Nobody can
turn on a blush—as they can turn on, say, a stammer or an
appropriate sort of laugh. A blush—at least if it is only a
faint blush or flush—is a perfectly manly thing, and
seems to witness to ingenuousness of intention. 'Forget it,'
the young man said. 'Or—dash it!—no. Consider it, give
it a chance, for just a moment. It's *not* absolutely awful.
I'm a perfectly respectable character. I'm in the perfectly
respectable pensione next to yours. I noticed you going
out this morning.'

If Gloria felt this was a little too much fuss she hardly
registered it. She was thinking that very faintly in her
head the young man rang a bell. Had she noticed him
lying in bed as she trundled her tea-trolley through a
ward? It seemed improbable. He did have 'London' somehow written all over him, but he didn't have written all
over him what was still sometimes called 'hospital class'.
She certainly hadn't seen him on a rugger field; he wasn't
the type that plays for Blackheath or has ever collected
an important Cap or a Blue. Perhaps she'd glimpsed him
on television, talking about polyphonic music or the future
of the pound sterling. It could only have been a glimpse,
since she always turned that sort of programme off. In any
case, she wasn't going to make a talking point of the thing
now.

'All right,' she said. 'And we'll meet outside the cinema
just before the film starts.' However right Kirstie was
about escorts, she was herself determined absolutely to
decline the need for one while walking through Venice of
an early evening.

'That will be most—'

'Oh, look! Somebody's climbed on one of the horses.'

This was Kirstie's interruption, perhaps made merely
from an impulse to create a diversion: she had to take
in the new situation. But there could be no doubt about
the horse. The great bronze creature now had a rider. High

above the Piazza though he was, he could be distinguished as a young man of the wandering, long-haired sort—but even with a leg-up from a friend he must own considerable athletic skill to have made his present perch. He didn't, however, at all suggest one of the four splendid youths Gloria had lately imagined, since he was so out of scale with his mount that he looked like a more than usually shrunken jockey, or even like one of those unfortunate monkeys clinging on for dear life during an equestrian turn in a circus. The neighbouring horse had the appearance of turning its head to give him a glance of disdain. Gloria was just going to laugh at this when her new acquaintance burst into surprising speech.

'Good God! It's an utter outrage. They'll allow anything, absolutely anything. What they're not actively corroding with fumes and acids from their beastly factories they're simply allowing to sink and slide into the lagoon. Those horses are as precious as anything surviving from the ancient world. And the next thing we'll see is yahoos like that carving their names on their flanks.'

Gloria—apart from considering this last an improbable prognostication—was astonished by the vehemence of the prospective cinema patron's tone. And a moment later she had caught in it something more: the note of high indignation against the general Philistine cast of things in the modern world that she associated with certain of her mother's visitors to Nudd. Persons professionally concerned with the arts, they had commonly been. And suddenly a clear memory came to her.

'Do you know?' she said. 'I think we've just glimpsed each other once before.'

'Have we?' For a brief moment the young man was taken aback. 'It's quite possible, Miss Montacute. For I think you are Miss Montacute, aren't you? I've been to your house, as a matter of fact.' His manner had become grave and candid. 'I haven't mentioned it, because it was on the day your mother died. It seemed an awkward thing to speak of, straight away.'

'You drove down with another man.'

'Yes, indeed: Lambert Domberg, the head of my firm. My name's Octavius Chevalley. What an odd encounter this is.'

'It's all of that,' Kirstie Anderson said crisply.

14

ROMANCE IN A GONDOLA

CHEVALLEY HAD STARTED at a disadvantage. There had been an element of dissimulation in his approach which, although surely insignificant, Gloria Montacute's friend had firmly underlined at once. But he had extricated himself deftly enough, since hesitation in referring to Mrs Montacute's still recent demise had been both credible and creditable. Certainly Gloria (as was her habit) had given him the benefit of any doubt she may have entertained.

For a start, *Il Prigionero di Zenda* had been a success. It was a predictably romantic affair, sporting as many cloaks and daggers as one could imagine, but the young man had enjoyed it in a thoroughly uncondescending way. As a film it could hardly be called groovy; it was unaware of either the Ken Russell or the Andy Warhol angle; the scenario might have come from the talented and facile pen of Barbara Cartland herself. But Octavius Chevalley clearly liked Anthony Hope's hero—almost aspired towards him, one could feel—so that Gloria soon ceased to fear that she had beckoned him (not that she *had* beckoned) into the viewing of a childishly naïve spectacle. After the show they had gone to the sort of *trattoria* Kirstie and she would certainly not have found for themselves, and there enjoyed a supper—a wantonly extra meal—of a sort that boarding-houses on the Zattere would judge it impolitic to set before an Anglo-Saxon clientele. And Chevalley had taken it for granted that they'd all three go Dutch.

During the succeeding few days it did sometimes come

to Gloria as surprising that she had rapidly arrived on
terms of some intimacy with a young man whom Harry
Carter had promised one day to belt until he snivelled.
She had to admit to herself—for she had a considerable
command of sober realism—that she could see Octavius
Chevalley snivelling. He wasn't a husky type. But she
was humbly aware of herself as a person living on the
mere fringe of the civilized. Nudd, or the parties at Nudd,
had been a good deal frequented by phoneys; yet she
hadn't been unconscious of the occasional presence of
persons of a genuinely finer grain. And Octavius belonged
to them.

That he had *become* Octavius within twenty-four hours
wasn't in itself remarkable; if one accepts a new acquaintance at all one also accepts the conventions of one's
time. Kirstie, indeed, had stuck out for 'Mr Chevalley'
for long enough to intimate a reserve, but she had abandoned this before it approached singularity. As a trio
they were soon getting on very well.

At the start, Gloria didn't, indeed, as they went around
together, do a great deal of thinking about Octavius. She
did rather more thinking about Harry. She wondered how
he was getting on as a full back. He had a dogged quality,
she felt, that augured reasonably well for that place kicking. If he would only practise it from every angle—particularly the awkward ones—with the grim pertinacity of
a top tennis player getting up his backhand drive there
was no telling how far he mightn't go. She'd been unable
to resist saying this over again on one of her postcards—
although she'd only sent the postcards at all out of a sense
of guilt, or at least compunction, at having done a luck-
less belting act herself. On that dreadful evening Harry
had behaved very well, and he'd scarcely deserved so
sharp a rebuff in answer to an almost unconsciously straying hand. She found it impossible (could it conceivably
be disturbingly impossible?) to imagine Octavius's hand

behaving in that way. But then Harry was a simple creature, and to be accepted as such.

Not that Octavius didn't have his own boldness. He must have been aware that his two chance-met companions weren't exactly aesthetes, but he took it pleasingly for granted that in Venice everybody looks at pictures. He was himself here to look at pictures in what was no doubt a learned and recondite way: there seemed to be absolutely nothing he didn't know. This was particularly true of Vittore Carpaccio (he was able to remind Gloria that there was a Carpaccio at Nudd), and it turned out that Carpaccio was extremely entertaining even for people who weren't learned at all. Carpaccio seemed to have invented the comic strip—only he told stories each episode in which was a vast and crowded painting, so that a set of them were sufficient to clothe the walls of a large room. They weren't, of course, actually comic, except perhaps the one called *St Jerome Leading his Lion into a Monastery*. It was a different sort of lion from St Mark's, but so extravagantly benevolent that the perturbation occasioned in the monastery was very funny indeed. It didn't look as if Carpaccio had taken religious occasions or the legends of saints all that seriously. But he had certainly done a most devoted job on the city of Venice.

'In all these pictures,' Octavius said instructively, 'one sees people making an everyday assignment of holding the gorgeous East in fee. You chuck your carpets casually over your balcony to air, but they're spoil from Trebizon and Samarkand. The same with your washing. The stuffs are so splendid that you can hang them out of the windows of palaces, and leave them there during even the most imposing state occasions.'

'Did they wear their best clothes always?' Gloria asked.

'Oh, they only had best clothes. So they had to wear them for the most humdrum ploys. For no end macabre ones too. You might be sent out with your pals to martyrize a queen and her ten thousand attendant virgins. A gory bow-and-arrow affair. But you preserved an extreme of elegance in your *tenue*. Just look.'

In her childhood Gloria had been told so often just to look that it was remarkable how unresentfully and even zestfully she was doing so now. She even made her own discoveries.

'The lap-dogs and the chimney-pots,' she said. 'He remembered to get them in.'

'The lap-dogs have changed a little—but the chimney-pots not a bit. You can still see them in Venice today. I expect you could buy one, Gloria, and take it home as a souvenir. It would be something you haven't got at Nudd already. You have some of the silks and velvets Carpaccio painted—perhaps the very ones, which is an awesome thought—but not his chimney-pots. Or what about a Moor? Let's stroll down to the Riva degli Schiavoni and see if we can pick you up a Moor cheap.'

'Was there much racial prejudice?' Miss Anderson asked. Her inbred Scottish seriousness frequently surfaced by way of reaction to nonsense.

'Well, of course the principal piece of evidence is Shakespeare's *Othello*, and unfortunately it can be read in different ways. But look at the black man who's just going to take a header into the canal. It's his own idea, wouldn't you say? Nobody bullying him. But is he a shade undernourished, perhaps? Kirstie, you ought to have a professional eye for that.'

As he produced this slightly persevering gaiety, Chevalley glanced not at Kirstie but at Gloria. And suddenly he was blushing again. Gloria perceived this with a shock. It took her mind straight back to something that was worrying her from time to time. There was a gap—it might be thought of as a credibility gap—between Octavius Chevalley now and Octavius Chevalley as she had first glimpsed him: the young man who had momentarily

eyed her from a big car with what could only be remembered as amused contempt—the young man, in fact, for
whom a belting lay in store. He had seen a fat girl ludicrously intertwined with a scramble of puppies, and his
manners had deserted him at the sight. Because he had
said something about an under-nourished Negro, he was
himself remembering the occasion now.

Well, it would be ungenerous to hold it against him,
Gloria thought. A fat girl is a fat girl. Only it was just a
shade humiliating that this particular aspect of herself
remained distinguishably vivid in his mind. She now had
the key to another moment—here in the Accademia—
only half an hour before. There was a painter her mother
had called Palma Vecchio, but whom Octavius called
Jacopo Palma. Octavius had pointed to a rather boring
picture called a Sacred Conversation by this man, and
said he'd had a special line in female saints characteristic-
ally Venetian in their ample charms. And as he'd uttered
this quite amusing phrase he'd suddenly and awkwardly
pulled himself up. There was now no misunderstanding
that. The important thing to hold on to seemed to be
that he was a sensitive young man. He probably woke
up in the middle of the night and did this blushing business in bed.

They moved on rather abruptly to Tintoretto now, and
looked at an enormous thing called *St Mark Rescuing a
Slave*. Octavius seemed to feel Tintoretto fairly safe. Tintoretto, on the whole, went in for spare and elongated
forms.

It would be extravagant to claim that, with the learned
Chevalley as cicerone, Gloria was belatedly embarking
upon an artistic education. She wasn't one of those Anglo-
Saxon girls, seemingly sensuously inert, who are awakened
at the touch of the warm South to new potentialities of
response and perception. Or not quite. But she was cer-

tainly seeing things more vividly than before, and wasn't unaware of it: at times it struck her particularly as she came out of a gallery or a church. Here, outside, was something continuous with things she had been dutifully viewing within. This hadn't used to happen when she walked out of Nudd in quest of fresh air.

Octavius made no jokes about artistic education. He said that Gloria and Kirstie (for he seldom said anything about Gloria that he didn't say about Kirstie as well) were developing a historical sense. He also said that they were extremely good shoppers—and he accompanied them more than once, and with every appearance of enthusiasm rather than indulgence, down the winding course of the Mercerie for this purpose. The multiplicity of beguiling boutiques in these narrow streets defies computation, and if many turn out to sell precisely the same wares as others there is at least the possibility of exciting novelty in every one. Both young women thought of a surprising number of friends for whom small presents might appropriately be taken home, and they spent their money accordingly. What you had bought here in the *cinquecento*, Octavius said, had been silks and damasks and cloth of gold. But he flinched at absolutely nothing directed to a more modern taste, and even commended to Kirstie a diminutive plastic gondola which could be pleasingly illuminated through the agency of an equally diminutive electric battery.

Gloria didn't trust this enthusiasm a bit. She could even imagine some of the derisive things Octavius would say if describing these purchases to somebody of his own sort —his employer Mr Domberg, for example. The girls had filled a small portmanteau with objects suitable for raffling in an institution for the blind. That would be the kind of fun Octavius would produce. The thought of it didn't offend Gloria in the least. She was even coming to feel that, in the past, she had perhaps too regularly written-off this particular sort of young man. Why shouldn't one enjoy the society of people with quite different tastes from oneself? And if one didn't mind being less clever than clever people (and Gloria didn't feel she *did*) couldn't one get a great deal of entertainment from them? This second question was receiving an affirmative answer all the time. The Italian holiday had livened up a great deal during the past week.

Of course the turning up of any other lively young man might have had the same effect. But there was another thing about Octavius Chevalley which was much more of an individual matter and dimly portentous. He'd never again come to give Gloria the kind of glance he'd given her from Domberg's car.

Gloria's knowledge of this was intuitive—and like much knowledge intuitively come by it had a disturbing quality. The narrow little shops in the Merceria di San Giuliano or the Merceria di San Salvatore have entrances correspondingly narrow. Gloria had to exercise some care in slipping through them. But the fact that this didn't produce a flicker from Octavius was not a consequence of his minding his manners better than on a former occasion. Nor was it simply that he'd ceased to bother his head with her physical presence, in a way that she knew a young man can do when he has made a familiar companion of you and has no other views whatever. Octavius *was* aware of her—aware of her, one might say, still in terms of the scales and the tape-measure. But his attitude to the reports these brought him had somehow changed. She wondered obscurely whether this had something to do with Palma Vecchio and (for that matter) Titian. She also wondered—but this brought her to ground yet more obscure—whether Octavius was at all an effective young man in point of the sort of activities these thoughts adumbrated.

This was the state of affairs when Kirstie made her

rather surprising suggestion that they go out in a gondola.

It was surprising because made somewhat in the face
of social convention. Young people are very conscious of
what, as an age-group, young people do or don't do. And
they don't, on the whole, potter around the canals of
Venice, or voyage at large on its lagoon, in gondolas.
Gondolas are expensive, tortoise-like, and really rather
dull; they are also sticky with bogus romantic associations.
Elderly Americans, the sort whose garments are lined
with travellers cheques, go around in gondolas, solemnly
whirring their movie-cameras as they glide. Kirstie was
aware of all this. She knew she was poor; she suspected
Octavius of being poor; she divined that Gloria had come
abroad partly in order to escape for a little longer from
the poor-little-rich-girl business which was creeping up on
her. But Kirstie said that in Venice one sailed in a gondola. As she was undoubtedly right, her insistence deserved better fortune than it actually met with.

Octavius, entering agreeably into the spirit of her enterprise, gave the proposal a good deal of thought. It
seemed simple enough to Gloria; you merely walked down
to the Molo and stepped into one of the things as if it
was a taxi. But Octavius started the idea that he could
borrow a craft of superior comfort and consequence from
an elderly Italian lady resident in Venice; there would be
the further advantage of the trip's being for free, apart
from the handsome tip to the two liveried servants who
would provide motive power. But on this proposal he went
progressively vaguer as the day wore on—perhaps because
the *contessa* or whoever she was existed only in his imagination; more probably (Gloria felt shrewdly sure) because he had developed misgivings about showing off.
That misgivings distinguishably tenanted a good many

odd corners of Octavius's mind was one of the attractive things about him.

However this may have been, its consequence was that the project became a nocturnal one. That was what Kirstie really wanted: she pointed out there was a moon. The stickiest romance of all attends, of course, upon gondolas by moonlight, and Gloria felt she must by no means counter or abridge this small enclave of adolescent *Sehnsucht* in her almost undeviatingly rational friend. (Gloria didn't, indeed, employ this sort of language to herself. But chroniclers have their occasional privileges.)

Octavius supported the new idea. It would add, he explained on an easy and brotherly note, thirty per cent to the bill. But it would undoubtedly be worth it—at least if it didn't turn too chilly. He would have the chap clap on the *felze*, he learnedly added, instead of the *tenda*, and then they'd be as snug as need be.

The *felze* proved to be a kind of portable wooden shed, and Gloria felt that the effect was of being in a floating chicken-coop. This was at least better than being in a floating coffin, which was how gondolas, perhaps on account of their sombre hue, commonly struck her. At least their gondolier bore no resemblance to an undertaker. He was a young man and almost wickedly handsome. He cultivated—for professional purposes, no doubt —the appearance of a corsair. And he sang.

Having formed the opinion—erroneously, and because the gentleman spoke Italian—that the ladies were cultivated persons, the gondolier sang Monteverde. Gloria found what are called unprepared dissonances startling, but concluded that the lyric was being intervolved with those weird alerting cries which those who hire gondolas expect to have thrown in for their money. Even although there was singing elsewhere on the water—quite a lot of it—the set-up was all mildly embarrassing. She knew perfectly well that the man wasn't singing because he felt that way. He'd had a long day senselessly standing in for a simple out-board petrol engine; he was probably very considerably bored, and looking forward only to a final stupefying swig of *grappa* and to tumbling into bed.

Octavius must have caught hold of the mortuary suggestion, since he announced that they were going where the cold sea raves by Lido's wet accursed graves—a thought from the poet Browning which neither lady was in a position to appreciate. The expedition modulated into success, all the same. The moon was there, and so was Venice. And to this combination of circumstances it was impossible not to respond.

Gloria responded, whether relevantly or not, by advancing Octavius further in her regard. She still gave a thought from time to time to Harry (of whom she had been reminded, indeed, by certain aspects of the gondolier's physique), but it was by way of thinking how different Harry was from Octavius, and Octavius from Harry. She wasn't consciously disposed to put these two young men in an order of merit. What was chiefly attractive in young men—she had come to feel—was the unlikeness between one and another; their diversity made for interest rather more than did what they seemed monotonously to be liable to have in common. Even when you had only one at all substantially in your head it was still in his distinguishing signs and traits that the fascination lay. And now Octavius in the foreground drew an additional charm from a contrasting Harry who had withdrawn into the middle distance. Yet even at this degree of relegation, it may be, Harry had for Gloria a residual small clear meaning which was the sharper for Octavius's standing where he did.

In fact, of course, Octavius was sitting—side by side with Kirstie in their little floating room. He had put an arm round Kirstie. Or, if not precisely that, he had put an arm *behind* her. Gloria could have stretched out her own

arm and touched either of them, and this made it odd
that she couldn't hear what Octavius was saying. But
then Octavius was murmuring rather than talking—and
murmuring into Kirstie's ear.

This was a sudden discovery, and it was a second or two
before Gloria was quite clear that her feeling before the
spectacle was the correct feeling of benevolent amusement.
It was entirely in order that Octavius should mildly flirt
with Kirstie, since Kirstie was a very attractive young
woman. And she was glad, she told herself, that he wasn't
trying to flirt with *her*, at least in a chicken-coop. *Madame
Bovary* had never come Gloria's way, but her own experience had made her think poorly of amorous advance in
hired conveyances.

Not that Octavius was *doing* much. Within the shadowy
felze it wasn't easy, and of course it wouldn't have been
proper, really to *see*. But Gloria had a strong impression
that decorum—it didn't occur to her as anything more
fundamental in Octavius than that—was imposing a
marked brake on the proceedings. Since she was now
distinctly jealous of Kirstie—amusement, sad to say, had
been evanescent humbug—she ought to have found some
satisfaction or at least solace in this continence. Strangely
enough, it irritated her and increased her uneasiness. If
Octavius felt that way—and, once more, why shouldn't
he?—he ought to be able to get on with it.

The gondolier had stopped singing. Perhaps he felt that
with his barcarole he had brought about what was required of him—not that, from his perch astern, he could
do more than divine the conduct of his incapsulated
clients. The gondola carried a little lantern; so did others
on the water; the general effect was of a slow-motion
nature film dealing with the life cycle of the firefly. Behind Gloria was a little window embellished with unnecessary curtains smelling of salt water and dust;
through it she could see the outline of their private cor-

sair dimly against a phosphorescent wake. They were now
being heaved or spooned or waggled—for the motion of
the oar was an extraordinarily subtle one—back towards
the Piazzetta. There was still a cluster of lights there, but
much of Venice had gone dark. On their left the island of
San Giorgio Maggiore showed in silhouette against a
luminous southern sky; directly above its campanile, as
if at the tip of an invisible mast, hung a single star. Gloria
felt disoriented. She tried, quite without success, to remember what had put this entire Italian journey in her head.
She recalled, as a comforting circumstance, the small
number of hours separating her by jet from Heathrow,
the East End of London, and the new job she would presently be taking up there.

It was thus that the water party ended in an atmosphere
of some constraint. Neither Kirstie nor Octavius appeared
to have taken satisfaction in whatever had passed between
them. Octavius paid the bill briefly and without airing
his Italian to the corsair at all. And as the corsair parted
from them without cordiality it looked as if Octavius had
even allowed his sense of displeasure to reflect itself, most
unjustly, in the size of the *mancia*. They could easily
have been put down at the Punta della Salute. But
Octavius hadn't thought of it, so they tramped through
devious and deserted *calli* and *salizzade* to the Ponte
dell'Accademia. Octavius tried to enliven their progress
by explaining that, although gondolas are of enormous
and even mysterious antiquity, the recognized way of
moving about Venice used to be on horseback. But the
young women—themselves unjustly, this time—supposed
this to be a feeble joke, and Octavius sulked for several
hundred yards as a result. They reached the Zattere,
passed the Gesuati (from the façade of which they might
have reflected that there gestured at them statues of Prudence, Justice, Strength and Temperance), and so reached

their twinned boarding-houses. They paused outside for
a few moments to assure one another that it had all been
great fun—just as if they were forty-year-olds at the end
of a party that hadn't quite come off. Gloria found this
the evening's most depressing moment. But not being in
fact forty-year-olds, she and Kirstie weren't glum for long.
They had regained their normal good spirits—or something very like them—by the time they got up to their
room.

'You can have first bath,' Gloria said obligingly, and
sank down on a bed which stood up to her very well. She
added at once: 'Was that young man making passes at
you, or was I tricked by moonlight?'

'Yes, I suppose he was. He must have felt it to be the
thing—when in a gondola like that.'

'Perhaps he felt that you felt it to be the thing—when
in a gondola like that. The gondola was your idea, my
girl.'

'So it was.' Kirstie had gone into the bathroom and
was turning on taps. 'But he couldn't,' she called back,
'have felt I felt anything of the kind. Because I didn't.'

'He must have got a false impression. I think he's much
too sensitive to have any notion of making what he could
feel might be unwelcome advances.'

'Do you, now?' Kirstie appeared again, and began
peeling off her clothes. 'What I feel is that he gets things
out of books.'

'Out of books?' It was clear to Gloria that this had
been offered as an adverse judgement upon Octavius Chevalley; and she had an instant, if odd, impulse to defend
him. 'He's certainly not an ignorant gnome, like you and
me.' Gloria had a certain weakness for picking up passing
slang. 'But just what has he been getting out of books this
time?'

'I don't feel I quite know.'

'We're both doing a hell of a lot of feeling.'

'Then let's unfeel. No p. m.'

'Very well.' Gloria had to agree at once that no *post-mortem* would be held. 'And you just hurry up.'

Kirstie disappeared again, and splashed. Gloria wrote a couple of post-cards, of which one was her third to Harry Carter. The bath gurgled out in the alarming way baths can gurgle out in Italy. When Kirstie returned to the bedroom in her pyjamas she was looking unexpectedly troubled.

'Listen,' she said. 'To go back, after all. To recur. To analyse.'

'Just a minute.' It was because Gloria too was now inexplicably disturbed that she deferred further conference until she had filled her own bath. She was careful not to fill it too full. This was because of another thing about Italian baths. They can behave badly when an unexpected degree of displacement befalls them. 'Well,' she presently demanded, kicking off her shoes, 'what are you analysing?'

'I suppose it's Octavius's motive in making those eyes at me. It *was* just eyes, you know. And a kind of mooing and cooing. You heard.'

'Murmuring would be fairer.' Gloria's instinct was again to defend. 'Still, it *was* murmuring. I give you that.' She returned to the bathroom and immersed herself with caution. 'Come and talk here,' she said. 'When I've finished I want to go to sleep.'

'All right. But you do know what's going on?' As she fired off this question, Kirstie returned to the bathroom, sat down on the lavatory seat, appeared to judge this inelegant in view of the matter in hand, and instead perched on the end of the bath. 'It's one of those sudden holiday things. The young man's in love with you.'

It was perhaps the seeming extreme inconsequence of Kirstie's announcement that induced in Gloria what felt like a spasm or contraction round the heart.

'You're dotty,' she said.

'Or this Chevalley is.' Kirstie now spoke with a calmness which Gloria recognized with dismay as masking extreme resentment. 'Or he's been reading a book about the technique of seduction. In Italian, I don't doubt.'

'What a disgusting thing to say!' Gloria had sat up—like a very Venetian Artemis surprised by Actaeon, or some such mythological character, when bathing in a secluded silvan spring.

'He was making you jealous.'

'He was doing nothing of the sort.'

'I mean he thought he was. Going by the book.' Kirstie paused. She might now have been an actress admirably schooled in delivering her lines. 'Octavius Chevalley is a very oblique young man.'

'Oblique?' This unusual word quite grounded Gloria.

'Or let's be charitable. A confused young man, if you like.' Kirstie made one more pause—and then burst, amazingly, into a mysterious Doric. 'But what I'd call him, Gloria Montacute, is a fair scunner!'

'Just clear out for a minute.' Gloria had managed to be calm. 'Or I shan't have room to dry.'

To flirt with one young woman by way of stirring up another—Gloria thought, when left alone—is certainly a bookish wile. It probably happens in Jane Austen, and people like that. It's silly and a bit inferior, but you couldn't call it infamous. Kirstie, of course, had a right to feel annoyed, if she really felt it was this that had been going on. But why was she so thoroughly angry? It was almost as if she felt that—all into the bad bargain—she'd been merely messed around with; offered not so much what was aimed at someone else as what wasn't honestly there at all.

But Gloria didn't go to sleep before she had decided to think poorly of such a speculation. She returned Octavius, so to speak, to Miss Austen's innocent world. And after that she slept like a heroine with some agreeable destiny before her.

15

THE BAD CONSCIENCE OF
OCTAVIUS CHEVALLEY

OCTAVIUS CHEVALLEY ROSE early, and with difficulty conquered gloom sufficiently to order his breakfast.
The rolls hadn't arrived, and he had to distribute his two
pats of butter over some rusks which must surely have
been manufactured for the purpose of promoting teething
in the very young. He scarcely noticed, for he was feeling
bad.

He went out and prowled the slowly awakening city.
Women were splashing water on walls and pavements—
here in Venice just as they would be doing in Holland.
World-over, the presence of canals must encourage such
domestic lustrations. He gravitated towards the Piazza
San Marco—one always does when wandering aimlessly—
and surveyed it sadly. A few wretched old men—the low-
est form, he supposed, of Venetian servile life—were
swabbing down the café tables. The pigeons, being more
privileged creatures, weren't yet on duty. The Basilica
looked gimcrack and absurd; it might have been run up
for some ephemeral purpose by Metro-Goldwyn-Mayer.
The campanile was much more substantial. He crossed
over to it; was mysteriously appalled by his own ant-like
presence at the root of its raw red upward thrust; turned
away, and hurried down to the Molo. Although the dull
green waters he now surveyed constituted the theatre of
his late ineptitude he sat for a long time on the chilly
steps of St Theodore's column and stared at them. His
dim idea was to make an honest attempt at sorting himself out.

He remembered a novel—for he was very much the

bookish young man of Miss Anderson's penetrating regard—in which somebody not unlike himself had arrived
in Venice with designs upon a great heiress. The heiress
hadn't been at all like Gloria Montacute. But had he
himself, nevertheless, really been nursing a plan like that?
He didn't know. It was all very mixed up.

He looked at his watch, and to his surprise saw that it
was half past nine. This meant that refuges were open to
him. He got up, found his way to the Ponte dei Greci,
and was soon standing before the Scuola di San Giorgio
degli Schiavoni. It was a grand name for a very modest
building, but not too grand for what lay inside. He'd
brought Gloria and that other girl here, so it held uncomfortable associations. But he went straight in—absent-
mindedly paying a fee, although in his pocket he had a
ticket admitting him to the whole lot. And now he was
at home.

For we here arrive at the underlying fact, the simple,
fond, not (at the start) dishonourable truth about Octavius.
Venice went to his head—and also to his heart and intellect.
Venice was the sole originating occasion (a recording angel
would have pronounced) of his being in Venice now. He'd
jumped at something that would get him here: something
not too beautiful, yet not positively sinful in terms of this
imperfect world. Comberback and Domberg were giving
him leave of absence for his trip; they were even putting up
the money for it; and in return he was to make himself
agreeable and persuasive to a possible client. Looked at now,
it seemed a pretty shabby notion, anyway—chumming up
with the owner of the Nudd collection in the interest of a
sale. And—fatally—it had put another idea in his head, or
nourished there what had been no more than a casual
fantasy foreign to his nature. So from one sort of fake—it
was the truth he now confronted—he'd become a deeper
fake still.

Octavius went into the Oratory, where Carpaccio's pictures are, and for some minutes just wandered around. He had talked a good deal of nonsense about them to the young women, and in his present mood he was even ashamed of that. Carpaccio mightn't be the very grandest of the Venetians. But he was his, Octavius's, painter, on whom he'd already published two modest papers. And one ought to be serious about one's own thing.

He paused before St Jerome, the lion, and the bolting Dominicans—this chiefly because it was the picture that had most amused Gloria. There were three Turks in the background, which didn't seem quite right in a monastery, but then Carpaccio got his Turks in everywhere: you could see this identical trio in his early *Adoration of the Magi* (if it *was* his) in the National Gallery. Octavius offered himself these reflections in a perfunctory way; he wasn't, at the moment, really interested in Jerome and his pet; what he had a date with was *The Triumph of St George*. Standing before this, you could test out your visual memory pretty extensively. There was a preliminary drawing in the Uffizi, and a number of things had happened between that and the painting before him now. An oddly gesturing Saracen borrowed from a woodcut in Breydenbach's *Description of a Journey to the Holy Land* had taken Carpaccio's fancy at first, and in the drawing he had clapped him in directly behind the slain monster. But the Saracen's arms, oddly cramped in comparison with the free-flowing posture of the Saint, had irritated the composition, so in the painting there was an extra horse instead. But you also had to call up from Reeuwich (who was Breydenbach's illustrator) the Mosque of Rama, Solomon's Temple in Jerusalem, and two Mohammedan women. The Mosque and the Temple came through pretty well intact, but there were other drawings that showed Carpaccio playing around with the women, and one of these had even changed sex in the painting.

Having thus desperately and ingloriously bolted to his

own thing, Octavius was able to finish up before *The Vision of St Augustine* in a state of very simple aesthetic delectation—not even bothering to reflect on the astounding metamorphosis of the dog as revealed by the drawing in the British Museum. But then he looked at his watch again, and saw that it was nearly eleven o'clock. On two days running he'd met Gloria and Kirstie outside Quadri's at that hour, so it was reasonable to regard it as a fixed thing. If they were there now, he just mustn't funk facing up to them. He hurried out of the Scuola in confusion and almost ran through the narrow streets.

Perhaps, he told himself, there was nothing that couldn't be retrieved. Perhaps he was exaggerating his last night's ineptitude: the vulgar notion that he might make Gloria jealous by a little getting off with her companion. But he knew in his heart that it had all been more alien to him than he'd reckoned, and that he'd somehow managed simultaneously to overplay his part and to underplay it, so that he'd just been both offensive and ineffective. Could he apologize to Kirstie? Could he pretend he'd been tight? No—to start making speeches to her would be impossibly heavy-handed. But he'd have to make some sort of speech to Gloria. He'd have to tell her—confess to her—a great deal.

It was his having conceived a high regard for Gloria—one of those from-afar sentiments, it might have been called—that brought Octavius Chevalley to this good resolution. Like many good resolutions, it was not, perhaps, a good idea.

16

A TRIP TO TORCELLO

GLORIA WAS ALONE, and in front of her on the table stood an *espresso*. To Octavius's eye the minute cup, not quite filled with the blackest of black coffee, bore an austere and even forbidding appearance. He realized that he was going to be very easily unnerved.

'Hullo,' Gloria said, and dropped a lump of sugar into the cup. She could only just have arrived.

'Hullo.' Octavius tried to take heart from Gloria's not going in for a formal 'Good Morning'. But probably she never did. 'Where's Kirstie?' he asked. As he didn't much care where Kirstie was, and had no intention of dishonestly continuing to simulate interest in her, he'd perhaps put this question rather too soon. And he'd even asked it with anxiety—although the anxiety was only a kind of spill-over from an adjacent area of his mind.

'You sound quite breathless, Octavius. Have you been running, or something? Do sit down.'

'I thought you might be here.' Octavius had liked being called Octavius in this normal way. 'But I was back on Carpaccio, and I'd rather forgotten the time.'

Gloria nodded—briefly, but with seeming approval. What she was approving of, perhaps, was the general proposition that men should put their work first. Gloria was the superior sort of girl, he told himself, who takes a serious view of life.

'This way of doing coffee,' Gloria said, 'you'd think was about right for a cage of canaries. But even a small swig of it is bracing. You'd better order one.'

Octavius ordered one, thereby admitting that he needed to be braced.

'Kirstie has broken it up,' Gloria said casually.

'Broken it up!' The alarm in Octavius's voice disconcerted him as he detected it. But it seemed faintly to amuse Gloria.

'Oh, just for the day,' she said. 'She has gone on a steamer to a place called Chioggia. The book says it's the principal fishing port of Italy, and Kirstie said it would do her good to see a spot of honest labour going forward.'

'She'll do that, all right.' Here was the theme of work again. Octavius was intelligent enough to be aware that both these young women worked hard themselves, and liked it. And if that's your disposition, a holiday tends to fold up on you after three or four weeks at most. They'd probably both had about enough of Italy. 'There's a kind of second-rate Lido effect near by, but at Chioggia itself they do land plenty of fish.'

'Is there anything by Carpaccio at Chioggia?'

'Oh, yes!' By this inquiry, which seemed not mischievously intended, Octavius was quite touched. 'There's a St Paul in the church of San Domenico. And Kirstie will have a nice trip there.' His spirits were rising. 'The boat touches at two islands entirely populated by lunatics. And there's a third, which your guide-book describes as "verdant", reserved for the extremely aged. You see the bright eyes of the ancient creatures peering out at you through the undergrowth as you sail past.' Octavius paused, and suddenly decided that this all-is-forgotten note of levity was quite wrong. 'Gloria!' he said urgently, 'I want to—'

'And what are *you* going to do? Today, I mean.' Gloria's tone didn't acknowledge the slightest consciousness of having interrupted. 'For it's rather a gorgeous day.'

'I'd like you to come to Torcello with me.' To Octavius's surprised sense, this had uttered itself like an inspiration. 'It's just the day for that.'

'What's Torcello?'

'It's another island.'

'With lunatics?'

'Of course not. It's in the other direction.'

'Not where they make you buy lace or glass?' Gloria plainly felt she had bought enough of these commodities.

'No, no—that's Murano and Burano. You stop at them, but there's no need to get off. Not if you're on the ordinary *vaporetto*, and not on one of those shocking tourist affairs. And Torcello itself is really very nice.' Octavius's vein of inspiration continued. 'There's almost nothing there at all.'

'Nothing?' Gloria was visibly attracted.

'Well, there's a more or less abandoned cathedral, which is very splendid; and a more or less abandoned little church, which is very beautiful; and there's a very good restaurant, which won't be all that crowded at this time of year. And—Gloria—I'd be awfully pleased if you'd come to Torcello with me, and lunch with me there.'

These were, or seemed to be, accents which it is not for a young woman to mistake. What chiefly struck Gloria— what touched her to an extent she recognized and, some-how, accepted without surprise—was the fact that she was being *invited* out to lunch. Octavius was poor, and it was useless to pretend she wasn't rich, but he wasn't this time talking about going Dutch, all the same. It made the situation serious, but she didn't think she was afraid of that.

'Thank you very much,' she said, and waved to the waiter. She would at least pay for her own *espresso*. 'When do we go?'

'Oh, we can set off at once.' Octavius looked happy, but also rather alarmed; he was feeling, she supposed, that some die had been cast. 'We just walk over to the Fondamente Nuove, and with luck we shan't have to wait ten minutes.'

Gloria felt that there would now be a longer wait than that before Octavius came out with what he had to say. He had, she guessed, some particular setting in his head— or perhaps a favourite building or picture or statue from the presence of which he was proposing to draw support in a crisis. That would be extremely like Octavius, she told herself with as much confidence as if she had watched his development from childhood. And how enormously different he was from Harry—and, in a way, how very much more mysterious! She found it perplexing that anybody quite young should go in passionately for art. Of course she knew that this was only because her mother's art-loving associates had without exception been elderly and very plainly money-loving as well. All the great paint-ers had themselves been young once: Octavius had ex-plained that Raphael (whom she remembered her mother disapproving of) had done some of his best stuff when of positively tender years. She must revise her ideas. She made a start now by telling herself that Octavius would certainly be the world's top authority on Carpaccio be-fore he was thirty. And that this was quite something to be.

These thoughts (which point the sombre fact that loy-alty and susceptibility constitute a hazardous combina-tion in a young woman) took Gloria across Venice now. She was glad that Octavius wasn't rushing anything, be-cause she did very sensibly feel that she had real thinking to do. There were people to whom it would be of no account whatever that Octavius was your only coming oracle on Carpaccio, and there were people to whom it would similarly be of no account whatever that Harry might become your only possible choice as a full back for England. That was one way to put her problem to herself —but of course it could be expressed in other terms. You played for England on the strength of a certain radical masculinity which wasn't a bit relevant when deciding whether a Sacred Conversation, or a Madonna with Donors, or a Saint Somebody in his Study, was by this artist or that.

They had paused in what she knew was called a Campo, and before an equestrian monument. For a moment she wondered whether this was going to be Octavius's supporting presence. It was plainly a tremendous thing. And if you wanted radical masculinity, the man on the horse was it.

'Who is he?' Gloria asked.

'Who is he?' As he repeated her question, Octavius stared at her much as if, standing on Westminster Bridge, she had uttered some such words as, 'Please, what river is that?' But at once he recovered himself. 'It's Bartolommeo Colleoni,' he said, 'and it's by Verrocchio. Only he didn't live to finish it.'

'What was he?'

'Verrocchio?'

'No. Whoever you called him. The man on the horse.'

'I'd say he was pretty well nobody at all. A run-of-the-mill ruffian, or small-time bandit. But the statue just happens to be the greatest thing of its kind in the world. Which is odd, I suppose. But then art can be like that. Verrocchio was told to do Colleoni. But he did an idea instead.'

'Yes, I see.' And Gloria did see. 'I was thinking,' she said suddenly, 'there ought to be riders on those horses on the church. But naked, and not with terrific armour and helmets and all that. Like the ones in the British Museum.'

'Splendid notion.' If it came into Octavius's head that this reference to the Elgin Marbles perhaps represented Gloria's first-ever incursion into the field of comparative criticism, he didn't betray the fact. 'Come on,' he said. 'We're going to look at things much less arrogant.'

The *vaporetto* was crowded with country-people. At least they looked like that, although Gloria supposed the islands they were going out to counted as no more than suburbs of this watery city. They pushed past you vigorously, but with polite outcries of *'Permesso!'* and *'Scusi!'* such as you wouldn't get on a London tube. Some were going to the cemetery, and at the cemetery a funeral party was arriving as well. So here was a gondola that really was a Ship of Death: an outsize affair exuberantly adorned but pervasively inky, as if Styx or Acheron, or similar nasty rivers one had been taught about at school, had coated it in their own hue. Over the top of fortress-like walls an army of cypresses, answeringly black, peered curiously at the new arrival. The cemetery island must be so crammed with corpses that it was surprising there was any room for trees. Gloria asked whether it was inhabited, and Octavius said there was a large population of cats.

Once past Murano, they were out on the lagoon. It had a loneliness that had nothing to do with distance. You could count the planes at the airport on the mainland; and here and there, all the time, you came on little islands with brick buildings crammed on top of them. The buildings didn't look at all old, but they did look derelict; some of them were blind and blank structures which Octavius—although without giving much impression of authority—declared to have been powder-magazines. The fact of so much being deserted made for melancholy, and so did the unnatural stillness of the water. Torcello, when their wandering course eventually got them there, at first seemed melancholy too, but Gloria took to it at once. The canal and lagoon smells (which in fact she had by now rather taken to as well) were mingled as soon as you landed with something faintly aromatic, which might have come from herb gardens abandoned long ago. Commerce was represented by only one old man, who had a forlorn little stall on the quay. As they were the only voyagers to disembark, he naturally looked at them with expectation, and Octavius pleased Gloria by stopping, holding one of his Italian conversations, and buying a small and gaily enamelled bangle at the substantially reduced price which the right sort of Italian conversation secures. The old man wrapped it up carefully in tissue paper—rather as if (Gloria thought, recalling a stray reminiscence by the well-travelled Guise) he had been a goldsmith on the Ponte Vecchio in Florence, with some really high-class jewellery at his command.

'It's for you,' Octavius said, and handed her the minute parcel with a subdued flourish which one of Carpaccio's well-bred young Venetian gallants might have learnt from. That the gift had cost less than a pint of beer or a packet of cigarettes pleased Gloria still further, and she would have unwrapped the bangle and slipped it on at once if she had been quite confident it would clasp over her wrist. 'Just as many ghosts here as on San Michele,' Octavius said.

'San Michele—the place there's a story about?' Gloria, although not a literary character, had recalled Axel Munthe's celebrated book.

'Well, no, that's another one—near Naples.' Octavius was amused, and Gloria found she quite liked amusing Octavius. 'The cemetery island is called San Michele. But, you see, this one—and it's really quite tiny—had about 20,000 inhabitants at one time. Their ghosts are bound to be around. You're going to adore Torcello.' Octavius produced one of his attractive, because rare, displays of confidence. 'It has a kind of enchanted effect. Sleeping Beauty stuff.'

This was true. They walked along the margin of a

narrow canal to a tiny basin, and in front of them there distinguishably appeared the vestiges of a piazza which must have been, at some remote time, the centre of a flourishing town.

'How many of the 20,000 are left?' Gloria asked.

'119.' This was Octavius's confidence again—founded, although Gloria didn't know it, on his possession of a guide-book of his own. 'All changed, changed utterly: a terrible beauty is born.' He seemed, rightly, to judge this too mysterious. 'But it's lunch time, don't you think? And we can look round a bit afterwards.'

Gloria wasn't too excited to enjoy her lunch in what proved to be an open-air restuarant. But she *was* excited —and also, for some reason she couldn't get down to, puzzled as well. Of course she was puzzled, for a start, by the spectacle of what was apparently happening to her. Apart from a brief and not agreeable impression which itself wasn't exactly far back in time, she'd known this young man for less than a week. And nobody outside one of Mrs Bantry's novelettes—she thought, recalling books she'd picked up in the kitchen at Nudd—totters on the verge of serious commitment on the strength of an acquaintanceship of quite that brevity. You'd have to belong to the most casual sleeping-around crowd to think of getting cracking at such a pace.

But then, she had to ask herself, *was* there what could be called a serious commitment in question? She now liked Octavius Chevalley very much—a good deal more, oddly enough, than before his bad behaviour on the previous night. But she wasn't at all clear about what kind of liking it was. She was still interrogating herself about this as she ate something called *mascarpone*, which Octavius had discovered on the menu and triumphantly declared to be the perfect close to a meal. It was certainly very good. But it didn't answer Gloria's question, which was simply whether she was in love with Octavius. And she failed to reflect—after all, she was very young—that it is a question which those who *are* in love don't often have to ask themselves.

Yet however she wondered about herself, she wondered about Octavius a good deal more. When he wasn't being gay he was being very nervous. And although this was right and proper—or at least was right and proper in a story-book way—there was something about the quality of it that was disturbing. He seemed less a man with something on his mind than a man with something on his chest. But that, of course, must be his folly on the gondola. If he was going to tell Gloria that he loved *her* (and by now she hadn't a doubt that he was going to do just this), then he certainly had an awkward fence to take. The episode could no doubt be played down, passed off as a piece of fooling which had turned out a flop and in bad taste. At any rate, Octavius certainly felt he had to speak about it.

Gloria would have preferred him not to. She had now accepted Kirstie's explanation of the affair, and was finding it touching rather than either offensive or even absurd. Octavius must be a very inexperienced young man to have fumbled after so odd a stratagem. Perhaps he *did* get things out of books, just as Kirstie had suggested. But that was rather appealing, really. It made him, somehow, as vulnerable as a boy—say, as a clever boy, without the resource of physical robustness, tumbled into the bullying and bewildering life of a big school.

There was very little lucidity in these thoughts of Gloria's, and she certainly didn't go on to ask whether they might hint a substantial element of the maternal in the hovering relationship between Octavius and herself. What she did go on to was to acknowledge that her whole speculation wasn't quite in the target area. Octavius was certainly going to declare his passion (as Mrs Bantry's authoresses would have put it). There was no question in her mind as to what. But he was also going to say she just didn't know what.

17

A CONFESSION

THEY LOOKED AT the cathedral. It had been a good deal altered—and mainly for the worse, Octavius said—in 1008. Gloria gazed with proper respect at a fabric which had been monkeyed with (as a rapid calculation informed her) 58 years before all that about William the Conqueror. When at school she had been taken on appropriate cultural expeditions to various English abbeys, roofless and inanimate. ('Bare ruined choirs where late the sweet birds sang,' she recalled the English mistress quoting between explanations of the mysteries of night-stairs and reredorters.) But a cathedral still very much roofed but entirely unworshipped in was unfamiliar and disconcerting. It looked almost as if something extravagantly splendid had been dredged out of the lagoon. There were great marble columns, not hard-veined but softly shimmering like water, and fading towards their base into a kind of seaweed green. There was a floor like an ocean floor upon which foundered galleons had split out a treasury of plundered gems.

'The superannuations of sunk realms,' Octavius said softly—thus obeying (although Gloria didn't know it) the same impulse as the English mistress. 'But did you notice that they've turfed out Attila's chair?'

'Attila's chair?'

'Of course it has nothing to do with him. It used to be in here, but now they've dumped it in the little campo. We passed it coming in.'

Gloria ought to have noticed this. But she didn't worry. What she was aware of was that Octavius wasn't showing off; it was just that all this was his thing.

'Do you like the peacocks?' Octavius suddenly asked.

She did like the peacocks. They were carved on a marble panel beside a big pulpit: long-necked creatures stretching up to reach a kind of bird-bath at the top of a tall pillar. Of course they suggested the same sort of puzzle as the horses on St Mark's: there seemed to be no reason why there should be peacocks in a cathedral.

'Do they mean something?' she asked, commendably concerned to solve this small enigma.

'Oh, yes.' Octavius was flushed and pleased. 'It's a chalice that they're drinking from—which tells you they're the human soul grown incorruptible through the mystery of the Eucharist. It's a Byzantine symbolism one meets with all over the place. Only this is the finest example I know. Just look at the tendrils of the vine.'

Gloria looked—at this and presently at much else. There were vast mosaics: over the apse a Virgin and Child surrounded by old gentlemen, and at the west end a Last Judgement conceived by an imagination you couldn't call exactly comfortable. It was alarming that there had ever been people who devoutly believed in an occasion of that sort. Perhaps it was all true, Gloria thought—and immediately conceived of herself as tumbled naked into an uncompromisingly bubbling cauldron.

'You can put 100 lire into one of those tape-recorder things,' Octavius was saying, 'and listen to a spiel about the history of the place. But there's something in Torcello that I like better. So will you. Come on.'

They went into the second church, which was a much smaller one. It would have been insignificant altogether, Gloria thought, if it hadn't been the only other considerable building still extant on the island. She was just going to ask Octavius why it had been necessary to have a little church next-door to the big one, when Octavius spoke first.

'And this is beauty,' Octavius said. 'The real, the absolute thing.'

For a full minute Gloria produced no reply. She knew Octavius must be right, because it had become an article of faith with her that he was always right about these high and mysterious matters. But she wasn't seeing what he was seeing, and it was another article of faith with her —and one of much longer standing—that one didn't pretend about them for the sake of polite conversation. This church—it was called Santa Fosca—seemed to be nothing much at all: a humble little blunted Greek cross in shape, and in fabric constructed from rough brick—the colour of the pale sort of salmon that comes out of inexpensive tins. There were eight marble columns corresponding to the simple octagonal plan, and it was true that they ended in rather splendid capitals of what she remembered were the Corinthian order. But what these supported was dark wooden beams with the marks of the adze on them, and these reminded her of an old barn. The one running north and south in front of the business part of the church had a row of sharp iron spikes on top of it, such as might be put up to keep you out of a dangerous area in a zoo. There wasn't much to look at anywhere—unless it was another couple of those talking-machines into which you put a 100-lire piece. The plainness extended to what she remembered were called the Stations of the Cross, which are commonly revolting strip-cartoon affairs not a bit like Carpaccio. Here they were just small carved crosses let into the walls. She wondered whether poor unassuming little Santa Fosca had been plundered at some time or other.

'It's a pity about the mobile,' Octavius said.

Gloria followed Octavius's glance and saw that he was looking at a kind of candelabrum thing hanging from the flattish wooden cupola. 'Mobile' had been a joke—a rather uncertain joke, as if Octavius was preparing to defend himself against some Philistine response to the place which she might herself put up. But she saw that the object he was referring to was somehow not quite right; it was too like the gimmicky electrical contraptions that hung in hideous hugger-mugger in Italian lamp shops.

It was when she had seen this that Gloria suddenly saw the whole thing. Here, of course, is a vague phrase—but it must be vague since it has to cover a good deal. Gloria's perception that Santa Fosca *was* beautiful to just the degree that Octavius had declared was also her perception that they had arrived where Octavius had all the time intended. This was his place, his particular place, his inner sanctum within what was plainly his larger home, the city of Venice. And he'd had to bring her here. Considering these patent facts, Gloria was also constrained to admit that her perception of Santa Fosca as beautiful was, yet again, also her perception of a rather deeper hinterland to her feelings about her new acquaintance even than those which she had candidly been owning to herself.

'Let's sit down on those steps,' Octavius said suddenly. 'I don't think anybody else is going to come in. Gloria, I've something I must tell you.'

Gloria was visited by an inconsequent memory of sitting down on baled straw. The straw had been prickly. The marble was cold. But, of course, the memory *wasn't* inconsequent. The two occasions held both similarities and contrasts. She didn't, however, have leisure to work these out. She had to listen to Octavius. Octavius, who had turned extraordinarily pale, was saying something about Nudd.

'Nudd?' Gloria repeated. She didn't see how Nudd could come into the matter now so plainly in hand. She herself had scarcely thought of Nudd and its perplexing riches for weeks.

'I think you know that—on that day I hate reminding you of—I went down with Lambert Domberg. He's my boss. He takes a tremendous interest in the collection. He has strong views on what it would be wise to do about it.'

'Quite a lot of people have that.' With an obscure dismay, Gloria realized that Octavius, for some unaccountable reason, had embarked on a prepared speech. Not that he had much chance of getting to the end of anything of the kind. He was much too agitated. But he did manage to get out what were—although Gloria didn't yet grasp it —the crucial words upon which, however confusedly, everything else must follow.

'It's why I came to Venice.'

'You mean this man Domberg sent you?'

'Not exactly. In fact, I suggested it myself—I suppose just because I like getting here.'

'I see.' Suddenly, Gloria saw much more. 'Do you mean that our meeting—there in the Piazza—wasn't just chance?'

'Your solicitor told Domberg where you were staying.'

'Mr Thurkle is almost the only person who would know.' Having made this inessential remark, Gloria at once came out with something very essential indeed. 'Octavius, why do you have to tell me this? Why aren't you just carrying on with the plan?'

'With the plot.' These three words came from Octavius in a voice Gloria didn't like. A book would have called it a strangled voice. Octavius was launched on a scene of abasement. It was something he'd have a flair for. 'It's very complicated,' he said, and gave Gloria a hopeless glance.

'It sounds quite simple to me.'

'Well, yes—in a way. I was to make friends with you, and suggest what would be a good line to follow. A big sale, you know.'

'At least we *have* made friends.'

'Yes—you, me, and Kirstie.' Octavius's voice now trembled. Gloria, who knew that inflexible justice was the absolutely essential thing, told herself this wasn't a turn. There was *that* saving grace to it. Octavius was terribly moved. She hoped he was going to have the manhood not to weep.

'All right,' she said. 'Kirstie. I don't quite see the relevance of your performance last night. Not if a brisk business discussion was the idea.'

'I think I had another idea, too.'

'Octavius—hadn't we better drop all this? We've made friends, and that's it. I think the next *vaporetto* would be the best thing. No p.m. That's what Kirstie would say.'

'A filthy venal notion. And now I have to tell you.'

'Octavius, you have told me. No need to spell everything out.'

'I'm just frightfully sorry. Because I do so tremendously admire you, Gloria.'

There was mingled in this what taxed Gloria a good deal. What Octavius's last words chiefly carried was what they finally excluded. That she is tremendously admired is not what a girl in a certain state of feeling—or who has been verging on that state—precisely wants to hear. But Octavius had arrived at honesty. And he might have failed to do that. She might have had to find him out, yet more painfully, later on. She wondered whether the pervasive chill she felt was just seeping up from the cold marble of Santa Fosca. Whether this was so or not, it would be sensible to stand up and get moving. But suddenly Octavius said a very strange thing.

'Gloria—it's not that I don't find you physically splendid.'

She stared at him, and saw that he was, so to speak, taking time off her humiliation to peer in a puzzled way

at his own. And that was about enough: how right Kirstie
was to put a ban on any sort of p. m.

Gloria rose abruptly to her feet. Then, obeying a sudden impulse, she stretched down a hand to Octavius, as
one may do to a lazy companion in such circumstances.
He took it with a wondering look, and without speaking.
Still in silence, they left the little church. It was very
warm outside, and there was a smell of dry hay. She
noticed what must be Attila's chair. But she didn't want
ever again to have the antiquities of Italy explained to
her.

Yet she oughtn't simply to write Octavius off; to give
the effect of ordering him from her presence with an
indignant mien and a flashing eye. He'd deeply wounded
her—but how could he have known he was going to do
precisely that? Did he even know it now? Had he much
notion of having touched her heart—touched it in the
way he'd been shamefully proposing to pretend that she
had touched his? All the same, whatever he'd felt or believed, his clean-breast-of-it resolution hadn't been ignoble.
Yet perhaps it hadn't been sensible or even sensitive either.
When he'd discovered he was up to something it wasn't
in him to bring off, or that was too contemptible to go
on with, he would perhaps have done best simply to
organize an unspectacular fading out. For in that case
he'd have left behind him in Gloria's memory nothing
that couldn't be classified as what Kirstie had called 'one
of those sudden holiday things', an attraction that hadn't
developed, an incipient love-affair that hadn't come off.
As it was, she was left with a feeling she found it hard to
put a name to—but she thought of it as related to the
feeling you get if you go up to your room and discover
it has been burgled. And she hated the fear she had that
she might later come to nourish a mean resentment, to
tell herself that she'd been humiliated and hurt just because Octavius Chevalley, having chickened out of an

enterprise (or brace of enterprises) he hadn't the nerve for,
had salved his vanity by turning on a bit of theatre. This
would be a foul thing to come to believe, because it
wouldn't be really true.

They walked back to the quay still without speaking.
There was no sign of a *vaporetto*, and Octavius muttered
something to the effect that their wait might be up to
half an hour. Gloria very much wished that she was clever
enough to be able to think of the right things to say.
She had a notion of what they were, but no words for
them. She wanted to tell him that they were both young;
that when young one flounders about, seeing oneself as
this or that, getting into false positions every second time
one steps out, alarmed and trying to kid oneself if one
finds oneself without some impulse or ambition or standard which convention takes for granted. She wanted to
say things like this, but in fact she wasn't able to say
much. For one thing, she simply knew far too little about
the inner nature of this acquaintance of a week. And she
wasn't likely ever to learn more. It was true that, by the
time the little boat did come, they were managing to
smile at one another ruefully, and that when half-way
across the lagoon they were exchanging civilized remarks.
But treachery remains treachery, and can't be more than
briefly scotched by remorse, compunctions, or generous
feelings. Gloria knew very well that she and Octavius
Chevalley were already each a painful episode in the
other's past—and that, forty years on, they still wouldn't
be too pleased by an accidental meeting at a party.

Octavius must have felt this too, for when they had
landed and walked a little way into the city he excused
himself in not very intelligible terms and vanished. It
wasn't gallant but it showed good sense, and Gloria didn't
resent its happening in a quarter where she wasn't very
sure of her bearings.

She carried neither a guide book nor a plan, so it wasn't

surprising that she was quite quickly lost. Just at the moment, it was a condition there was something to be said for, since it reproduced the state of affairs she was conscious of inside her head. She thought of the people you read about as found wandering because they've forgotten who they are. She was a bit like that. She'd been calling herself a young woman, and it turned out she was really a bank account and a collection of pictures. Perhaps she ought to have been prepared for it. She remembered Harry telling her—rather brutally soon after her mother's death—that she'd be a tremendous catch and God knew who would be after her. Well, Octavius Chevalley had turned out to be one answer. And it had been careless of her—conceited of her, in fact—not to think of it.

Perhaps, however, she'd better un-lose herself. It wasn't wholesome, deliberately cultivating a forlorn state. She could stop any stranger, any female stranger, in this unknown *salizzada* she was walking down and simply say 'San Marco?' on an interrogative note. There would be helpful gestures, pointings and smiles, and when she'd repeated the process two or three times she'd arrive on home ground, more or less. Or she could stop an elderly man. She could even stop a *young* man. Gloria made this last announcement to herself experimentally; it was to discover if she could so much as entertain the thought of a young man ever again. She decided not.

It was just at this moment that a young man stopped her. He did it by jumping up from a table outside a little café and planting himself before her.

'So here you are,' the young man said. 'You won't remember me. I'm Jake.'

18

INOPPORTUNE REAPPEARANCE
OF OUR HERO

'I'M JAKE,' JAKE said—and waited to see what coin, if any, dropped.

None did. So it would have been natural for Jake to amplify—using some such words as: 'I'm your cousin, Jake Counterpayne'. But for several moments he said nothing more. He was looking at Gloria attentively—much more attentively than she was looking at him. Gloria appeared to be having difficulty in emerging from a brown study, which was something he wouldn't have reckoned she had the habit of falling into. But if this was unexpected, nothing else about her was. So Jake told himself he had been right about this girl. It was something it wouldn't be easy to present in a sensible light, since their acquaintance over a dozen years hadn't been exactly extensive. Still, this was it.

'I last saw you the day your mother died,' Jake said, without awkwardness. 'Of course, we didn't manage much talk. But it was a reunion, all the same.'

'Yes, of course ... Jake.' Gloria put out both hands, and for a moment clasped both his. It was more than Jake had expected; he was delighted but he was puzzled as well; suddenly he had a very queer perception that she'd done it simply to stop herself from turning and running away. 'How odd to meet in Venice!' Gloria said, and appeared to remember something. 'I suppose this *is* a chance meeting?'

'Oh, not a bit.' Jake found the question unexpected, but it seemed a good lead in. 'I thought I'd hunt you up.'

This remark was not a success. If Jake, abruptly assuming the form of a bug-eyed monster, had incontinently yelled 'I thought I'd hunt you *down*' he might have reckoned to affect Gloria much as he now seemed to have done. She was certainly upset. It occurred to him that she might be exhausted by the sort of sight-seeing people are conned into in a place like Venice.

'Let's get some tea somewhere,' Jake said cheerfully, 'and talk for a bit. That's what I'd like.' Feeling this last statement to be egotistical, he added: 'If *you* would, that is.'

'Yes, of course.' Gloria smiled. It was the smile—Jake perfectly clearly saw—of a princess who, when ready to drop, must still do the right thing. This was discouraging, and even alarming. But at least it was a challenge, and there is always something in that. 'Only,' Gloria was saying, 'I don't know this part of Venice at all.'

'They've been keeping you in the posh places, I expect. As a matter of fact, this caff I've been sitting in isn't too bad. So let's just stay put. I haven't ordered anything yet. Only just decided on a tea-break. Haven't felt like taking much time off.'

'From what?' But now Gloria had at least sat down.

'Finding you, of course. It's quite something, quartering a city like this. *Due te con limone, per favore.*' Jake's Italian, although atrociously pronounced, was of the carefree sort that is always understood. 'Of course, I'd no idea of your hotel.'

'It's a boarding-house. Didn't Mr Thurkle tell you the address?'

'Thurkle?' Jake was puzzled. 'I've never heard of him.'

'Then how did you know I was in Venice at all?' There was no urgency in Gloria's question. There wasn't even the lively curiosity that Jake would have liked. He had to face it, he told himself. She was making conversation until she could get away. Jake (although he wasn't really a conceited young man) found this bewildering.

'I knew it was Venice,' he said, 'because I was told by a chap called Harry—Harry Carter, isn't it?—when I went down to Nudd to look for you.'

'Oh, I see.' For a moment Gloria again seemed quite uninterested. And if she was abashed, she certainly didn't show it. But now she frowned, as if absent-mindedly perplexed. 'How did you come to talk to Harry about me?'

This was difficult. Jake, in a man-to-man way, was pledged to silence about the little matter (which was how he now saw it) of the rustic trollop in the barn. So he couldn't begin from that. In not doing so, he was in fact telling a lie. He saw that keeping faith with a girl meant cutting out that man-to-man stuff, and he made a note of this for future use. But now he prevaricated.

'It had to do with a tea shop,' he said vaguely. 'And muffins.'

'You won't get muffins here.' This was the first flicker of life Gloria had shown. As it died away, Jake faced the conclusion that there was really something wrong. 'How did you travel?' Gloria asked politely.

'I've got a van. I shoved it in that big car-park for a night—but they wouldn't let me sleep in it, and it cost the bloody moon. So I've got it on a nice bit of swamp near Mestre now, and I can nip across on the train for a bob.'

'Jake, I'm afraid I don't even know what you do.'

'Do? I'm a painter.'

'If you're interested in art, I suppose you're very fond of Venice.'

'No, I'm not.' Jake had for a moment supposed that there must be something malicious in the suggestion of his being 'interested in art'. But he realized that Gloria's mind didn't work that way. 'Are *you*,' he asked as the tea arrived, 'very fond of Venice?'

'No, I don't think I am.'

'Then you're quite right.' This hint of common ground encouraged Jake. 'It's a dying organism—which isn't a very cheerful thing to be crawling round.'

'I rather liked Torcello, and in a sense it's *quite* dead.'

'No harm in being dead. It's the preliminaries there's no sense in hungering after. If you were going to write some sort of death-wish thing, you'd do well to set it in Venice. Thomas Mann did a superior job at just that. Change and decay in all around he saw—and a spot of cholera thrown in for good measure.'

'I haven't read it.' Gloria was still being polite, and she had started drinking her tea. 'If you don't like Venice,' she asked, 'why have you come here?'

'I've told you. To hunt you up.'

'That's why you *came*?'

Jake realized that, up to this point, Gloria had failed to get the message. And there wasn't anything gratifying in her manner of taking it now. She had, indeed, exclaimed in a tone of astonishment which might have been all right in itself. But it hadn't been like that. 'Incredulous horror'—Jake told himself—were the words a dispassionate observer would apply to Gloria's reaction. In short, and for some mysterious reason, he had quite an assignment on his hands. He sought for some changed approach.

'Tea all right?' he asked. 'Would you like an ice?'

'It's very good. No, thank you.'

'Ice-cream is something the Italians are supposed to be tops at. I'm researching into the subject. Because I'm going to make some.'

'Ice-cream?' Gloria was managing to be politely interested again, although it was evident she was still controlling something. And this time, she didn't sound surprised. A world in which young gentlemen dedicated to the more liberal professions periodically tipped themselves into manufacturing pursuits for financial reasons was obviously familiar to her. So Jake decided to enlarge on this ground.

'It's going to be quite good pay. I had to borrow some money from my father not very long ago. And as he puts in a lot of time feeling the bread-line lapping up on him, it's the fair thing to get it back to him pretty soon. I don't think you've met him since we were kids. He's quite a decent old chap.'

If Gloria was asking herself in her heart whether she could ever have said of her mother, in that throw-away fashion, 'She's quite a decent old girl', she didn't betray it. The poverty of the Counterpaynes, however, might conceivably have been opening up for her some further vista. She gave Jake a look that troubled him. It might have been called a hardening look—such as you might get if you'd been barefaced or impudent. As these were not among Jake's numerous failings, he was left rather groping about.

'Does your father,' Gloria asked, 'feel he's been hardly done by in a family way?'

This, for a change, didn't trouble Jake at all. He had a notion of conversation as something that should get you where you're going as quickly as may be.

'Oh, yes!' he said. 'There's nothing round-the-bend about him, exactly. But he has his dotty side. I can see he's the last man who ought ever to have handled his own investments, and so forth. But, in fact, he's made a disastrous full-time job of it. When he could have been breeding trout, or conserving the countryside, or any harmless ploy of that sort. I rather think he imagines he's going to go bankrupt, and all that. Bailiffs, and so forth.' In what might be called the innocence of his heart, Jake was almost enjoying painting this picture of Counter-payne penury. 'And he'll certainly die while thumbing over the butts of old cheque-books.'

'I'm sorry that your father should be worried by these things.'

'Well, it's his life, in a way. And at least he won't

worry *you*. His bark's much worse than his nibble.' Jake paused. His sense of misgiving was mounting. On the other hand, he did now seem to command Gloria's attention. He resolved to carry on with this mild family fun for a while. 'And he can be entirely at sea. You know your Velazquez?'

'No.'

'Don't be silly! Of course you do.' Jake wasn't standing for waywardness. 'The small Spanish boy on horseback.'

'Oh, yes. It's said to be very valuable.' As she said this, Gloria looked merely bewildered. 'What about it?'

'My father thinks it would be nice if you sent it to him as a Christmas card.' Jake suddenly saw why he was saying all this. 'There *are* a lot of imbecile family feelings I'd hate to see take you by surprise, Gloria. But they're not bad feelings, really. Only batty ones. And they're not what you and I ought to be thinking about, at all. I've come to Venice because—'

'Jake, would you mind telling me the way to the Zattere?' Gloria had stood up. 'If you'd just point it out to me. No more than that.'

'Yes, of course.' Jake had stood up too. 'But I want—'

'I don't know *what* you want. But saying you've come to Venice to find me is quite fantastic.' Gloria's desperation was suddenly extreme. 'You've been thinking something up—some sort of horrible double bluff. I don't want to hear more. I can't take more. Perhaps I've got everything wrong. But it's enough for today.'

'You go straight down this street.' Jake might have been described—in a figure appropriate to the place—as having gone as pale as Desdemona's smock. 'There's an archway. You go under it, and are in the Piazza. Then—'

'Then I'll know. Good-bye.'

Jake found this extravagant scene took some recovering from. He was aware that he must have been nervous, and gone off on a silly tack as a result. But whatever the puzzle was, there was a big chunk missing from the middle of it—and just where to put his hand on what would make sense of the surrounding mystification he didn't at all know.

He did know he mustn't pursue Gloria now. It was the sense of pursuit that had rattled her. Having told her the simple truth of why he'd come to Venice, he ought to have gone dead ahead from that. It would have been easier if they'd had, the two of them, at least a few meetings even of the most fleeting sort in the years between childhood and now. Not, he sensed, that the crux of the matter had lain in that. He'd have carried the staggering fact that he was simply in love with her but for this hidden thwarting thing. But you can always get an apple-cart on its wheels again, and he had a clear saving sense that brainstorms don't last. And he did now know that he'd never, never let go.

Jake strode through Venice—scowling at it even more ferociously than he'd ever scowled at Lambert Domberg of Comberback and D. He *blamed* Venice. Whatever had put it in Gloria's head to come to the beastly place? It wasn't her sort of place in the least. An 'abhorrent, green, slippery city'—that was what D. H. Lawrence had called it; and Lawrence, although a bit given to creating, had been a thoroughly sensible man. Had somebody brought her here? It didn't seem likely she'd come entirely on her own. He'd find out tomorrow. It had better *be* tomorrow. He just mustn't push in on Gloria again until she'd slept something off. Unfortunately that meant that there was the rest of today.

He paused in front of another café, a rather bigger one. If you didn't go to those idiotic tourist places and sog yourself in disgusting music purveyed by execrable bands, you could at least get your drink tolerably cheap. The immediate solution lay in that. He sat down at a

table. But he saw Gloria looking at him—although only
in his disturbed inward vision—and jumped up again. He
glanced at his watch, although quite without taking anything in from it, and just walked on and on.

Eventually he came to the Piazzetta, and sat down on
the steps of one of the great columns. In front of him
was a broad expanse of marble patterned like a chess-
board gone mad. Beyond that was the sullen water of the
bacino. A big ugly freighter, which you'd have supposed
had gone hopelessly astray, was nosing out of the Canale
della Giudecca. It was sending up smoke that blotted out
almost the whole of San Giorgio Maggiore. Very incon-
sistently, since the whole place was so beastly, he felt
this to be an outrage. There was another young man,
obviously an Englishman and not an American, similarly
sitting on the steps a few feet away from him, and equally
obviously nursing much the same feeling. As the young
man was a total stranger, Jake was surprised to hear himself speak.

'What are *you* doing here?' Jake asked gloomily.

'God knows.' The young man wasn't bothering to wonder why he'd been addressed. But he took a look at Jake.
'Well—Carpaccio, I suppose,' he said. 'I needed to have
another look at him.'

'Anecdotal character.'

'Yes.'

The conversation lapsed. On Jake's other side a woman
was having something or other explained to her by a guide.
She was the sort of wealthy woman who announces to
heaven knows whom that what she expects in a male
guide is that he should be young and good-looking—and
who gets what she wants. From this depressing spectacle
Jake turned back to his neighbour.

'Come and have a drink,' he said.

They went and had a drink, punctuated by a few more
perfunctory remarks. They both had their troubles, but a

common code, perfectly understood, assured them that these, like their personal identities, would remain anonymous. Ten minutes later, they parted with a casual nod. It isn't recorded that they ever met again.

19

A VERY NICE GIRL

ON THE FOLLOWING morning Jake felt ready to tackle his problem anew. But there were really several problems, and the first was to discover Gloria's whereabouts. She had wanted to be directed to the Zattere, so she was presumably in some sort of hotel or pensione there. At least there weren't two sides to the Zattere, as it ran along the verge of the crazy place's broadest ditch. Still, there was nearly a mile of it, and he might have rather a hunt. He decided to begin by going to a tourist office and getting a list of hotels and so forth in that part of Venice. This took quite some time, and was probably a mistake. The Zattere proved not crammed with hostelries you could imagine Gloria staying in. And the second one he entered immediately struck him as hopeful.

'*Buon giorno*,' he produced to a woman behind a desk—but with an impatience of this initial civility which made it sound not at all right. '*E a casa la Signorina Montacute?*'

The woman gave a shake of the head which, although perfunctory, conveyed quite a lot—for example, that Jake's Italian vocabulary, accent, syntax and whatever were about as pitiful as could be. She seemed quite a decent woman, and he supposed she must be having a bad day. But he hadn't time to feel discouraged before somebody else spoke from behind him.

'Miss Montacute isn't here now. Not any longer. She left after breakfast.'

'Oh—thank you very much.' Jake had turned round and seen that the speaker was a young woman—a very pretty young woman—more or less of Gloria's age. She had a Scotch accent and the appearance of being more competent than, perhaps, it is wholly desirable that a pretty and promising girl should be. Jake, however, being in the condition he was, regarded her without the shadow of an improper thought. 'Do you mean she's left Venice?'

'Yes.' The pretty Scotch girl came to a full stop on this monosyllable. Jake gathered that he had to produce credentials before communication could be carried further.

'My name's Counterpayne,' he said. 'I'm Gloria's cousin, as a matter of fact.' (For the moment, Jake forgot his conviction that second cousins aren't cousins at all.) 'If you're a friend of hers, I expect you may have heard of me.'

'No.' The pretty girl had no doubts in the matter. 'I never have.' She looked at him consideringly. 'I'm Miss Anderson.'

'How do you do?' It struck Jake as extremely funny that anybody should say 'I'm Miss Anderson'. But no doubt it was quite the thing in North Britain. 'Have you been travelling with her?' he asked.

'I suppose so.' Miss Anderson seemed to have discovered something answeringly funny for herself. 'Although it's rather a grand word for it. We haven't exactly been to the sources of the Nile.'

'Of course not.' Jake was a shade intimidated, or he wouldn't have made this weak reply. He rallied. 'Will you come out and have some coffee?'

'Yes, if you like.' This reply surprised Jake. He'd been undergoing a scrutiny to which it hadn't occurred to him that he was standing up all that well. 'There's a little place just beside the Accademia,' Miss Anderson added.

'Then come on.' Jake led the way out of the pensione with alacrity. If he wasn't going to be baffled—or baffled at least for a time—his only chance lay in chatting up Gloria's friend. Gloria might have gone off abruptly, but it wasn't likely to have been to an unknown destination. 'Had you arranged to split up?' he asked when they were in the open air. He tried to put this question casually, but it turned out not to be the kind of question that can be spoken that way. It must be perfectly evident that he was in a state about Gloria.

'Sooner or later, we were going to. In a few days, in fact. My parents are at a place called Ortisei—that's up north—and I'm joining them for the rest of their holiday before going home.' Miss Anderson seemed prepared to be communicative, at least about herself. 'I've got to be back at work, the Monday after next. I'm a nurse.'

'And Gloria has to be back at work too?'

'Oh, yes.'

'Giving out tea, isn't it?'

'She's changing jobs. She's going to run the Admin. canteen.'

'I see.' Jake hadn't much idea what an Admin. canteen was, but it didn't sound exactly glamorous. The important thing, however, was that he'd gained some sort of footing or tolerance with the Anderson girl. He nursed this carefully with occasional becoming remarks until they reached the café. 'My name's Jake,' he there thought it possible to announce.

'I suppose that's really James? I'm Christine, but generally called Kirstie.' Miss Anderson seemed instinctively to compensate for this moderate advance in familiarity by putting a certain distancing into her tone. 'Did you and Gloria meet yesterday?' she abruptly asked.

'Yes, we did—just for a few minutes.' Jake was taken by surprise. If Gloria had mentioned their meeting to Kirstie, Kirstie wouldn't now be asking if a meeting had taken place. If, on the other hand, Gloria hadn't mentioned it, what was putting the question into Kirstie's head? The only possible answer seemed to be that Gloria had arrived back at her pensione still distinguishably in a state to need accounting for, but had offered no explanation to her friend. And then—this morning, indeed only a few hours ago—she had bolted from Venice, still leaving Kirstie in the dark. And here was the explanation of Kirstie Anderson's having agreed to come out and have coffee with him in this way. She suspected he held some key to a mystery, and was resolved to get hold of it. And he, in his turn, was in the same position in relation to her.

It was a tricky situation, Jake thought. But he didn't approve of making things trickier than they had to be, and he decided to take the initiative with a few direct questions.

'Has Gloria gone home?' he asked.

'Yes. She's gone off in an *Alitalia* plane by way of Milan. It was the first offering.'

'You mean she was in a great hurry? Had she had bad news from England—anything like that?'

'I don't think so. She mentioned nothing.' Kirstie had left Jake's first question unanswered. She seemed disposed to turn reticent again. But Jake had a feeling that this was a temporizing process, a holding operation while she studied him. She wasn't doing this in quite the way that he'd sometimes been gratified to notice in girls; for instance, she seemed less interested in his eyes or his mouth aesthetically regarded than in how he looked and spoke. It was a bit of character-appraisal that was going on. He wished she'd step on it.

'Do you think she's gone back to Nudd?' he asked.

'I suppose she may have. I think she rather feels she's been putting it off—her problem there, I mean.'

'Her problem?' For a moment Jake took this to refer to nothing less than the dangerous Harry Carter himself.

'What she's going to do about all the valuable things there.'

'Oh, I see!' Jake was much relieved. 'She'll liberate them, if she takes my advice. Scatter them around—so that there will be a nice bit of this or that here and there. That's how everything of that sort ought to be—don't you think, Kirstie? The Russians made a frightful mistake after their Revolution—just embalming everything in the same pompous old museums and palaces and places. In China—'

'Did you air these views to Gloria when you met her yesterday?'

'No, I didn't—but I expect I shall. Not that it's all that important, really. Museums and picture galleries have their points, I suppose, even although I don't happen to care for them myself.' Jake was being entirely reasonable. 'You can nip in whenever you please, and nip out with precisely what you've wanted ten minutes later.'

'If everybody did that,' Kirstie said stiffly, 'there soon wouldn't be much left.'

'You've got me wrong.' Jake was much amused, but immediately became serious again. 'Look!' he said. 'I don't know Gloria all that well. I haven't, I mean, *seen* her a great deal. But she's terribly important to me, Kirstie. And clearly she's upset. She's gone off in a state. Isn't that so? Be honest. I want to know.'

'I wouldn't call it a state. Gloria's a controlled sort of person. But it's true that she'd rather suddenly had enough of Venice.'

'Why? What was it?'

'I think it's her that you ought to ask about that.'

'But she's probably over Mont Blanc by now! And I want to *know*.'

This urgency had at least the effect of causing Kirstie to stir her coffee thoughtfully. The café—or the open-air part of it—was on the restless side: close to the Accademia landing-stage, with *motoscafi* scurrying and *vaporetti* loitering in and out all the time. Jake, who didn't possess much historical information, wondered what imbecile impulse had induced people to build up a city in which you had to slop around in this way. It wasn't dignified, as in Gentile Bellini's State occasions set here; or at once idealized and lively, as with Carpaccio whom that chap yesterday evening had been on about; or all dissolved into such lights as never were, which had been Turner's notion of coping with the scene. Turner's Venice—it came to him suddenly and brilliantly—was Venice in the second that the bomb dropped: visually enthralling, and in the next instant it would be gone for ever.

Only here it still was—busily engaged in sinking into the sea, according to some authorities on the subject. But that, quite obviously, was no more than a hoax or a racket. The place was destined to go on mouldering for centuries. Of course you could fall in love with it in a necrophilous way. He saw that clearly enough.

These thoughts—which illustrate the fact that professional preoccupations can be irruptive even within states of considerable personal urgency—left Jake scowling at Miss Anderson in a fashion which had the sudden effect of swinging her to his side of some invisible but significant fence.

'Then I'll tell you,' she said, 'just what I know. But it really isn't much. You might put it that Gloria has been pestered by somebody.'

'What do you mean by that?'

'I mean a young man pursuing her to Venice and pretending a romantic interest in her, when he was really just after what she's inherited.'

'She couldn't believe—!' Jake was for a moment utterly at sea. Confusedly, he saw his yesterday's encounter with Gloria, and the idiotic line of talk he'd developed in it, as perfectly supporting some mad and low accusation. '*You* might think ... but Gloria could never think—'

'Somebody we've been tagging about with for a week.' Kirstie had looked at him round-eyed, and spoken very quickly. 'I'll tell you his name. Octavius Chevalley.'

'Never heard of him.' Jake had taken a deep breath. 'Does he know Gloria well?'

'Oh, no. I don't think she'd ever heard of him either.'

'It sounds crazy. What's his line?'

'He works for some firm that has to do with pictures and things. I remember he said something about a man called Domberg.'

'Then he's had a first-rate training as a parasite and blood-sucker.' Jake announced this with robust conviction. 'Anyway, he's been exposed.'

'I wouldn't call it that. He exposed himself.'

'He—?' Jake almost got this one wrong too. 'Just how?'

'He had a change of heart, or something, and thought it wasn't nice.' Kirstie didn't speak as one who professes charitable feelings. 'He explained his unworthy designs, and withdrew.'

'When?'

'Oh, just yesterday. When Gloria and he went to Torcello. I'd gone to Chioggia.'

'And Gloria told you about it afterwards—when she'd got back here in the afternoon?'

'Yes. It had been a shock to her.' Kirstie paused. 'A bigger shock,' she added grimly, 'than it damn-well ought to have been.'

'But she didn't tell you about meeting me?'

'No, she didn't.'

'Don't you think that was a bit odd?' Although he tried to conceal it, Jake was dismayed.

'Oh, I don't know.' Kirstie considered this coolly. 'It was just a casual meeting with a cousin—and when she had something else very much on her mind.'

'There was nothing casual about it for me.'

'So you've rather conveyed to me.' Kirstie regarded Jake gravely. 'The question is, what did you convey to *her?* Did you *pretend* it was a casual meeting—as Mr Chevalley did a week ago?'

'Of course not.' Jake was aware of something unusual happening in his blood stream; a fuss or flurry liable to produce anger or a flare-up of injured pride. 'Not that it wasn't *difficult*.'

'Difficult?'

'The trouble is that we don't—do we?—believe in love at first sight. As a generation, I mean.' Jake was speaking carefully. 'Lust at first sight, yes. You know? I'm bloody well going to lay that girl. You hear it said.'

'You may. I don't.'

'Sorry. But you see what I mean. Instant lust's in order. But not the other thing.'

'The Romeo line, as it were?' The question came so drily from Miss Anderson that a detached observer might have suspected her of being, despite herself, a little affected by this turn in the talk. 'The point is, you came clean?'

'I certainly didn't say: "Oh, Miss Montacute, how surprising to meet you here"—which is what this filthy Shubunkin seems to have said.'

'Chevalley.'

'All right— Chevalley. I mean that I simply told Gloria I'd come to Venice to find her.'

'And dower her with your hand?'

'If you like to put it in that offensive way.'

'I don't believe *you* were offensive.' Kirstie came out with this handsomely. 'But you mayn't just have been—'

'All right—don't I know it? The question is what I do now.'

'Then I can give you the answer, if you want it.'

'Of course I want it.'

'You proceed as planned.'

'Faint heart never won fair lady?'

'Very occasionally, perhaps. But not much of a lady.'

'Then I'll go right ahead.' Jake was much heartened.

'But can I give you a lift to Ortisei? It's only a few hours, and I can go home over the Brenner.'

'But you'd lose a day that way. So I think not.'

'Kirstie, you're a very nice girl.'

Part Four

20

INDIGNATION IN GRAY'S INN

'IMPOSSIBLE!' DOMBERG SAID.

'It's surprising, I agree.' Mr Thurkle, ensconced behind his own broad desk, deprecated perturbation. 'But, like it or not, that's what he calls himself. The Montacute Curator.'

'The thing's outrageous. Can't you get rid of him?'

'My dear sir, I am not this man Guise's employer. It appears that he has been at Nudd for a very long time. Longer than the Montacutes themselves, in fact. So I certainly can't do anything rash. It is very possible that he enjoys a considerable measure of my client's confidence.'

'He's certainly acting as if he did. And where is that confounded girl, anyway?'

'Miss Montacute?' Thurkle had raised his eyebrows at the unseemly cast of this enquiry. 'It is possible that she is back at Nudd by now. I have written to her, and am awaiting her next instructions. I can't bully her, you know.'

'Nor influence her in any way?' Domberg stared glumly at the lawyer. 'That's what Chevalley seems to have decided, too.'

'Chevalley?'

'The young man you met in my office. He suggested to me—most resourcefully and perfectly properly—that he should go out to Venice and contact this ... and contact Miss Montacute. Have a chat with her about the future of the collection, and so on.'

'He may be said to have gone to Venice,' Thurkle blandly asked, 'in the character of a tout?'

'Confound it, Thurkle, that's a most uncalled for way of putting it. Comberback and Domberg were—informally, of course—Mrs Montacute's professional advisers in various artistic matters for many years. It was—'

'I don't recall anything of the kind appearing in the lady's accounts. No doubt you acted in an honorary capacity.'

'That goes without saying.' Domberg made the gesture of one whose whole life-style vindicates his aloofness from monetary considerations. 'But about Chevalley. He has behaved damned oddly. He hadn't been in Venice more than a week—and on the firm's cash, mark you—when he wrote in throwing up his job with us. He says he has hopes of a junior lecturership in the history of art in some outlandish provincial university. What do you make of that?'

'It is no doubt natural that he should seek to better himself.' Thurkle appeared to offer this opinion without malice. 'Would you care for a cup of tea?'

As the tea had actually been brought into Thurkle's room and placed on Thurkle's desk, Domberg was hardly able to refuse. Kitchenmaid's tea, he told himself ill-temperedly, in chipped kitchenmaid's cups. It was unfortunate that the late Mrs Montacute had chosen as her solicitor one so blind to all aesthetic decency.

'I suppose you agree,' he said, 'that this fellow Guise, whether enjoying the young woman's confidence or not, must be off his head? Criminally, for that matter. "Montacute Curator" is sheer imposture.'

'Is that so?' Thurkle was urbane. 'I am not, of course, particularly conversant with criminal law. In this office, as you can imagine, it doesn't often come our way. But I have a fancy that the point you raise would depend for its validity entirely on Miss Montacute. If she is aware that Guise is calling himself that, and sees no reason to take any steps about it, then he *is* that. We might find Counsel to produce another opinion, I suppose. But then one can find Counsel to produce pretty well anything. I ought to have asked whether you take sugar. There may well be some in the office.'

'Thank you, no. What earthly title—'

'Well, it appears to be Guise who has got those people lined up. We can't blink *that*. Once one has come to think of them they're a most obvious resource. Which is something *you* appear not to have done, my dear Domberg.'

'Stuff and nonsense. I clearly recall its being in my mind on the very day Mrs Montacute died. And *before* she died. I mentioned it to somebody. To that unprincipled Chevalley, in fact. He pointed out—and he was absolutely right—that the American universities and foundations and so forth are simply no longer spending money in that way. They haven't got the dollars. It sounds incredible, but it's the truth. Big new foreign-campus ventures—which were always just prestige stuff —are out for an indefinite time ahead. You could travel from coast to coast, my dear Thurkle, without finding anybody who'd be prepared to go beyond the million dollar mark on such a venture. However, the Japanese are said to be becoming interested. I heard of one the other day who has more than half an eye on Blenheim. But that's scarcely relevant to our problem.'

'Miss Montacute's problem. What I was saying, however, is that Guise has in some manner educed expressions of interest from at least two reputable seats of learning in the United States. One of them has even had architects and surveyors down at Nudd, looking into the possibility of extensions to the house—dormitories and so forth.'

'Dormitories? Are they thinking of starting a prep school?'

'No, no. Recollect, my dear Domberg. "Dormitory" is a word used by the Americans, very absurdly, to describe

what we should call a court, quad, or even hall of residence. Not that there would be any intention, I imagine,
of housing droves of undergraduates in Nudd. It would
be for scholars in all that sort of thing—your sort of
thing—at a high academic level. With the collection—or
the entire inspiring *ambience*, as one might put it—left
entirely as it is. I'm bound to say it appeals to me as a
very convenient way for Miss Montacute to dispose of
her property. If the price is right, that's to say.'

'Have you any idea why this man Guise should concern himself with the matter, whether one way or another?'

'It is certainly not conduct at all usual in a butler. Or
so I should judge. I cannot say that I have ever retained
one in my employment.'

'It must obviously be self-interest of some kind. Perhaps he simply hopes to keep his job if Nudd remains a
going concern.'

'Possibly so. But on my visits there he has struck me—
the Montacute Curator—as rather an unusual man. He
would have to be, come to think of it, to assume such a
title.'

Domberg, who had now drunk as much of his tea as
civility required, did not dispute this proposition. On the
contrary, he seized upon it.

'Exactly so. The mildest thing one can possibly say is
that his conduct has been extremely eccentric. And he's
in complete charge down there?'

'That was Miss Montacute's arrangement, and it holds
until she returns to Nudd herself—which, as I have said,
she may now have done. I myself put in a word only
upon one or two points of security. Locks and keys, in
fact. Insurance companies are always happier when there
are plenty of those in use.'

'Insurance companies? I'd be uncommonly surprised
to learn from you, Thurkle, that the collection is insured

for anything like its full value. The premiums would be prohibitive. Am I right?'

Thurkle frowned—signalling thereby that professional discretion must not be impaired, and that his client's dispositions in this matter were no part of Domberg's business. Here he was undoubtedly right—the more so in that his visitor had turned up on him without invitation. And now he replied only obliquely to Domberg's question.

'The collection is undoubtedly an anxiety. If Miss Montacute were devoted to it, I would make every endeavour to find means of keeping it, or the greater part of it, in being, and as her property. But we are agreed, I think, that her interests lie elsewhere. That being so—'

'That being so, your own responsibility is the heavier.' Domberg offered this proposition in what was itself a thoroughly heavy way. 'The security of the collection must be very much your concern. I confess that I am concerned about it too.'

'That is most obliging of you.' Thurkle wasn't taking to being taught his business.

'And I hope my concern is entirely disinterested. I am simply conscious that it would be a tragedy if the Nudd collection were lost.'

'Lost, Domberg! What the devil do you mean? Is it going to be carried off in pantechnicons by an army of thieves?'

'Even that isn't totally impossible nowadays. But I am still thinking of this fellow Guise. What if he's a maniac?'

'My dear sir—what if you are a maniac? It's an idle question, which one can ask about anybody. Why should Guise be a maniac?'

'Because he has an *idée fixe*.' Domberg suddenly spoke as a man inspired. 'His conduct isn't motivated by any rational consideration whatever.'

'I understood you to be advancing the view that he

was obviously governed by some form of self-interest.'

'Well, it may very possibly be only in the most crazy sense. He's determined to keep Nudd exactly as it is. And if that isn't lunacy, what is? Rather than see the collection dispersed, he'd take some positively maniacal action. Burn the whole place down, perhaps.'

Thurkle was plainly impressed by Domberg's voice of doom. Being a conservative person, he was probably addicted to reading Victorian novels, in which great houses fairly regularly go up in flame in the last chapter. And a place like Nudd was eminently combustible. Where would an adequate fire-fighting force have to come from? Gloucester, perhaps, or Swindon, or even Oxford. Thurkle was appalled.

'You seriously think,' he asked, 'that the man may do this at any time?'

'Certainly I do. But I believe the likeliest moment to be upon the occasion of Miss Montacute's return to Nudd. He will be cunning enough, you know, to seek to give some colouring of accident to the thing. And remember that she will be arriving for the first time as owner of the estate. It will seem very proper that an old family retainer —such as we understand this demented Guise to be— should make preparations to celebrate the occasion. With the loyal tenantry joining in.'

'There aren't any tenantry, loyal or otherwise.' Thurkle was making a first attempt to rally. 'Only a single home farm.'

'No matter. Guise will be a host in himself. He will have arranged fireworks—'

'Fireworks!'

'Fireworks, and a bonfire, and little paper lanterns festooned all over the house. In these circumstances, arson will be simplicity itself.'

'My dear Domberg, what ought I to do?'

'Ah!' Domberg's exclamation held a hint of glee. Too often had he been snubbed by this wretched little lawyer. Now he was giving him a bad half-hour. 'In the first place, you ought to send down somebody of your own at once. A confidential clerk, or person of that sort. Thoroughly able-bodied, if possible. He can pretend to be making an inventory, or sorting out papers—and actually he can keep an eye on this rascally butler. But the important thing, of course, is to apprise Miss Montacute.'

'Apprise her?'

'Of the constant risks to which a collection such as hers is exposed. Guise is only an instance, you know—nothing but an instance. Impress upon her—'

'That the sooner she disperses the collection and banks the money the better?'

'Precisely so. You couldn't give her better advice.'

'Not, certainly, in your interest.' Thurkle had made an effort, and was himself again. The momentary scales had dropped from his eyes, and Domberg was a shark once more. 'I will certainly make proper inquiries about the man Guise and his courses. An explanation is undoubtedly required. But his American contacts, however come by, are not to my mind to be rejected out of hand. There may conceivably be powerful interests behind them: the Carnegie people, the Rockefeller people'—with these august names a just confidence returned to Thurkle's voice—'or other of the great foundations to which such short-term financial stringencies as you were speaking of are, in my judgement, unlikely to apply. I may communicate with you again in the event of nothing coming of them.'

'Then I wish you all good fortune in your quest.' Domberg had risen to his feet with dignity, as if proudly determined to take this dire decision—and deplorable folly—well. 'It is what a man needs, my dear Thurkle, when he goes after fairy gold.'

And having delivered himself of this powerful commination upon the Almighty Dollar, the active half of Comberback and Domberg treated Thurkle to a commiserating shake of the head and hastened to quit the dusty purlieus of Gray's Inn.

It had been the occasion—one might have said—of Domberg's Last Throw.

21

SOLITUDE AT NUDD

BACK AT NUDD, and with a week in hand before starting her new job, Gloria applied herself to sorting out this and that. But neither this nor that was among her more intimate affairs. These, whether wholesomely or not, were proving elusive, or had gone to earth for a time. She sorted out Mrs Bantry's sister, Mrs Pottinger, who had been waiting for a bed in the local hospital longer than was tolerable; and she sorted out the gardener's boy, who had conceived an antipathy towards a probation officer and was in some danger of receiving the renewed attention of the magistrates as a result. She even sorted out the vicar, a nervous man unable to decide whether Mrs Montacute's death was yet sufficiently in the past to render appropriate some rustic merrymaking or other in the village hall.

When not involved with these matters Gloria did a good deal of thinking about the Admin. canteen. It needed a spot of sorting out, too; and this was no doubt why she had taken it on. She had misgivings as to whether it was really her sort of thing. She could do it, she knew; but she wasn't clear about it in terms of job-satisfaction. Job-satisfaction had been explained to her by somebody as important. Drop your job-satisfaction-quotient too far and it was mathematically—or was it psychologically?—impossible to do the job well. This worried her. There had been a lot of j-s in being a tea lady in a great hospital—so much as to make her feel almost guilty. She could recall—because her mother had been fond of the recreative resource known as a 'cruise'—those men who, in not quite spotless white dungarees, ceaselessly prowled around the vast engine-rooms of more or less obsolescent liners, applying here and there, from oil-cans answeringly vast, some humble but essential emollient drop. Precisely this was a tea lady's line.

Midway between professional and wholly private matters came the problem of the collection. She didn't want to think about the collection at all—much less go round looking at it. Even little Don Balthasar Carlos, of whom she had been rather fond, was to be avoided. He reminded her of the more disturbing of the two disturbing young men who had turned up on her in Venice. Her cousin Jake had said something about his father wanting Don Balthasar as a Christmas card. She hadn't understood him in the least—or why he had suddenly been sitting in front of her in that little café, saying such extraordinary things. She would have to be clever, she obscurely felt, to understand Jake—cleverer, oddly enough, than to understand Octavius Chevalley, who himself went in for being clever much more obviously than Jake did. Thinking about these two young men made her remember (as she'd resolved not to) that there had lately been not two but three young men in her life. It was a bit much, that. As for a distinction between them, she could see that Jake and Harry held about equal shares in something Octavius hadn't got. It was surprising that she was coming to think quite affectionately of Octavius, and that she didn't feel in this way about either of the others, at all.

None of the three was entirely isolated from the problem of the collection. Nor was somebody else—and that other person was Guise. In this there *wasn't* a surprise, although there was certainly an element of the mysterious. For almost as long as she could remember, Gloria had known that it was Guise who really understood the pictures—and, for that matter, the camels and the pots and jars and the scraps of velvet and nuggets of jade and

the *fontana minore* itself. Nobody else had appeared to
know this; and, what was more, she didn't believe that
Guise knew that she knew. Her mother had sometimes
talked about Guise's taste—but only to visitors, and with
a great air of advancing an amusing paradox. In fact if
you were observant, and even although you weren't yourself remotely with it art-wise, you couldn't miss the simple
truth. It emerged in the way that Guise, seemingly just
buttling round, would unobtrusively move one object six
inches towards, or away from, another object. It had
occasionally emerged in the frigid deference he would
accord to some of his employer's gushing and chattering
guests.

This endowment of Guise's had never struck Gloria as
all that important; and the extent to which it was something out-of-the-way in a butler even seemed to her a
measure of the extent to which Guise might be mildly
dotty. But Guise had always been nice to her, even
although she had been (she somehow knew) a disappointment to him. It wasn't her intention that Guise shouldn't
have his due. All these circumstances made her particularly annoyed with Mr Thurkle's strange letter.

Mr Thurkle's letters were invariably circumspect,
which meant that they were hard to make much of. What
he had chiefly on his mind was estate duty, and the
diminished extent to which, nowadays, being clever
enough to own works of art instead of stocks and shares
gave you any edge over others when confronted by this
iniquitous imposition. Gloria failed to see it as iniquitous
in the least. If you'd enjoyed, in whatever form, a whack-
ing fortune during your life, it seemed to her fair enough
that, at your death, a sizeable chunk of it should be carried
off and used to build a school or hospital or something of
that kind. But Mr Thurkle had given her to understand—
although with a very great deal of circumspection indeed
—that this was, if laudable, yet an immature and in-

sufficiently informed view, and that nothing but ruin lay ahead of a society giving countenance to it. Mr Thurkle also had a lot to say (surprisingly enough) about charities, and about the blessings that attended being able to involve one's affairs with activities and institutions classifiable as such.

Gloria didn't follow much of this, but she was arrested by the way in which, in Mr Thurkle's last letter, Guise's existence had cropped up. There was, it appeared, a praise-worthy side to Guise. There were initiatives which, al-though not properly his to take, he had been taking with a certain ability. Nevertheless Gloria must observe caution in her relations with Guise, and anything the man advanced to her Mr Thurkle would be obliged if he might have reported to him immediately.

It all seemed very great nonsense to Gloria, and she was disposed to speak to Guise about it at once. Unfor-tunately, although she didn't in the least want to be cautious towards Guise, Guise did seem disposed to be cautious towards her. Where Mr Thurkle was circum-spect, Guise was wary. He gave an effect of biding his time. Moreover, in addition to this, something seemed to have happened to Mrs Bantry. Mrs Bantry was adopting towards Gloria an attitude of unnecessary solicitude. It might be accounted for by her sense of her young em-ployer's recent loss. It took the form, however, of an ex-pressed conviction that Gloria was 'out of sorts' and 'run down'—an undesirable state of affairs which she mono-tonously attributed to 'all that kickshaw foreign food'.

This wasn't the less annoying because Gloria *did* feel by no means a hundred per cent. She didn't suppose her-self entitled to be aggrieved by the mere fact in itself; her Italian journey could be described, she supposed, as hav-ing ended in a mildly trying way; and in any case one's ups and downs shouldn't be too much attended to. But there was no denying that Mrs Bantry wasn't exactly a resource, and it was even possible to suspect that her fussing was a cover-up for something else. She had a good deal to say in a dark and gossiping fashion about 'goings-on' in one or another supposedly respectable gentlefolks' house in the neighbourhood. Gloria wondered whether there could conceivably have been 'goings-on' at Nudd.

All this had the effect of making her feel rather alone. She wished she could have brought Kirstie Anderson home with her, even although Kirstie's presence would have been a standing reminder of one or two things she wanted to forget. She had thoughts of returning to London at once, and of occupying her time until the Admin. canteen claimed her by decorating her flat. But when a girl does that she is widely supposed by her acquaintance to be in retreat from some unsatisfactory affair of the heart. Gloria felt she would resent any such inference about herself—whether justified or not.

And then she remembered a social duty which was incumbent upon her. Mrs Carter had been kind to her on the night of her mother's death. Mrs Carter, moreover, was a thoroughly sensible woman. It would be a good idea to walk over to the home farm and have a talk with Mrs Carter.

Gloria put this resolve—which can be seen as wholly admirable in itself—into execution at once.

22

AVOIDING THE HARVEST BUGS

WHAT WAS NOW called Nudd Manor was a mansion of considerable antiquity, and would undoubtedly be described by the estate agents as 'mellow' should Miss Montacute decide to sell it up. Even so, the centuries behind it were not nearly so numerous as those behind the home farm. The farm, in fact, had been the original manorial dwelling, and was still not without suggestions of its former feudal consequence. For example, the kitchen —familiar to Gloria for as long as she could remember —was as large as the hall in which the late Mrs Montacute, posed beside the playing or piddling *fontana minore*, had been accustomed to receive her guests. And from the kitchen you could look out on a grove of oaks. Mr Carter (who was now blind and never seen in the fields) had always been proud of the oaks and of their having been let stand where corn might grow. Gloria could recall his telling her, when quite a small girl, that the oaks were as old as England.

There was a lane to traverse and a stream to cross; Gloria paused on a foot-bridge to survey the scene. She was without much grasp of leases and tenancies, but she did know that she owned the farm quite as definitely as she owned the manor. The knowledge somehow troubled her. The farm was quite clearly the Carters' farm, and yet in law it was nothing of the kind. If old Mr Carter suddenly went mad and ordered the cutting down of the oak trees she could stop it at once. Mr Thurkle would take this sort of proprietorship for granted, but it seemed strange to her that she should have any sort of control over mature people who for generations had been doing just what they were doing now: conjuring wheat and turnips, milk and wool, out of the quickened earth. It put her in an unsatisfactory relationship with the Carters —with *any* Carter. The money-thing—which was also the class-thing—would always make itself felt.

But why, after all, should it matter? Without being particularly prompted to articulate an answer, Gloria walked on. She had done so for only a dozen paces, however, when she was brought to a halt by a loud whistle from not far behind her.

If a whistle brings you to a stop, it may be expected to make you turn round as well. For a moment, at least, Gloria didn't do this. She was occupied by the amazing discovery that it was Saturday, and that on a Saturday Harry was quite likely to have come home for the week-end. She felt properly disconcerted at having chosen a Saturday afternoon to call on Harry's mother. Not that she had made any resolve to shun Harry or ignore his existence. She acknowledged to herself, on the contrary, that he occupied some rather urgent corner of her mind—and that he was quite clever enough to break free of it, if given half a chance, and roam about as he pleased. It was just that he required thought. There was some dimension to Harry that she hadn't at all grasped, and which it was important that she should.

Meanwhile, the whistle was repeated. It was a rural whistle; a whistle, indeed, such as you might hear from a shepherd who is bringing a dog to heel. Gloria turned round. Harry was doing his wood-god act. In wholly decent areas, that is to say, he was naked; and where he was naked he was splendidly bronzed. On an afternoon full of lingering autumnal warmth this was entirely in order. So was the implement he carried: a wicked-looking, gently-concave blade on a long pole. It was a billhook, she supposed, and he had been thinning out a coppice with it. She thought, however, of pictures she had been seeing in Italy in which saints major and minor—and young and handsome as well as old and with elaborately crimped beards—stroll negligently around carrying the instruments of their martyrdom. But that was not quite what she was really seeing. There was something more elusive and teasing, something from farther back, that she was being reminded of. It was an illustration in a history book used at school. Had it been about the French Revolution—or about Jack Cade, and people of that sort? Certainly it was with improvised weapons just such as Harry was carrying now that persons of a plebeian order had been represented as advancing threateningly upon their betters.

This recollection, totally irrelevant as it seemed, struck Gloria less than the fact that, having twice whistled, Harry was standing quite still on the path behind her. It was almost as if he expected her to trot obediently back to him. But this effect lasted only for a moment; it was a minute calculated joke made possible only by that nice sense of timing which a good rugger player must possess. Harry was advancing at a run, with his billhook high in air. Its carriage in this fashion was a simple safety precaution; at the same time he might have been a charging Zulu or the like out of a boy's artless imagining.

'Gloria, my dear!' Harry said. And he was standing laughing in front of her.

'Hullo, Harry.' Gloria spoke with a calm hollow even to her own ear. She had realized instantly how very definitely Harry was out of that corner and roaming. 'I was going over to have a chat with your mother.'

'Chat' was a word unknown to Gloria's natural vocabulary, and although she wasn't normally sensitive to extreme linguistic nicety she recognized it as another sign that she mightn't be going to do too well. She noticed, too, that she had used an unfortunate tense—and it was a

slip which Harry's swift grin showed he hadn't missed
either. Yet Harry's intuitions couldn't, in these few
moments, have been sharper than hers. Fleetingly she
found herself in two places at once—with neither of them
a field-path near Nudd. One was inside Nudd itself, and
she was walking round the house with Harry in the dusk
of a fatal evening, looking at pictures: an uncomprehending couple, but not indisposed to join hands. The
other was the Accademia, and she was having pictures
explained to her by Octavius. These two imagined places,
remembered occasions, belonged to different universes.

Or not quite. And here she was confronted by—or,
rather, peripherally aware of—something very difficult
indeed. Harry's impact owed a little of its momentum to
Octavius, and rather more than a little of its momentum
—absurd as this was—to her cousin Jake. In fact she'd
been put on skids, got on the run. Or she was like a ball
in one of those idiotic gambling machines men fool
around with in pubs. Down she went, bumped from one
pin to another. Once started, just that happened. And
there wasn't much the ball could do about it.

'Oh, my mother's gone out,' Harry was saying easily.
'She won't be back till supper time. You must come to
tea with her tomorrow. We always have a tremendous
tea on Sundays.' He glanced around him, as if admiring
the afternoon. 'We'll go for a walk.' He tossed the billhook carelessly on the ground. 'And I shan't need *that.*'

They went for a walk, climbing rapidly to the down.
Harry pretended that Gloria went too fast for him, and
puffed and blew. He pretended they had a leash of puppies
with them, and disentangled them from Gloria's feet.
But he appeared not to have in mind any recapitulation
of a former occasion. For when they arrived in front of
the ruined barn he hesitated and then shook his head.

'No good there,' he said decisively. 'Full of harvest bugs

by now. In half an hour you'd be scratching at your tummy like mad.'

It was characteristic of Harry that, having conjured up this not wholly polite image, he didn't cap it with anything further in a similar vein. Gloria wondered whether his talk was equally impeccable when he was out with village girls. The thought of village girls was displeasing —but what it gave rise to, she had to admit, was a jealous rather than a misdoubting reaction. There were a good many frank-hearted young women in the neighbourhood, and she had come to acknowledge that it would be silly to think of Harry Carter as a virginal soul. Of course he'd been with some of them. She found herself wondering whether Octavius Chevalley had ever been with a girl at all. But these were gross speculations, which she resolved not to pursue.

'Harry,' she asked abruptly, 'how's Australia?'

'Australia?' For a moment Harry seemed uncomprehending. 'Oh, yes! It may come to that yet. But at least not for a while.'

'It sounds attractive in some ways. Marvellous surf.'

'Not if you're hundreds of miles in the interior, wrenching your guts out clearing scrub.' Harry had glanced at her swiftly and curiously, as well he might. It was mysterious to Gloria that she had brought this subject up.

'I think you should go,' she said decidedly. 'And take care not to get married first. An Australian wife's essential, if you hope to settle down.'

'Nonsense!' Harry shouted this word to the winds. His spirits were rising, and she sensed him as very sure of himself. 'I shall marry you, my dear. And, as you're a great heiress, we'll buy a sheep station six times the size of Warwickshire, and live happily ever after.'

There was something about this that, at least for the moment, disconcerted Gloria very much. She couldn't quite make out why. Of course she had herself turned on

a flippant note—under an impulse rather like that which
makes one grab at a slipping shoulder-strap. So perhaps
it was no more than that Harry was being flippant in
return. It was certain that, no time ago, he had seemed
serious in his wooing her with talk about Australia. Now
he was making a joke of it, and she felt it to be a joke
beneath which there lay nothing substantial at all. What
had happened in the interval? Well, she had indeed become, with unexpected promptness, what Harry called a
great heiress. Perhaps he was saying—being so cockily
confident as he was—that they'd marry without buying an
Australian sheep station; that they'd make do with buying Warwickshire instead.

But that was quite wrong. For there were two things, and
two things only, that she confidently knew about Harry.
The first was the simple one that he had for her a powerful and specific appeal of a sort which she'd been brought
up to regard as perilous to maidenhood. The second was
just coming back to her now. She'd never buy Harry
Warwickshire, or anything else in a big way. He wouldn't
let her. Some principle of pride in him—and it couldn't
be of a Satanic sort—insisted that her wealth was an
irrelevance with which he'd have nothing to do. Even if
there was something perverse in this—sub-Satanic, say—
there was something very heady as well. Gloria had fled
from Italy, having been hunted, however indecisively and
ineptly, for her gold. Harry was a hunter, without a shadow
of doubt. She believed he was also a suitor, which is a
different thing. And her possessions didn't come into it.

These two pieces of knowledge which Gloria had, or
believed she had, about Harry Carter had only to run
together to render her very vulnerable indeed. If Gloria
had a Guardian Angel (although she had perhaps never
so much as heard of such a being) he was certainly alerting himself for rapid downward flight as he watched this
walk on a Saturday afternoon.

23

HAZARDS OF CHECKING UP

THIS TIME, THERE was no question of a stockade, or of a sofa and chairs whimsically constructed out of straw. Harry was making love to her on the open turf. Only it was so decorous a love-making that it would scarcely have been awkward if the vicar himself, or a whole crocodile of schoolgirls, had come wandering by. Harry didn't issue commands (whether about chocolates or anything else) and prepare to pounce if they were disobeyed. His fingers didn't—as upon that unfortunate nocturnal walk down the drive at Nudd—grossly misbehave. They didn't misbehave at all. He had kissed her once—very decisively but not for alarmingly long. And now he seemed to be feeling that eternity ought to be spent holding Gloria lightly and chastely in his arms, while occasionally engaging in lazily affectionate conversation. It was, she supposed, how a man, a man who really loved you, would behave after love-making rather than before it. She wasn't herself in a state of calm, nor was it clear to her how the occasion was, so to speak, to be switched off. That, she suspected, was something simpler for a man than for a girl.

'Do you know,' Harry was saying idly, 'that the hippie came down to Nudd?'

'The hippie?' Gloria stirred very gently. It was undoubtedly a luxurious thing to do. 'What hippie?'

'The one who was here the day your ma died, and who said he was a cousin or something.'

'Oh, yes—Jake.' Gloria stirred again, but this time to a different effect. 'Yes, of course. He told me he'd come to Nudd to ... to call on me.'

'*Told* you?' As if he had sensed Gloria's very small withdrawal, Harry made a more pronounced, but entirely casual, movement of his own. In fact he rolled over, smacked her inoffensively on the bottom by way of inviting her to sit up, and sat up himself. 'Where did he tell you, my dear?'

'In Venice. Jake came out to Venice.' Gloria felt that, until thus announcing this circumstance to Harry, she had somehow failed to face up to its full surprisingness. 'And I remember now that he said it was you who told him I was going there.' Gloria paused for a moment. 'How very odd,' she added, and was conscious that this was a vague and feeble comment.

'Odd? Oh, I don't know.' Harry had found a stray blade of rye grass, and was sucking it with his baffling air of relaxed and appeased sensuousness. Looking at his lips engaged thus, Gloria was aware of wanting to be kissed again. The discovery made her tell herself, although without full conviction, that all this had better stop—had better stop, that was to say, until Harry's intentions became explicitly honourable. And perhaps there was really something wrong. Perhaps it was a sign of something wrong—was a small red light—that a prudential notion of that sort should come into your head.

'Oh, I don't know.' As Harry repeated this, he called his most rustic, his most arrogantly non-U, burr into his voice. 'Although he did say that a bus fare to Margate would be beyond him at the moment.'

Gloria almost said: 'But he arranged to make ice-cream'. But she didn't. Harry, even although he'd kissed her continently but with staggering effect, wasn't entitled to that sort of information about the tiresome (yet reassuringly forthright) Jake. But this discrimination so disturbed Gloria somewhere at the very bottom of her mind that what she did say was entirely crude.

'But the Counterpaynes aren't all that poor, although Jake's father pretends they are. They could find more than a bus fare at a pinch.'

'Then that would be it.' Although with an air of leisure, Harry had spoken before Gloria realized she had said an unjust and vulgar thing. 'A penny to land a pound, my dear. And your Jake certainly led off with a good nose round Nudd.'

'What do you mean by that?'

'Well, it came through on the grape-vine by way of your Mrs Bantry. Hippie Jake didn't content himself with inquiring for you at the front door. He did another tour of the house, more or less. You can ask Guise, who kept an eye on him.'

'Why should Jake want to do that?'

'He's some sort of artist, isn't he?' Harry didn't sound as if he had any particular interest in discussing Jake Counterpayne. 'He'd know whether it's fourpence or fivepence that Titian's tarts or Velazquez's little Don Thingummy are likely to rate at. And some chaps—even hippies—like to get their sums just right.' Harry chucked away his grass-stalk, stretched himself, yawned, and sank back supine on the turf. He straddled his legs, stuck his eight fingers in his breeches-pockets, and regarded Gloria across the flat of his belly.

Gloria, who didn't want to think about Jake at all, found herself thinking that Jake wouldn't do precisely this. Jake wasn't at all like Octavius, but Jake wouldn't look at you with a kind of mocking innocence over his own crutch. Harry, who had great airs of spontaneity, was a virtuoso in contrivance and calculation. Only he oughtn't to repeat identical effects.

'Stop that stupid seduction stuff,' Gloria heard herself say. 'And sit up.'

Once more, as they walked down the hill, Harry gave

no sign of bearing malice. Perhaps it was commonplace
to him that action can seesaw to and fro across a battle-
field. Perhaps he subscribed to the comfortable Terentian
view that the quarrels of lovers are the renewal of love.
Gloria, although without considering either of these pro-
positions, was honestly shaken by his unimpaired confidence. He had believed himself (which was extremely
absurd) to be threatened by Jake Counterpayne as a rival,
and he had at once moved rapidly and decisively into
the attack—which was just what might be expected of
him. The attack hadn't quite paid off. For reasons obscure
to Gloria, Gloria had reacted against it. Probably, she
thought, it was the class-thing, and unfair to Harry. Harry
hadn't obeyed some code which Jake or Octavius would
have obeyed unthinkingly. Something about not being in
a hurry to tell tales.

And perhaps there was something else in the same area
—something that now came to her in that image of Harry
charging at her and waving what might have been a pike.
Her fortune didn't count with him; there was a strand in
him that forbade that. But her mere position did. The
tenant's son felt he owed it to himself to capture and
humiliate the lady of the manor. And his assurance was
formidable. Despite this further check, he believed he
had her where he wanted her. It was because he believed
just that that he was feeling—as he obviously was—
extremely friendly and well-disposed. Put more crudely,
and in the disgusting sense of the term men used, he knew
he was going to have her, as certainly as he'd known it
(she now convinced herself) of half a dozen girls round
Nudd.

These weren't pleasant thoughts, and the fact that she
could entertain them without their instantly rubbing out
all sense of Harry's attractions was a discovery which
alarmed her a good deal. A mature counsellor would
probably have told her that there was no occasion for

panic; that she had unconsciously absorbed from the spirit of her age an exaggerated estimate of the awful potency of the drives of sex. It wouldn't have followed that she was making an unnecessary bogy-man of Harry as she walked down the hill with him. That he was quite a wicked youth was, as a mere statistical matter, very much on the cards. Only she *was* perhaps making an unnecessary bogy-girl of something inside herself.

They parted amicably. Almost, indeed, they parted in a face-saving way, so that the occasion bore a faint kinship to her parting with Octavius—with the difference that Harry plainly wasn't giving up. To her parting with Jake it bore no kinship at all.

At least there was one point on which she could check up. All she needed was the telephone, and she went straght to it as soon as she entered Nudd.

'I was coming to call on you this afternoon,' she told Mrs Carter over the instrument. 'But I met Harry, and he told me you were out.'

'Yes, of course.' Mrs Carter's reply was unhesitating but thoughtful. 'I was going out, but something prevented me.'

'It's a long time since I've seen you.' With Harry thus unmasked in cold fact, it was surprising that Gloria's voice remained perfectly controlled. 'Perhaps I might drop over now?'

'Would you mind Spot?'

'Spot?'

'My terrier, Miss Montacute.' (Gloria was rather struck by this manner of address.) 'I was just going to take him for his run. So perhaps we might come over to you?'

'Yes, of course,' Gloria said. It was evident that Harry had gone home. He'd have plans for later in the evening, she told herself with remorseless realism. After the recent course of things he'd have an itch for some sort of satisfactory round-off to the day, but no doubt he was going to have a bite of something first. 'Yes,' she repeated. 'Do please come. Both of you. I love Spot.'

Mrs Carter talked about one thing and another. She wasn't being evasive, or shilly-shallying. But conceivably she had a certain amount of experience at interviews of this kind, and was waiting for a lead-in that would spare Gloria's feelings. At length she decided to go at it straight.

'I thought I'd come over here,' she said, 'because Harry will like to have the place more or less to himself if his *fiancée* drops in.'

'I didn't know. But how very nice.'

'Yes.' Mrs Carter seemed to feel better. The two women looked at each other with a level gaze. 'Harry is very impressionable, Miss Montacute.'

'Gloria—*please*.'

'Harry is very impressionable, Gloria, and very susceptible.'

'I know.'

'And not always properly thoughtful about the feelings of others. He has been an anxiety to us. So we are most relieved. It's an entirely suitable match.'

'Do tell me about it.' Gloria was hearing her own voice as if from very far away.

'The Mercers own their farm. They bought it when the Gracechurch estate was broken up, and the mortgage isn't too heavy. Of course there is no son. Only Beryl. So it all fits very well.'

'How splendid! I'm extremely happy for Miss Mercer.' Gloria wasn't bookish, but it must have been out of a book that she rather nobly managed this old-fashioned expression of courtesy. 'Has it just been settled?'

'Oh, no. For business reasons, we've had to keep it very quiet. But it has been a fixed thing since—let me see— shortly before your mother's death.'

24

IN BELMONT IS A LADY RICHLY LEFT

THAT EVENING GLORIA sat numb and dumb at dinner. The numbness needs no explanation. The dumbness followed from the fact that Guise, although always willing to converse when waiting at table upon domestic occasions, very properly expected the initiative to be taken by his employer. Gloria didn't feel up to this—and the less so because there was still an obscure oddity in Guise's manner. She wondered whether he was proposing to give notice. With no more parties at Nudd—whether magnificently musical or unassumingly dedicated to the plastic arts—he must be having a dull life.

And there would never be parties again. Gloria, as if taking breath before tackling her central perplexity, reflected on the strangeness of her condition in this presumably exceptional house. Perhaps it had never been very securely a home because it had always been so uncompromisingly a museum—and a museum so much less satisfactory than others she had sometimes wandered in. Pickled whales, doll's houses, lavish recreations behind glass of the haunts and habits of Stone Age Man, motor cars of almost similar antiquity, galleons made out of mutton bones by prisoners of war: these had appeared to her, from a tender age, as objects of rational curiosity. But the fine arts (as Octavius Chevalley and others had from time to time found out) were somehow not her thing. And here lay just one more reason—she swiftly asserted to herself—for disregarding the perplexing attentions of her cousin Jake. Jake was an artist. It would be absurd to marry a man whose pictures one would be liable ignorantly to hang upside-down on the wall. And—what was the immediate point—it would be almost equally absurd to take up permanent residence as the mistress of a wilderness of treasures one's natural attitude to which had become a defensive inattention. She didn't even try to imagine herself standing beside the *fontana minore* and receiving guests like Mr Lambert Domberg of Messrs Comberback and Domberg. No more parties: she was at least certain of that.

Mrs Bantry, as if aware of spiritual crisis and the uses of material recruitment, had sent in her favourite final dish—known in her nursery long ago as a light steamed pudding with a jam sauce. Gloria did her best to do it justice, and she even let Guise fill her glass a second time with whatever modest wine he had judged appropriate to her solitary situation. That it was also a forlorn situation was the only distinguishable consequence of her drinking it. She would be feeling not quite so bad, she was sure, if she had returned firmly to her flat in Bethnal Green and was there opening a can of beer. And in that event there would not have happened what *had* happened that afternoon.

Harry Carter had almost possessed himself of her—on a tump of grass on the open down. She faced this resolutely now. It was staggering, but true. It would have happened if Harry, for his own pleasure, hadn't been playing some connoisseur's delayed-action game. And if he hadn't mentioned Jake and started crabbing him.

This last fragment of analysis was so bewildering that Gloria turned away from it at once, and thought instead to entrench herself in the sternest of attitudes by meditating the subsequent revelation of Harry's perfidy so deliberately (and kindly and wisely, no doubt) made by Harry's mother. She immediately arrived at the discovery, more staggering still, that the revelation had quite failed of its intended effect. On the contrary, it had been what a psychologist (or was it an economist?) would have called counterproductive. There was only one conclusion it was possible to draw. She was jealous of Miss Beryl Mercer and her prospective felicity.

At this point Gloria's thoughts went, if only briefly, quite haywire. Harry had intended to evoke just such a jealous reaction. A Machiavellian seducer, long practised in such subtle guile, he had actually put his mother up to her brutal disclosure. It was all a plot.

The idea remained with her for the full minute during which Guise removed the remains of the pudding and set before her some nuts and a bowl of fruit. (Guise was remorseless in such matters.) Then she recognized it as nonsense—this not because of what she knew about Harry, but because of what she knew about Mrs Carter. Nature, perhaps in compensation for creating her so helpless before the tactile values of Giotto and things of that sort, had endowed her with a reasonable sense of human character. She knew that Mrs Carter, far from being a procurer of disreputable enjoyments for her son, was a perfectly honest woman.

She also knew at least some things about herself. For example, she now knew that she was *not* jealous of Beryl Mercer. That young woman—on whom she supposed she had never so much as set eyes—just wasn't in the picture at all. If Harry still had his appeal, if at this moment he had mysteriously what was even an enhanced appeal, some other explanation must be found. So just what had happened? What had Mrs Carter's disclosure set squarely before her, if only she ventured to look at it?

She reiterated the answer to herself as she dutifully cracked a nut. There was something she had always instinctively felt about Harry, which the discovery of his present intentions made wholly certain. Harry could do with £40,000. But they weren't going to be Gloria's £40,000. That particular need was going to be supplied

by the Mercers' prosperous acres, and this had been clear
to Harry from the first. He'd get the girl in the big house
if he could, and talk nonsense about Australia as part of
his design. He was, it was true, going to marry where
money was. But the girl would be of his own sort, and
he'd remain within the context in which he'd been brought
up.

Gloria told herself it had to be reckoned admirable in
its own way. She also told herself that he might have
wanted her as a social scalp or trophy on the cheap, but
that at least he hadn't viewed her as a winning coupon
in the pools. It was because Mrs Carter's disclosure confirmed the second part of this proposition quite as much
as the first that it had produced not exactly the reaction
it ought to have. If she had rather a considerable kindness
for Harry at the moment, she suddenly thought, it was
because it's better to be hunted for one's self alone (or at
least for that plus the pleasure of successful class-warfare)
than for one's Titians and T'ang camels.

In these confused speculations Nature again doubtless
bore a part. The great creating goddess contrives what
the human intellect can interpret as compensations, as
checks and balances, but contrives ironies as well. She
surrounds with peculiar perils the girl who is beautiful and
glamorous—but she surrounds with perils too the girl who
is plain, who is ungainly, or who believes herself to be
either or both of these. If Gloria Montacute had been in
demand as a model by the major fashion houses of Europe,
or even paintable as a remarkably pretty young woman,
the inglorious conclusion to the episode of Octavius Chevalley might not, even for a time, have been as upsetting
as in fact it was. Nor would she have viewed with
muddled suspicion a second youth, awkwardly constrained by his situation to urge anything so unlikely as
love at first sight. There is a girl in a poem who sighs for

a man who will love her for herself alone and not her yellow hair. Gloria was heading for the conviction that almost everybody must be after her not even for her hair but for her bank balance. Harry Carter had been rather dramatically proved a perplexing special case.

She had been given to understand that, in a literal sense, the bank balance was not at present very remarkable. It was a consequence of her mother's fanatical devotion to the collection that almost everything was locked up in it. She could survey her total fortune in the course of a fifteen minutes' stroll through Nudd. And it was this that, as soon as she had risen from table, she now undertook.

From the walls, the cabinets, even the carpeted floors and gilded ceilings, her affluence surveyed her. That she lacked the knack of appreciating works of art made the effect, somehow, very much that way on. It was uncomfortable. She was like a newly acceded monarch, most horribly inadequate in terms of every personal endowment, who must run the gauntlet, stretching through endless apartments of state, of contemptuous courtiers ranked with mocking deference on his either hand. The camels, of course, were always supercilious, but tonight their insolent nonchalance had communicated itself to Buddhas and mandarins, to gipsy girls and infantas and homely nudes in bath-tubs. Even little Don Balthasar Carlos was infected. She had often paused before him in aesthetically illegitimate appreciation—feeling, that is to say, that it would be very jolly indeed to bear and rear so radiant a child. But now he seemed to be regarding her with a precocious regal disdain, so that she was constrained to a defensive fault-finding in return. She didn't like the obtrusive pedigree effect of his chin and his upper lip, or the absurd elaboration of his attire, or the miniature marshal's baton he was balancing so confidently on a hip.

But of course it was something else that had destroyed

the charm of this incredibly valuable square of canvas. Hadn't she gathered from Jake Counterpayne that his family believed they had a claim to it? Her memory wasn't clear, but it had been something like that. Her memory wasn't clear now because her head hadn't been at all clear then. There had been Octavius, and her just not knowing whether his confession had been honourable or shameful—but knowing very well that it had been humiliating and painful in a fashion she'd never experienced before. And then at once there had been Jake, and she had felt like a hare that doubles from the one greyhound to tumble under the muzzle of the other. Perhaps that hadn't been fair to Jake. But finding out what Jake really had in his head—she obscurely felt—would have been very much easier if she hadn't become the owner of Don Balthasar Carlos and all his shadowy company. It was no doubt a mildly shocking thing—but the plain fact was that she would do nothing but rejoice if the entire Nudd collection went up in smoke. Or at least departed in one way or another. It would be a satisfactory start, for instance, if the portraits—English or Italian, French or Flemish—behaved like those in the old whisky advertisement. Once they had stepped out of their frames, she would certainly encourage them to pack their bags and clear off elsewhere. If they chose to ride away on the camels, that would be all to the good.

These fancies may have hinted a Gloria who was recovering her spirits, but it would be rash to conclude that beneath them no deeper current of feeling flowed. And of something of the kind it is conceivable that Guise was aware. That she was not walking round Nudd as a rich man rejoicing in his own (nor yet as a poor man like Guise himself, rejoicing in the sole possession of a seeing eye) was apparent enough. When she had taken her after-dinner promenade through the whole place (thus reproducing a habit of her mother's, although she had forgotten

this) she might have been aware of a mingling of com-
miseration and apprehensiveness in the regard with which
her butler accosted her in the hall.

'Your coffee is in the library, Miss Gloria.' (Guise had
once or twice tried out 'Madam' on Gloria, but had
gathered without admonishment that she didn't much
take to such a form of address.)

'Thank you, Guise. Please tell Mrs Bantry it was a splendid pudding.'

'She will be very pleased. Would it be convenient, Miss
Gloria, if you and I were to have a short conversation?'

'Yes, of course. Come back to the library now.' Gloria
wasn't paying any very close attention to Guise, since
her own thoughts were still of an insistent sort. But she
was dimly aware that he was taking some sort of plunge.
'Is it about what you wrote to me when I was in Italy?'

'Yes, Miss Gloria. It is very decidedly about that.'

25

A REPORT FROM THE CURATOR

GLORIA COULDN'T RECALL ever having heard her mother ask Guise to sit down, but perhaps it had been her habit to do so when the two were closeted together over the domestic accounts. Anyway, she herself asked him to sit down now, which he at once did without fuss. There remained the distinction that she had coffee to drink and he hadn't. But as she could hardly suggest he fetch another cup, she drank her own coffee and let this be. She then saw that, although he had asked for the interview, it was his idea that she ought to offer the first remark.

'Were there many visitors,' she hazarded vaguely, 'while I was abroad?'

'There were a number, Miss Gloria. In one category and another.'

'I believe my cousin came down?' Gloria hadn't in the least intended this question. 'Mr Jake Counterpayne,' she amplified.

'Yes, Mr Counterpayne paid a call. A courtesy call, it might no doubt be called.'

'What did you think of him?' This further question was involuntary too, and Gloria was struck by Guise's not putting on any eyebrow-raising turn before its shocking impropriety.

'I formed no very pronounced impression, Miss Gloria.' Guise paused on this discreet reply. 'An impression of sorts, of course, I had arrived at on a previous occasion. On the day of Mrs Montacute's decease, in fact. If I may be pardoned for bringing it up.'

'Yes, I remember. He very kindly stayed to see me.'

'It was thoughtful, no doubt. I don't recollect that his name was on the list of invited guests.'

'Then it ought to have been.' Gloria was again surprised by her promptness in saying this, and a little upset by a sharpness of tone which might sound like an indecent stricture on her mother. Guise was a man to notice such things. 'However, it was neither here nor there.'

'I didn't venture to say it was. And his behaviour was very proper, I remember. When, that is, the sad news broke.'

'But not before?'

'The gentleman was perhaps a little free. *For* a gentleman, that is. One makes allowances for those who are not. But one can see that Mr Counterpayne is a public school man.'

'All sorts go to those places now.' Gloria was conscious that this, which was intended to cut down Guise's piece of portentous rubbish to size, had emerged as a socially confused comment. 'Just how was he free, as you call it?'

'A little concerned, perhaps, to make a show of rejecting the manners of his class.' Guise wasn't one to abandon a line lightly. 'Nothing to speak of, of course. And he was certainly very interested in the collection. In a slightly covert way, it may have been. The same as when he made this second call.'

'I see.' Gloria's heart sank. Guise, too, was crabbing Jake. She wasn't to know that he was speaking of somebody who had scandalously shouted 'Waiter!' at him.

'But he is an artist of sorts, it seems, and he was undoubtedly attracted by the pictures. Sensitive, too, I'm bound to add. He saw the point of a small adjustment I was prompted to make while in his presence. It was before what we'd like to think of as the Giorgione.'

'The what?'

'A small Venetian painting, Miss Gloria.' There was a

hint of grimness in Guise's voice. He was perhaps recalling what he was up against. 'But my point is that the
young gentleman was observant, beyond a doubt. As he
walked through the house—for one of the women had
shown him into this library—there wasn't much he saw
that he didn't take note of. Or such was my impression.'

'It's what the things are meant for, I suppose.' Gloria
felt she didn't want to hear more about Jake from Guise.
'And who else has been here?'

'That brings us to business, Miss Gloria. If you will per-
mit me, that's to say.' Guise paused. 'It's a liberty,' he said.
He paused again, and spoke in a new voice. 'Miss Gloria—
my anxieties are very great.'

Long before receiving his mysterious letters while in
Italy, Gloria had been aware of Guise as no common
butler. So she wasn't surprised by the avowal just made
to her.

And certainly she wasn't disposed to distrust Guise.
Mr Thurkle—who had also written mysteriously—appeared to be in two minds about his client's butler. And
as it is an undeniable social truth that butlers may not
properly concern themselves with the proper manner of
disposing of a deceased employer's estate, the significant
fact must be that Mr Thurkle hadn't advised the firing of
Guise off-hand.

This shrewd view of the matter hadn't, however, taken
Gloria very far. If she had feelings about Guise, it was
without ever having arrived at any very distinct ideas
concerning him. But she did know something that he had
always shared with her mother: they had both thought a
great deal less of her than of the collection. She even
knew, if in a totally unformulated way, that the collection
existed for Guise (as for her mother it didn't quite do) in a
sphere elevated above all personal connections. Yet to
Gloria herself, since childhood so lamentably lacking in

aesthetic responsiveness of any sort, he had always been extremely decent. On the art-front he could never have kidded himself that she was anything but a dead loss. Nevertheless he had also recognized certain other facts of her condition, and been kind to her in various ways. So Gloria liked Guise, and would if it came to a crunch be rather far from disposed to letting him down. If he was dotty about the pictures and things, that was all right by her.

Until the present moment, this was as far as Gloria's notions of Guise had gone. Now he had uttered a few words not particularly striking in themselves. Anybody may tell you he has great anxieties. But Gloria had heard this manner of utterance before—heard it, say, from some stolid man, waiting patiently in a hospital reception area, who suddenly blurts out over his tea-cup that his wife has left him or that his daughter is dying of leucaemia. She braced herself to listen with attention and respect.

'It is my constant fear, Miss Gloria, that the collection may be dispersed.'

'Dispersed? But wouldn't it have to be, if there was a sale? I'm sure that's what happens with furniture.' Gloria was trying to be practical. 'Different people bid for different things they like or need.'

'Yes, Miss Gloria, that is so. And that is what would happen. But the collection is not just so much furniture. I do beg you to grasp that fact. It is what some of the gentlemen in London don't seem to know—or pretend not to know. But you must be different. You have grown up here. Even you, Miss Gloria, can't—' Guise broke off in confusion. He was so agitated—a condition disconcerting in so composed a man—that he had been about to blurt out something singularly lacking in tact.

'But, Guise, I do understand.' Gloria did her best to come to the rescue. 'You like everything just as it is. And of course furniture has nothing to do with it.'

'Oh, but it has, in a way.' Guise seemed now to be wondering whether he could ever make himself clear. '*Everything* is a part of the collection. Remove *anything*, Miss Gloria, and it *all* changes. It's *that* that's to be our tragedy.'

'Yes, I see.' Gloria could say nothing less than this before so emphatic a speech. She was a little bewildered, all the same. The conception that a particular arrangement or disposition of works of art can itself be a work of art eluded her. (This may have been an intellectual weakness in Miss Montacute—but it is a contentious point.)

'Nudd should remain as it is, Miss Gloria. But I do recognize the difficulties. I have recognized them from the first. They are of the financial order.'

'I'm afraid they are. Mr Thurkle has explained that to me. There isn't any money, really. There are just all the valuable things that are around us here. Guise, I'd *like* Nudd to remain as it is—perhaps almost as much as you would. If it could just stay put, and I could say good-bye for keeps to the whole—' It was Gloria's turn to break off, and only just in time. Having come, rightly or wrongly, to regard the famous Nudd collection as a millstone round her neck, she might have characterized it in terms which must have alienated Guise for good. 'Tell me,' she said abruptly, 'about those Americans. Does Mr Thurkle know about them?'

'Yes, Miss Gloria—and I believe his mind is not wholly closed to the possibility I have seen. It hasn't been so with some of the others. And that must excuse my presuming as I have done. Particularly in the matter of the Curatorship.'

'Of the what?'

'It appeared desirable, Miss Gloria, that I should assume a higher status—I believe that would be the word—if I were to carry any weight with the interested parties I had in mind. So, on certain occasions, I have ventured to describe myself as Curator. As Montacute Curator. And I hope I may be—'

'It's quite all right by me. You've been *doing* the curating, after all.' Guided to this view of the matter more by good sense than by semantic science, Gloria robustly brushed the point aside. 'But what does Mr Thurkle think?'

'Well, Miss Gloria, I can't claim to be in his confidence. He finds it difficult, I judge, to approve my taking any initiative in the matter. Quite properly, no doubt. It must seem to him much as if Mrs Bantry had done so.'

'Oh, I don't think Mr Thurkle can know anything about Mrs Bantry.'

'A mere *façon de parler*, Miss Gloria. Mr Thurkle naturally takes our own view of such things.'

'I'm not sure I have a view.'

'Our English view in general, Miss Gloria. It is noticeable that the parties from America have a more liberal attitude than the English gentlemen.'

'They're rather more free?'

'Not that at all.' Guise hadn't appreciated this mischievous equating of the parties from America with Mr Jake Counterpayne. 'Very good manners, they have—very good manners, indeed. Although without, of course, always knowing quite what's what. Most natural, that is—their republican tradition and the like being considered. But very reasonable people to work for, I consider they'd be.'

'I see.' This time Gloria really did see. 'If this sort of deal went through, do you think they'd keep you on?'

'I think it possible, Miss Gloria. Although the point is a minor one.'

'It's nothing of the sort. I wouldn't look at it, if they didn't promise to. And I'd make them use that word'—Gloria had to search for it—'that word Curator. The collection would be the Montacute Collection—I'd owe that to my mother, I think. And you'd be Montacute Curator for keeps. They'd make you a Doctor of Something in their university, Guise.' Gloria said this quite without amusement. 'And that would be just fine.'

'It's a thought, Miss Gloria.' Guise produced this uncharacteristic locution almost huskily; he might have been described by an indulgent novelist as deeply moved. 'And I'm very much obliged for your good opinion—very much obliged indeed, Miss Gloria. To give satisfaction has always been my aim.' Guise had quickly recovered his authentic professional idiom. Gloria found herself wondering how successfully he'd sink it if he really became the learned Dr Guise. Not that it would matter, if he had the sense to be frank about himself. There wasn't much doubt that he really knew quite a bit about Giorgione and all that. If he took appropriate occasion to explain from time to time that he had started life at Nudd as a knife-boy or whatever it had been, he would quickly become an exhibit in which his new employers would take a finely democratic pride.

'So we're getting somewhere,' Gloria said. 'Here's the way to save the collection as a collection. Nudd becomes a sort of college. Is that right?'

'I suppose it might be called that. Certainly a centre for the study of the fine arts in this country. There would be graduate students from the parent campus, no doubt. But eminent authorities would also be in residence.' Here, it might have been said, was a further professional jargon which Guise had been picking up.

'Do you mean they would be studying English art? Most of the things in the collection seem to come from other countries.'

'Very true, Miss Gloria.' Guise was patient (as he may have been reflecting he could now afford to be). 'Of course they would go around studying English art here and there. But world-wide activities would be going on as well. It would be a question of a setting, you might say. A dignified setting. Because that, you see, isn't easily come by in America. Over there, only the very old families have it. Only the very old families indeed.'

'Yes, of course.' Gloria had no occasion to doubt this sociological information, and vaguely supposed that the contemporaries of Christopher Columbus were in question. 'So which university is it going to be? If there are several after the place, I suppose it will just be the one offering most money. That's certain to be Mr Thurkle's view.' Gloria considered this point. 'And it would have been my mother's—don't you think? It's the sensible thing.'

'Certainly it is.' Guise hesitated. 'But there may not, it seems, be quite the scope I supposed. I mentioned difficulties to you. I ventured to describe them, I think, as of a financial order. One has to agree that great expense would be involved.'

'For the people proposing to buy the place?'

'Yes, indeed. Nudd as it stands—although one of the finest houses in the country, to my mind—is not precisely suited to the purposes proposed. There would have to be additions, which alone would cost a great deal. Architects have been down, Miss Gloria, and I understand they have spoken very plainly on the point.'

'At least it isn't *our* point.'

'It restricts the number of institutions interested. And that in turn, you will understand, limits what may be called our realistic expectations in the particular field we are considering. And it is the only field, so far as I can see, in which there is any hope'—Guise's voice suddenly trembled—'of saving the collection from dismemberment.'

'Then we must stick to it.' Gloria said this firmly, and without any particular sense of the momentous. She knew that she must part with the collection. Or, rather, she knew that she must part *from* it. It wasn't her thing, and therefore it oughtn't to remain the background of her life. The fact that it might fetch even considerably less than had been supposed didn't perturb her in the least. Indeed, it didn't *interest* her all that. The whole affair was something that her mind found itself straying away from. Only her regard for Guise was keeping her thoughts on the ball for even this long. She was rather surprised, as a matter of fact, that Guise was managing it. But this is a surprise which we are not obliged to share. Gloria Montacute didn't understand art. She did, however, understand dedication. From a point in her own particular sphere about as humble as Guise's own, she had watched quite a lot of it on the job. Guise had his thing, and it was around them now on these walls. There was nothing very surprising about Guise's singleness of heart. It was something not nearly so uncommon in the world as it was in the plays they took her to and the gloomy books they talked about. It was important, all the same. So Guise's disinterestedness claimed her serious regard, even although this had been an absolute field-day for more intimate problems of her own. 'We must stick to it,' she repeated. 'I'll go up to London and speak to Mr Thurkle about it tomorrow.'

Guise stood up—as he well might. A natural term had come to the interview—and it seemed a very satisfactory one at that. But Guise hesitated.

'As a matter of fact,' he said slowly, 'there's only *one* interested party left.'

'Only one?' Gloria was really surprised. She had been living, after all, in a private climate in which several contending parties (three, to be precise) had been jostling for a prize—although for just *what* prize had been agonizingly obscure. She had come to think of the world as consisting of small equivocal queues. 'Only one?' she repeated blankly.

'I'm afraid so. It seems that my sense of the matter has been a little out of date. Mr Thurkle, and the professional gentlemen advising him, have access to information it's hard for me to come by. The state of the market, one may say. So may I explain?'

'Yes, of course.'

At this, Guise sat down again, and talked for some time. Gloria heard him out in silence.

'We'll have to sleep on it,' she said eventually and with decision. Everything of her mother that she had in her—and it must have been something—was startled by what she had heard. 'But tomorrow I'll see Mr Thurkle, all the same. Would you say, Guise, that a rapid decision is required?'

'It would be desirable, Miss Gloria.' Guise again stood up. 'But you must do nothing in haste,' he said gravely. 'Nothing against your own deeper mind. And now I had better be going round the house. There's the security to see to. I should like you to know that I'm very careful about it.'

'I'm sure you are—dear Guise.'

'Thank you, Miss Gloria.' Miss Montacute's surprising butler produced what was rather more than a formally respectful bow. 'Is there anything you would require before retiring?'

'No. Nothing at all. Good night.'

Half an hour later Gloria was almost asleep—which was something of a tribute, perhaps, to the fibre of which she was composed. And then the telephone at her bedside rang.

'Gloria?'

'Yes.'

'It's me—Jake.'

'Oh. Where are you?' The question came from Gloria with something of the stunned inconsequence of Laertes answering 'Oh, where?' when told of the drowning of his sister Ophelia.

'I'm in London.'

'I thought you were making ice-cream.'

'Haven't begun. When are you coming back to town? I want to show you some pictures.'

'Pictures?' Gloria was bewildered. Pictures were about the last objects she ever wanted to hear of again.

'Yes. Some pictures. Quite interesting—although they're hardly the point. Except to me, in a way.'

'*Your* pictures?'

'Good God, no! I'm not mad.' There was a pause. 'Gloria, will you come?'

'Yes.' Gloria found herself trembling between the sheets. She had heard—she *believed* she had heard—a young man asking the question of his life. And she had made this reply. 'I was thinking of coming up tomorrow,' she said rather faintly. 'To see a lawyer. Probably in the afternoon.'

'Then in the morning. I'll tell you a pub where we can meet on the South Bank. That's where the pictures are. Listen.'

26

IL MIGLIOR FABBRO

HAD GLORIA BEEN obliged to give an account of herself to a dispassionate person—had she been going up to London, for example, on an unlikely visit to a psychiatrist —she would have found it uncommonly difficult to sort out her mental processes during the journey. She ought to have been bewildered that she was going at all. For she had simply been summoned by Jake Counterpayne—it came to that—whom she had met only twice since childhood, and who had, upon the second of these occasions, appeared to her in a confused way as the emissary of predatory relations and up to no more good than had been Octavius Chevalley. Even if she hadn't been summoned, even if that wasn't a fair way to put it, even if rather she was answering an appeal, it was still very odd that here she sat in a second-class carriage of what British Rail chose to call the Cathedrals Express.

Yet what she had to reckon with was the absence and not the presence of bewilderment. It was precisely this, in fact, that was bewildering. And such a complicated state of feeling was not one which she thought of herself as at all well equipped to analyse. The consequence was that she simply sat back and let Oxford and Didcot and Reading go by. What was happening was a fated thing. She had about as much choice left to her as a bride who has climbed into the hired Rolls-Royce with her papa—or, for that matter, as a corpse which has been firmly hoisted into the hearse. The train hurtled towards Paddington. A man came along the corridor to offer, in the spirit of an egalitarian age, even second-class passengers a cup of coffee in the dignity of their own compartment. It was all as commonplace as could be.

So was the tube. So was the pub. And so, in a disconcerting way, was Jake.

Jake had disguised himself—or such was her first impression. He was dressed in what other young men of her acquaintance facetiously called a gent's suiting. He answered almost perfectly, it occurred to her, to Guise's conception of a public school man. It was surprising that the effect wasn't crowned by a bowler hat.

This made for a bad start. (Jake Counterpayne was perhaps prone to bad starts.) Gloria felt that Jake had contrived this effect on a calculation that it would reassure her—which was injurious and absurd. She was an heiress and therefore, so to speak, an Establishment figure, prepared to be soothed by well-cut dark-grey clothes. It was something she just wasn't going to take. Being forthright by habit (a disposition in which there can be great blessing), she said so crisply and at once.

'I don't see,' she said, 'that you need have got yourself up like that.'

'Oh, but I always do. On these occasions, I mean.'

Gloria was appalled. Having so lately been in contact—embarrassingly close, if fortunately residually chaste contact—with one whom she now regarded as a kind of professional seducer, she took this as a shameless avowal that Jake thought of himself as in a familiar situation. Establishment heiresses were quite his line. He had a routine.

But Jake, even if given to unhappiness in love, was far from dim-witted. At least he marked the blankness of the pause his explanation had produced.

'For galleries, that is.' If he mumbled this, at least he got it out. 'I hate being part of a stage set.'

'A stage set?'

'Young artists doing their stuff. Prowling round the deliverances of their betters.'

'The what?' Gloria had to reckon with the fact that Jake even if untutored in literature by elderly persons, did from time to time frequent it. So he had at times an odd vocabulary, and a fondness for mysterious quotation, unknown in hospitals.

'You know what I mean. Budding geniuses with a crust in their pockets, posing as the hungry generation ready to tread Moore and Sutherland and all that lot down.' Jake must have been very nervous to continue with this rubbish, fully intelligible only to a close student of the poet Keats. 'And stared at by trippers and tourists.'

'Oh!' Gloria suddenly understood. And this glimpse of a strain of self-consciousness in Jake (which fleetingly reminded her of Octavius) at once softened her towards him. He was as young as she was. 'You mean you like to be invisible when looking at things?'

'At important things.'

'Aren't the things at Nudd important? You're said to have cut quite a flamboyant figure there.' By some curious infection, Gloria had found a wildly literary word herself.

'To your butler and that awful Domberg?' Tumbling like a flash to this, Jake produced for a moment an alarmingly breathtaking grin. 'Bitter?'

'Mild.' Being unaccustomed to mid-morning beer, had taken Gloria a second to realize that she was being offered a drink. But when the mild came she drank it gratefully enough. It gave her a space in which to collect herself.

'It has been most frightfully nice of you to come.' These conventional words burst from Jake without conventional effect. He brought out a rather crumpled packet of cigarettes. 'Smoke these things?'

'No, I don't.' It was from the tea lady (retired) that this reply came.

'I'll give them up when ... if ever I get married. One simple pleasure will be enough. Enough expense too, I expect. Do you object to them at *any* time?'

'Yes.'

'All right by me.' Jake chucked the packet in air as if it was a tennis-ball and smacked it with an open hand. It flew across the bar and landed in the lap of a stout lady drinking Guinness. Nobody seemed annoyed, least of all the stout lady. It was a friendly sort of bar. 'We'll be making tracks,' Jake said.

The gallery lay at the heart of an agglomeration of brutal concrete walls and parapets. Gloria judged the effect oppressive. It was as if the peaceful Thames-side hard-by was a stretch of savage Atlantic coast which, in Hitler's legendary wars, had been weighed down beneath fortifications so massive that they must endure to astonish savages in aeons yet to come. But it was a trendy quarter as well. Somebody had been round plastering it with stickers urging dispraise or boycott of somebody else's allegedly reactionary film.

'In here,' Jake said, and paid for two tickets. 'Penny plain first.'

One might have expected something like the interior of a gun-emplacement, but the gallery seemed rather good. There was still a lot of concrete in evidence, but they'd used the dodge of letting it set against a rough-grained wooden planking, so that it now itself looked like ash-grey wood. Gloria thought this rather clever. She felt she liked the whole place. It was plain without being bleak, which was more or less her idea of what places should be. The people wandering round were a bit like that too. They included some young women pushing perambulators. She wondered vaguely whether the occupants of these were infants of precociously aesthetic inclination.

But now she had to start looking at the pictures. At a first glance 'penny plain' seemed just right for them, since all were in black and white. The white seemed white beyond the wildest dreams of the advertisers of washing-powders, and the black was blacker than Indian ink. This notably held of her first picture: a big white canvas hung on a bigger white wall and spotted with a random scattering of small black discs in various sizes. Almost in the moment she looked at this, something began to happen. From the black discs white discs—whiter even than that unnaturally white background—detached themselves and floated lazily around the canvas. Then they drifted beyond the confines of the canvas to wander over the whole wall. Finally they seemed to break away from the picture-plane altogether, and fade and vanish like soap bubbles in the free air of the gallery.

'I like that one,' Jake said. He was plainly moved less by the impulse to make any verbal communication than by the duty civilly to fulfil some lay expectation. And the remark proved to be the only one of its kind that he offered during the visit. In fact he was rather like the white discs. You couldn't be sure quite where he was, or even if he was there at all. Gloria found this disconcerting conduct in a lover.

It turned out that all these black-and-white pictures did things. Gloria was sufficiently clear-headed—at least at first—to realize that the doing was all inside herself; that the way her pulse beat and so forth was dictating their delusive dance to what were in fact perfectly static objects on the walls. On the other hand, whoever had created the objects was dictating something to *her;* was dictating, really, that she helplessly confound appearance and reality. It was foolish to be dismayed. But when she came upon one or two pictures which (doubtless because of some imperfection in her neural organization) remained obstinately inert she had a relieved sense of momentarily coming up for air.

There was what was like a downward-moving escalator in the Underground up which a fine film of water was unnaturally moving; there was an affair of innumerable fine parallel lines from the surface of which sinuous ribbons of thicker parallel lines detached themselves, swam towards you, and gently oscillated against their background; there were undeniably flat surfaces upon which ranked or scattered blobs nevertheless emerged round curves or vanished round corners in a way that couldn't explicably happen in Flatland at all. There was a silky grey diamond covered with silver spots geometrically disposed, and over these spots there came and went a blush of blue here or there as your eye moved—which was the only hint of colour this whole stretch of the exhibition showed. For it was a kind of zebra universe, Gloria thought, into which she had been introduced. Not that lines and zigzags absolutely predominated. There was an infinity of these—but an infinity, too, of discs, circles, ellipses, cones, whorls, and figures she had no names for. Sometimes there seemed to be hundreds of them, thousands of them—and hundreds and thousands of hair-lines, whether straight or undulating, on a single canvas. Every picture was, whatever else it was, a nightmare or miracle of application. But what, Gloria asked herself, were they all *about*? They didn't have names, and it hadn't seemed to occur to Jake to buy a catalogue.

A catalogue might not, of course, have left her any wiser. And she knew she mustn't, in front of one of these things, simply ask Jake, 'What *is* it?' But some information she *had* to have—which was why she suddenly demanded, 'Jake—what's the name of the artist?' It was perhaps a vain inquiry from one who wasn't even clear about Giorgione, and she wondered whether this was why Jake for a moment looked at her vaguely, and why his reply came with the effect of his being a swimmer who had to take a couple of strong strokes before reaching her.

'The artist's Miss Gunga Din.'

'You mean they're by a woman?' Gloria had to decipher this bizarre reply in bits.

'Yes. Hadn't you spotted it? Divine patience.'

'Is that what you like in women?'

'One thing. And here it is. Michelangelo crawling upside down on the ceiling of the Sistine Chapel for years on end just isn't in it. Even although he was on the androgynous ticket quite a bit.'

Gloria didn't let herself be side-tracked by this incomprehensible remark. She was realizing that Jake knew as much about art as Octavius did, but that he didn't pause to explain things to the children. Perhaps this was a quite pleasing form of good manners. Or perhaps it was just that he was too absorbed in his own concerns to bother.

That what Gloria herself knew at least included a few familiar quotations was shown in her next question.

'Jake, do you mean Miss Gunga Din's a better man than you are?'

'For Christ's sake, Gloria! Of course she is. Nothing else like this in all Europe or America. I shan't touch it if I live to be a hundred.'

'Is it exactly what you'll want to be touching if you live to be a hundred?'

'Good question. Upstairs now. Twopence coloured.'

Upstairs the general principle seemed to be the same as down below. You could treat it all as parlour tricks of a dazzling (and it was certainly dazzling) cleverness—or more seriously as a kind of supernatural soliciting designed to convince you that nothing is but what is not. Gloria, having Macbeth's experience not exactly pat in her mind, didn't frame it precisely like this. But she had the idea. And if she didn't much worry about it all as art—since that wasn't her affair—she did feel it had to be thought about—this since it was Jake's affair. She believed—or was it hoped?—that Jake was a serious young man, and that she was here because he had conscientiously resolved she must be shown what might be called his context. Did this mean he was reliable? She had discovered—all within a scandalous twenty-four hours she had discovered—that just what Harry had Jake had too. Only, Jake had it plus something else. The something else consisted in his being uniquely Jake. Harry was no doubt uniquely Harry. But Harry's uniqueness was somehow not so near the centre of his picture as Jake's was. Here, once more, was the complicated sort of thing that she knew herself to be not too good at analysing out. She was left with instinct. This she did clearly know—as an instance, it may be thought, of the wisdom that young women savingly generate at times in a crisis of their fortunes. And she also knew (to go back) that a man must be reliable if it's to be any good at all.

The large rectangle of staring pigments she was now confronting was the antithesis of the reliable. It made some deep assertion of everything as flux, as in essence elusive and protean. (It didn't occur to her that a certain unschooled ability to arrive at such perceptions was the fundamental reason for Jake's chasing her up; that Jake had, in fact, a wisdom of his own.)

She looked at the picture—the biggest of the twopenny ones. On a white ground there were bright red diagonals, and down the middle of these red diagonals were thinner stripes alternately of green and blue. But wherever you held an area of the huge canvas only in peripheral vision the red faded to brown or to a sort of gold. You chased it round, and that was what happened. Perhaps it was again a small parlour trick. And perhaps there was a simple sensuous pleasure in it if you had the right reactions to colours, a pleasure as simple as coming on the ice-cream beneath the soufflé or the hot chocolate sauce. Only she suspected that something deeper was involved—a kind of verdict against the possibility of securely knowing anything at all. Certainly these things—all these things, for she was now circling the room—were far more powerful than a *bombe glacée*. Absolutely, they had to be reckoned with. But it was desperately unfamiliar ground. Carpaccio was kid's stuff in the comparison.

She tried further to attend to the coloured pictures—the more resolutely because Jake continued not much to attend to her. He was now, so to speak, right at the other end of the swimming-bath. He was floating where she'd never do other than flounder. She had to face that.

At this point Gloria, who had been rather at a stretch, realized she had shot her bolt. The pictures began to flicker, flash, come at her in a distressing way. All round her, innumerable multi-hued stripes in wavy parallel undulating like snakes, like the hair of Maenads, like railway lines melting or gone mad, were coming at her. Nothing was staying still.

'I think that will do,' she said. 'We'll go out.'

'No. There's one downstairs I want to look at again. Come on.'

She was about to resist when it came to her that Jake was no longer speaking more or less in disregard of her. He was very serious. He was presenting a small ultimatum related in some fashion to a blue-print he'd constructed of what he thought of as stretching before them to the grave. Men must work at whatever incomprehensible assignment they'd taken on. And women must weep —or at least put up with a headache. His idea was approximately in that area.

She followed Jake down.

Ten minutes later they were outside. They walked to a parapet, propped their elbows on it, and gazed out over the Thames.

'Well,' Jake said, 'that was it.' He gave Gloria a glance which she saw was meant to look mischievous, but which revealed itself as nothing of the kind. 'Do you think it might be all all right?'

'Yes.'

'I'm not an R.A., or anything.' As Jake made this foolish remark, his face was transformed. 'Gloria,' he said softly, and kissed her. He stood back. 'You can't have known for very long.'

'I think I found out in the train.'

'Romantic British Rail.'

Constrained to the idiom of their time, they looked at each other the more gravely. Just for the moment, they had to take out their feelings like that.

'We'll get some lunch,' Jake said. 'If your blessed solicitor can wait.'

'I expect he gets quite well paid.' Gloria was reminded of something as from very far away. 'Jake, what shall I do about the collection?'

'The collection?' It was almost as if Jake had to place this. 'I've told you, haven't I? Give it away. Do you like Chinese food? What a lot to learn!'

'Yes, I do.' Gloria wondered how much she still had to learn about Jake. She seemed suddenly to have enormous knowledge to be going on with. He was a perfectly ordinary young man, blundering round after himself, trying out tough airs and unrealistic political opinions. He was a little like Octavius in that sort of blundering. But whereas Octavius would find maturity and stability in an honourable profession and modest achieved goals Jake had this overmastering thing. It was possible—it might be, as they said, statistically probable—that its higher reaches would prove totally beyond him. In which case he might take alternately to drink and tranquillizers. Or he might go mad. Thinking these entirely sensible thoughts, Gloria caught Jake's hand in hers.

The restaurant proved, with a glorious absurdity, to belong to somebody called Young Young.

27

VETERIS VESTIGIA FLAMMAE

'GLORIA—MY DEAR!'

As the train made its first lurch out of Paddington Harry had tumbled into the compartment—an otherwise empty compartment. He looked unfamiliar. This was because, like Jake, he was in a gent's suiting. The suiting didn't suit him. But he was probably unaware of that. Although he must have known of his mother's disclosure of his affianced condition, he also appeared unaware of turpitude. He was looking at Gloria delightedly and unabashed.

'Yes, Gloria your dear: and I'm the most gorgeous girl.'

To make this remark was very wrong of Gloria. She did it partly because she was irresponsibly happy and partly because she was annoyed. She had jumped to the conclusion—probably quite unjustifiably—that Harry had lurked on the platform till the last moment, and thus secured her undivided company.

'Of course you are. What have you been doing?'

'I've been seeing a lawyer.'

'So have I—about some land.'

'Yes, of course.' Gloria pulled herself together. 'Harry, I'm very glad indeed about your engagement. I'm sure Miss Mercer is just right. Congratulations.'

'Thank you very much, my dear.'

'As a matter of fact, I've got engaged too.'

'You've lost no time.' As he produced this prompt and not very obliging remark, Harry's eyes had rounded. 'Congratulations handed back. No, that's wrong. Reciprocated. May I kiss you?'

Gloria allowed herself to be kissed. She was in a state of bliss making her feel, quite wrongly, that she owed Harry that. Harry's kiss was of the most unblemished brotherly sort. It was the end of the affair. At least in Gloria's mind it was that.

'What tremendous fun!' Having said this, Harry was distinguishably at a loss. 'Would it be a wild guess,' he asked, 'that it's your cousin?'

'Yes, Jake Counterpayne.' Gloria was now rather at a loss herself. She suddenly saw that she must appear an extremely inconstant person. She would have to explain that only yesterday her engagement had been a thousand miles away. She also saw the construction to which her incontinently changed state lay open. She might be held to have done something on what they called the rebound. Perhaps—she thought in momentary panic—she *had* Miss Mercer was the prime agent in the affair. It was as simple as that.

'If ever any beauty I did see, which I desired and got, 'twas but a dream of thee.' Harry's good grammar-school must have provided him with this wholly surprising shaft. 'Tell him that.'

'Harry, you mustn't be impertinent.' Gloria said this quite gently. 'Not if we're going to go on being friends.'

'As we are, my dear. And I'm sorry.' Harry could say the completely handsome thing. 'And Jake's a good chap. I have an idea he once wanted to lay me out—not that he'd have had much chance at it. But he's a good chap.'

'Why ever did he want to lay you out?' Gloria, although anxious to get off delicate ground, would not have been woman if she could have resisted this curiosity.

'He came on me in a situation he thought revolting in anybody who had anything to do with you.'

'I see.' For a moment Gloria was revolted herself, for she could make at least a rough guess at the sort of thing that must have occurred. But, after all, she had *known* about Harry. Of course she had! And it hadn't made Harry any less attractive. Nor did it do so now. Or not in certain obvious if superficial regards. Harry, for instance, was as good-looking as Jake—although Jake, in his turn, was happily as good-looking as Harry. They were equally upstanding young men, nicely formed—you could be pretty sure—all over. So in terms of the spontaneous response you make to that kind of appeal it would be dishonest to claim that Harry was, so to speak, suddenly drawing a blank with her. Did this mean that she wasn't really in love with Jake? Or that she was by nature a depraved, inconstant, or trivial person? Gloria had a moment of dismay, in which she confusedly felt that the memory of all those phantasmagoric pictures bore some part. At least what she had needed on this journey home had been to relax—into a deep contentment which was never going to leave her again. So Harry had been a bit much. And now Harry, with the clairvoyant power she had sometimes remarked in him, moved in with a question relevant to at least a part of these thoughts.

'Gloria, my dear, where did you get engaged?'

'Where?' It would surely, Gloria thought, have been more natural to ask *When*. 'Oh, it was outside a picture gallery. After Jake had been showing me some pictures he rather likes.'

'I suppose he likes yours too. He'll quite have glory, picture-wise. If you're going to live at Nudd. Are you?'

'No, definitely not.' It startled Gloria to discover that Jake and she hadn't remotely discussed where they were going to live, or how—or, for that matter, on what. She knew what they *wouldn't* be living on. The afternoon had seen to that.

'Did you like the pictures Jake likes?'

'I don't know. I'm not sure.' Gloria answered this innocent-seeming question even while she resented it. 'I didn't get the hang of them very well. Perhaps they're what people call problem pictures. I didn't know where I was with them really.'

'It doesn't matter, does it? Not since you know where you are with Jake. Or are he and the pictures a bit mixed up?'

Gloria wasn't exactly scared. She had a feeling that Harry was teasing her—and on the strength of some devilish acuteness which was as much his specific thing as becoming an artist was Jake's. She didn't want much more of this.

'Of course not,' she said shortly. 'It's not as if he'd painted them.'

If Harry found this odd reply interesting, the fact was perhaps attested by his appearing to indulge a certain absence of mind. He stared lazily out of the carriage window and into a gathering dusk. But presently he continued his inquisition.

'If you're not going to live at Nudd,' he asked, 'who is?'

'Americans.'

'Americans? Millionaires?'

'Not exactly.' Gloria hesitated. 'In fact, decidedly not.'

'But it will take a packet to buy Nudd lock, stock and barrel, won't it?'

'They're not going to buy it. They can't afford to. They've done their sums and they know they can't. It's a university. And it's a gift—with just a few conditions.' Gloria braced herself. After all, she was as of this present (as the Americans themselves would have said) Miss Montacute of Nudd still. 'I've given my solicitor his instructions.'

Harry appeared to admire this. He nodded with almost Mr Thurkle's gravity. (Not that Mr Thurkle had admired.) Then he stretched himself luxuriously in a way Gloria knew.

'Gloria, my dear, they'll make you a Doctor of Philosophy.'

'No. They'll make Guise that.'

'Guise?' Harry was at least pleasingly staggered.

'Yes, Guise. He's a very learned man.'

'He's a servant!' This came from Harry as from the heart of an outraged yeomanry. But he recovered himself. 'Well, well, well,' he said—and his interest in the conversation appeared about to lapse. He even picked up an evening newspaper he had brought with him into the compartment, as if prompted to discover what had been happening on the rugger-fields of England. But he had another question. 'Does Jake know?'

'Not yet.' Gloria had repressed an impulse to say something like 'A third impertinence, Harry Carter, and you're through'. This was because she had great faith in honesty. 'It's in line with his thought,' she added—and wondered that so odd an expression had come to her.

'But it's a kind of test, all the same, of the disinterestedness of his passion?' Simply because he was a conceited and confident young man, quick to over-estimate his chances, a glint had come into Harry's eye.

'I suppose it is in a way. But—'

'And you'll tell him he's passed with flying colours?' It was as if Harry believed that, at an eleventh hour, a small but still very attractive possibility had been tumbled into his lap. 'But of course you will. A lover—at least if he's a real watertight *fiancé*—can triumphantly be told things.'

'Naturally I'll tell him I saw it a bit like that.'

'Then that will be fine.' Harry Carter sat back contentedly. But then a very strange thing happened. Conceivably he recalled Jake Counterpayne and himself as sitting side by side on a bench, conscious of hostility, but conscious too of the mysterious satisfaction of simply being two young males together. 'Gloria Montacute,' he said, 'you're a damned decent kid. So don't be a silly little bitch as well.'

'Harry!'

'Who are you to go proposing tests to a chap like that Jake—who has the good sense to want to marry you? Pull yourself together, girl.'

Gloria stared at this transformed Harry in stupefaction —and stared, as with an inward eye and equal stupefaction, at her own muddled mind.

'Harry—just what am I to do?'

'Keep mum about it.'

'It?'

'Your bloody silly test, for Christ's sake. He just wouldn't take it. There would be hell to pay. He's a man, isn't he? Do you think he cares a damn about all those pictures— Don Thingummybob and whoever? He can paint his own, can't he? Pipe down. Tell him you're shut of the bloody collection, and that that's that. Can't you *see*?'

'Yes. And thank you very much. For your advice, I mean. It's right.'

'As a matter of fact, my dear, it rates another kiss. But I let you off.' Harry's face was radiant—not unlike Jake's, at an important moment, on the South Bank. 'Gloria, I like you very much.'

28

PLAIN ENGLISH

HARRY HAD A smart new sports-car parked at Kingham Junction—which showed how happily he was on the up-and-up. But he hung fire over offering Gloria a lift, so that she guessed he had an immediate date with Beryl Mercer. She was relieved by this. It wasn't that she was anxious to be rid of him. They could now get along very well. But some instinct suggested to her that it would be a good idea to arrive home alone. So she took her usual taxi, and sank down in it in bliss once more. She didn't count her blessings, since she was conscious of only one. Had she done so, she might have reflected that two young men, not henceforward to be very important in her life, had behaved by her rather well in the end. Equally she didn't reflect that one of these young men (whom she was always going to think of as poor Octavius) had been responsible for an experience which had almost been very traumatic indeed. But for the grace of God—and perhaps that stiff ticking-off by Harry—the hunted-heiress syndrome might really have mucked things up badly.

Her instinct had been right. As her taxi drew to a halt before the door of Nudd it confronted the parking lights of a small van. And out of this Jake tumbled at once. She could just see that he was grinning all over his face.

'Beaten you to it!' he shouted. 'I was afraid you'd polish off that solicitor too soon.'

'Well—I have polished him off.' She watched Jake—and it was an absolutely thrilling experience—advance and confidently pay off her driver. As the man ran an account with Nudd, he was mildly astonished. Fortunately he was too tactful to obtrude the fact. It was probably, she thought, Jake's last pound note. 'And all this, too,' she added.

'Do you mind my coming?' Jake asked. He had paid no attention to her last remark. 'I just couldn't not.'

'It was very nice of you.' Gloria was coming to understand the inadequacy of words. 'Come on in. Why didn't you *go* in?'

'Couldn't face Guise—not except under your wing. Into the ancestral hall.'

'It's nothing of the sort. Can you stay the night?'

'Yes, of course—if you'll have me. Although—by the way—I'm not going to sleep with you till we're married.' Jake said this as if it was the most extraordinary announcement in the world.

'I don't know that that's complimentary.'

'Don't you?' He took her in his arms. 'You damned well do.'

'Jake, I love you very much.' She freed herself. 'Drinks,' she said. 'And Mrs Bantry alerted to everything she can put on.'

'Didn't you have a decent lunch?'

'The best I've ever had, or shall ever have again.'

'I love you very much. And don't be pessimistic.'

'Jake, you'll be faithful to me—within all the real bounds?'

'Darling, I'm your true-telling friend.' Jake was very amused. 'As for Mrs Bantry, she's all very well. But can you cook yourself?'

'Of course I can.'

'Joy entire. I say—may I carry you in?'

They sat in front of the library fire. Dr Guise (if the small prolepsis be allowed) brought them sherry.

'I've parted with the collection,' Gloria said. 'And pretty well for free.'

'Good girl.'

'To an American university. It's going to be a centre for studying art and things.'

'Absolutely rotten. I told you to scatter it among the local hinds. You wait. When I've a girl I'll keep her in line.'

'I'll give you a good fight.' Gloria, unaware that Jake had merely made one of his random incursions into literary quotation, was a little startled. 'It's going to be very, very nice.'

'And very, very good. I'll be the nice and you'll be the good. Will Guise be producing wine?'

'Champagne—because I've told him about us.' As Gloria mentioned this festal beverage some memory made her blush. But there was only the firelight, and it passed unremarked.

'Then no more sherry. A temperate start.'

'Jake, I *have* been quite sensible. I don't see anything wrong with a bit of private income. Not if it's not enormous; not if it's just what used to be called a competence. So I've arranged it that way.'

'Well, I'm buggered!' Jake stared at Gloria in genuine astonishment. 'How much?'

'Five hundred a year.'

'Marvellous! It's an heiress I've had my eye on all along.' Jake said this with what Gloria could now only think of as his headiest grin. He was, in fact, relieved: largely relieved that the sum thus seriously named was so small, and a little relieved that it wasn't smaller still. The hazards involved in marrying millions, which had been so clear to his sister, may well have not been beyond Jake's own intellectual grasp. 'Your remaining fortune's enough to run the van—and for fish and chips at the end of the week, with any luck. It's a happiness I just don't deserve.'

'Jake, do be serious. We must really think, you know.'

'Time enough when we're married, darling. And that

won't be for six weeks. I've got to go and make all that ice-cream first.'

'Months, not weeks. I must stick to my new job, Jake, for at least that long. And not ice-cream. It's a useless thing, making ice-cream. I'll fix you up in the hospital for six months.'

'To move wild laughter in the throat of death?'

'Very much that.' Although unacquainted with *Love's Labour's Lost*, Gloria got the idea. 'Among the corpses, mostly. The pay's best at that.'

'Gloria, you're a practical woman. We'll do.'

The library door opened, and the Montacute Curator stood framed in it.

'Dinner is served,' Guise said.